SEBASTIAN DARKE

Prince of Fools

SEBASTIAN DARKE

Prince of Fools

PHILIP CAVENEY

LAUREL-LEAF BOOKS

Text copyright © 2007 by Philip Caveney
Illustrations copyright © 2007 by Bob Lea

All rights reserved. Published in the United States by Laurel-Leaf, an imprint of Random House Children's Books, a division of Random House, Inc., New York. Originally published in hardcover in Great Britain by Bodley Head Children's Books, an imprint of Random House Children's Books, a division of Random House Group Ltd, London, in 2007, and in hardcover in the United States by Delacorte Press, an imprint of Random House Children's Books, a division of Random House, Inc., New York, in 2008.

Laurel-Leaf and the colophon are registered trademarks of Random House, Inc.

Visit us on the Web! www.randomhouse.com/teens

Educators and librarians, for a variety of teaching tools, visit us at
www.randomhouse.com/teachers

The Library of Congress has cataloged the hardcover edition of this work as follows:
Caveney, Philip.
Sebastian Darke : Prince of Fools / Philip Caveney.
p. cm.
"First published in the United Kingdom in 2007 by Random House U.K."—Copyright p. cm.
Summary: Accompanied by his sardonic buffalope Max, seventeen-year-old Sebastian Darke meets a spoiled princess and a diminutive soldier who aid in his quest to become court jester to the evil King Septimus.
ISBN: 978-0-385-73467-7 (trade)—ISBN: 978-0-385-90465-0 (Gibraltar lib. bdg.)—
ISBN: 978-0-375-84643-4 (e-book)
[1. Fools and jesters—Fiction. 2. Princesses—Fiction. 3. Humorous stories.] I. Title.
PZ7.C29124Seb 2011
[Fic]—dc22
2006025262

ISBN: 978-0-440-24026-6 (pbk.)

RL: 6.0
Printed in the United States of America
10 9 8 7 6 5 4 3 2 1

First Laurel-Leaf Edition

To the hens in the coop . . .
and for Charlie, without whom . . .

SEBASTIAN DARKE

Prince of Fools

PART ONE

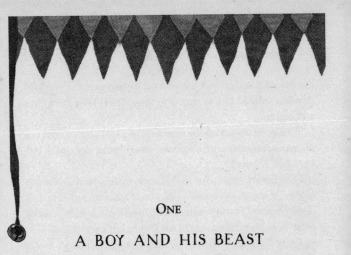

ONE

A BOY AND HIS BEAST

The ancient wooden caravan creaked slowly out from the cover of the trees and stopped for a moment on the wide stretch of plain.

If there had been anyone to observe the scene they would have noticed the words SEBASTIAN DARKE, PRINCE OF FOOLS painted gaily on the sides of the caravan. Those with a keener eye might also have noticed that the word "Sebastian" looked somehow different to the rest of the sentence. It had been added in a rather wobbly, amateurish hand, clearly over-painting another name that had already been there.

The sun was low on the horizon and Sebastian was obliged to shade his eyes with the flat of one hand as he gazed off into the shimmering, heat-rippled distance. The land ahead of him was flat, arid, featureless red earth, baked by the sun, with here and there the occasional bunch of scrubby grass thrusting tenaciously through the soil. He had no real idea how far it was to the city of Keladon, but a merchant he had met the previous day had warned him to expect to travel for at least three days and nights.

"It's a good distance," the merchant had told him. "And those plains are infested with Brigands. You'd better sleep with one eye open, Elf-man."

Sebastian was well used to this term, though he didn't much care for it. He was a "breed"—the son of a human father and an elvish mother. His tall stature and handsome features clearly came from his father's side of the family, but his mother's lineage was there too, reflected in the large jet-black irises of his eyes and his long, slightly pointed ears. His gangly frame was accentuated by the striped black and white costume he was wearing, complete with a tall three-pronged hat topped by jingling bells. The costume had been his father's and hung rather loosely on Sebastian, but he had steadfastly refused his mother's offers to alter it, saying that in time he would grow to fit the clothing. Fitting comfortably into the role of a jester might take a little longer.

Sebastian clicked his tongue and slapped the reins against the shaggy haunches of Max, the single buffalope that pulled the caravan. Max snorted, shook his great horned head and set off again at his usual leisurely pace. He had been in the Darke family for as long as Sebastian could remember; indeed, one of his earliest memories was of his father lifting him onto the buffalope's mighty back and leading him slowly around the paddock. Max was now of advanced years and had many gray hairs peppering the rich ginger of his shaggy hide. With each

4

passing day he seemed to grow more cantankerous, and he had never been slow in stating his dissatisfaction.

"I don't much like the look of this," he muttered now, as he started off across the plain. "We're going to need plenty of water."

"We've *got* water," Sebastian told him. "Enough for at least two days. And besides, there are streams out there. That merchant said so."

Max sniffed disdainfully. "Why you'd take the word of a Berundian oil-seller is quite beyond me," he said. "A man like that would sell his grandmother for a few croats."

"You suspect everybody," Sebastian chided him. "According to you, every person we meet is some kind of villain."

"That's because they generally are. I noticed the Berundian managed to sell you some lamp oil."

"So? We needed some!"

"Not at three croats a bottle we didn't. Daylight robbery! Back at the market in Jerabim you could get a bucket of the stuff for—"

"We're not in Jerabim now," Sebastian reminded him.

They moved on in gloomy silence for a while and Sebastian found himself thinking wistfully about his hometown, the place he'd lived for all of his seventeen years. He closed his eyes for a moment and saw the big bustling market in the town square, where prosperous merchants in their embroidered cloaks loudly advertised their wares as the townspeople moved past them. Suddenly a whole series of familiar images, smells and tastes assailed Sebastian's senses. He saw the richly decorated textiles and carpets that hung from wooden frames around the many stalls. He smelled the rich odors of the cattle pens, where people came to barter for buffalopes and equines. He tasted the delicious tang of the hot sherbet they served in the cafés, and savored the warm aroma of elvish coffee emanating from the many restaurants that lined the square. . . .

Then he had a vivid recollection of his mother's face on the day he'd finally left home—her red-rimmed eyes; her brave, forlorn attempt at a smile. Sitting up on the seat of the caravan, he'd called down to her that he'd be back just as soon as he'd made his fortune, that all her troubles would be over . . . but neither of them had really believed it.

"Take care of yourself, Sebastian," she'd called to him. "Remember, if things don't work out for you, I'll still be here!"

That had been three moons ago. He didn't like to think of her sitting alone at night in the shabby homestead, while the cold night winds sighed outside the window—

"This is tedious!" Max's whining voice broke rudely into his thoughts. "I mean, look at it. There's nothing out there, not even a hill or a tree. The least you could do is humor me with a little conversation."

"I'm not in the mood," said Sebastian. "Besides, most buffalopes know their place. They don't jabber incessantly at their owners."

"You're not my owner," Max reminded him. "That honor belonged to your father."

"He's been dead over a year now. I inherited the house and I inherited you. Accept the fact and shut up!"

"Oh, that's charming, isn't it!" exclaimed Max in disgust. "Downgraded to a mere possession. Well, at least I know where I stand."

Sebastian immediately regretted his words. "It's not like that. You're not a possession. It's more . . . you're more of a . . ."

"Servant? Chattel?"

"I was going to say . . . a partner."

Max seemed rather pleased with this. He lifted his head a little and walked with fresh spring in his step. "A partner," he mused. "Well, yes, let's face it, you wouldn't have got this far without my help. Who was it showed you the path through Geltane Woods? Eh? And it was my idea to take shelter in that pine grove last night."

"I'm very grateful," Sebastian assured him. "Really." The last thing he needed right now was a buffalope that didn't feel like walking anymore.

They moved on in silence, save for the creaking of the ancient leather harness, the crunching of the wheels and the tinkling of Sebastian's bells. He sat there asking himself, not for the first time, if he was doing the right thing.

Sebastian's father, Alexander, had been a jester, a very successful one. As Court Jester to King Cletus the Magnificent, he had lived a rich and privileged existence and had been able to keep his wife and young son in relative luxury for many years. But Cletus was already an old man when Alexander first came into his employ. Cletus's son and heir, Daniel the Doleful, had none of his father's love of wit and good humor. So it was clear that Alexander's good fortune was not going to last forever.

8

He had always harbored the wish that Sebastian would follow in his footsteps. From an early age the boy had done his level best to learn the jester's skills. But something wasn't quite right. He managed to memorize the jokes, quips and stories well enough, but somehow he didn't tell them convincingly. His timing was wrong, or he got some small detail mixed up. Where Alexander would be sure to get a hearty laugh, Sebastian could coax only a feeble chuckle; where Alexander would hold an audience spellbound with a story, Sebastian's listeners would quickly become restless and distracted. It was clear to Sebastian that he simply didn't have "the gift," as his father liked to describe it. But Alexander refused to accept this, insisting that practice would make perfect and that it was all just a matter of time.

Then King Cletus had finally died and Alexander had found himself without a patron. Attempts to ingratiate himself with other well-to-do nobles around the court were unsuccessful, and with no money coming in, he was soon obliged to offer his services to local taverns and music halls for a few croats a night. The family found itself in trouble as their income slowed to a trickle. Alexander tried everything he knew to find work, but it was to no avail. Then one night, in a tavern, a stranger told him about a powerful king in the city of Keladon, far away to the west.

"King Septimus is a fine and noble man," he had told Alexander. "It is said that his palace is the richest in all the world. He dines on gold plates and drinks from silver goblets encrusted with precious jewels."

"Does he have a jester?" Alexander had asked.

To which the stranger had replied, "Do you know, I don't believe he does!"

Alexander seized upon the notion as a drowning man clutches at a piece of driftwood. He became obsessed with making the long and arduous journey to Keladon, where he intended to offer his services to King Septimus. In preparation for the trip, he devised a completely new routine and practiced long into the night, every night, going over and over it, trying to perfect every word, every nuance, every expression on his haggard face.

He had not recognized the toll that the recent months had taken on him. He was undernourished and exhausted. One morning Sebastian and his mother had woken to find Alexander slumped unconscious on the tiled floor, pale and shivering. They carried him to his bed and Sebastian rode Max into town to summon a doctor, but it was no use. Alexander had been taken by a terrible fever, and within a week he was dead.

For Sebastian and his mother it was a desperate situation. The house and land was theirs but they had no income to speak of and the only option was to go begging in the streets. Unless . . .

When Sebastian had first mentioned it, his mother had been dismissive.

He was a mere boy, she pointed out. He could hardly undertake the long and hazardous journey to Keladon by himself. Sebastian had argued that Max would be with him and he challenged his mother to come up with a better idea, but she couldn't think of anything.

And so it was decided. Sebastian would take his father's

costume and caravan, he would take his father's jokes and stories and he would make the trip to Keladon in his father's place to seek employment at the court of King Septimus.

"What's the worst that can happen?" he'd asked his mother. "If they don't think I'm good enough, they'll simply send me on my way and I'll come back home again."

And his mother had nodded and forced another smile, but deep down in her heart she began to wonder if this was the beginning of the end; and she asked herself if she would ever see her beloved son again.

TWO

DOUBLE ACT

"Oh, come on, for goodness' sake, this is terrible. Tell me a joke!"

"What?" Sebastian came back to the present with a bump. He stared around at the seemingly endless stretch of dry, dusty plain and had to work hard to fight down a rapidly rising sense of panic.

"You heard me. Let's hear something from your marvelous repertoire."

"Er . . . not just now, if you don't mind. I'm thinking."

Max wasn't satisfied with this reply. "Is that what you're going to say when King Septimus asks you to perform? *Not right now, Your Majesty, I'm thinking!* That'll go down well, won't it? He'll probably have your head chopped off!"

"You have to understand," Sebastian told him. "I can't just turn it on and off at will. I . . . need the right setting. An audience—"

"*I'll* be your audience," Max assured him. "And I'll make

allowances for the setting. Let's face it, you won't have many other opportunities to practice, will you? The next time you perform it will probably be for the king and his court."

Sebastian swallowed. It was not a particularly encouraging prospect. "All right then," he said. "I'll try . . . but please don't interrupt until I've finished. And try to laugh in the right places."

Max rolled his eyes but refrained from commenting further.

"Well then . . ." Sebastian thought for a moment, then launched into his opening routine with as much confidence as he could muster. "Greetings, lords and ladies! I'm not saying it took me a long time to cross the plains, but I was wearing short pants when I set off!" He paused briefly, anticipating a laugh, but there wasn't one, so he continued.

"So . . . so this is the fine city of Keladon! I've heard so much about it. I heard that the merchants here are so prosperous, they've actually removed the padlocks from their dustbins! Of . . . of course, back where I come from, in Jerabim, things aren't quite as plush. I'm not saying it's squalid, but next week they're knocking it down so they can build a slum!"

No reaction from Max. Nothing.

"I . . . I had a very deprived childhood. Our family was so poor, we couldn't afford a fire in the winter. My father would chew pepper-root and we'd all sit round his mouth! And food . . . we . . . we could never afford to eat properly. Every so often my mother would send me to the slaughterhouse to buy a babarusa's head. And I had to ask them to leave the eyes in it— so it would see us through the week!"

Sebastian looked hopefully down at Max, who was plodding

resolutely onward, showing no signs of having heard anything. "A little encouragement wouldn't hurt," he growled.

"I'm sorry, I'm afraid the jokes so far are rather familiar . . ."

"That wouldn't have stopped you laughing if Father was telling them."

There was a brief silence.

"Your father had the gift of making the most unpromising material seem funny. Whereas you may have to work somewhat harder to achieve those results . . . but please, continue."

Sebastian gritted his teeth for a moment and then decided to weigh in with one of his own jokes.

"Did you hear the one about the two merchants who were walking to market? And the first one said—"

"Illogical," interrupted Max.

Sebastian stared at him. "What?" he snapped.

"Merchants never walk anywhere."

"Oh . . . all right then, they were riding to market. And one of them said—"

"I don't seem to recognize *this* joke."

"No. That's because it's one of my own."

"I see. And do you think it's a good idea to use your own material? Your father's jokes have at least been tried and tested."

"If you'd just let me finish!"

"Sorry. Do go on, I'm all ears."

"So . . . so one of them says, 'How long have we been traveling?' And the other one says, 'Three days. But to you, *two* days!'"

There was another achingly long silence, during which the creaking of the harness seemed unnaturally loud.

Then Max said: "Of course, there's nothing to stop you pursuing *other* lines of work. I believe they're crying out for builders in Keladon."

"It wasn't that bad!" protested Sebastian.

"No. No, it wasn't *bad*, as such. It's just that I failed to discern any actual humor in it. I mean, was it three days they'd been traveling or was it two?"

"That's . . . that's the point," said Sebastian. "You know these merchants, always trying to make you an offer? So, like, it's three croats, but to you—"

"Your father always used to say . . ."

". . . never explain a joke! Yes, I know. But . . . but then he didn't have you deliberately failing to see what he was getting at, did he?"

"I can't help feeling you're being a little oversensitive," said Max primly. "It's hardly my fault that you can't write decent material. Still, it's perhaps unfair to judge from one example. Please, continue—at least it's passing the time."

"Forget it," said Sebastian bitterly. He could see that the clouds on the horizon were darkening from red to a deep shade of crimson. Night came quickly here, and packs of wild lupers crossed the length and breadth of these plains, so it made sense to keep a decent campfire. Furthermore, they were approaching what must have been one of the only clumps of bushes he had seen on these flatlands. They were stunted and withered but would at least offer a little shelter. "We'll stop over there for the night," he told Max.

"Good thinking. My hooves are killing me!" Max expertly

maneuvered the caravan in beside the bushes. Sebastian jumped down from the seat and unhitched the harness. Max made a big show of shrugging his shoulders and stretching his legs. "Ah, that's a relief," he said. "It's no easy task pulling that caravan all day." He glanced at Sebastian hopefully. "And what delights have we for supper then?"

"Dried mulch for you," said Sebastian, trying to sound positive. "And elvish black bread for me."

"No, no, too much—you'll spoil me," said Max dolefully.

Sebastian ignored him. He went round to the back of the caravan and retrieved Max's nosebag, into which he threw a couple of handfuls of the dried food he had purchased in Jerabim. It smelled stale and unappetizing, but was probably preferable to the rock-hard chunk of bread that *he* had to look forward to. He carried the mulch round to Max, who sniffed at it disdainfully.

"My compliments to the chef," he said grimly.

Sebastian gestured to the nearby bushes. "You could always supplement your diet with those," he said. "Provided you leave us a little bit of cover."

Max looked downright offended by the very suggestion. "Good idea," he said. "A bout of dysentery is just what we need right now."

"You won't get dysentery," Sebastian told him; but then thought that Max was awkward enough to go down with it just to spite him.

He slung the nosebag around Max's ears and went back to the caravan for some of the dry kindling he had collected on his way through the forest. He had accumulated quite a pile in the back—enough, he hoped, to see them through a couple of nights on the plain.

"Go easy with that stuff," Max warned him, his voice muffled by the nosebag. "We don't want to run out."

"We can always resort to the bag of dried buffalope chips," said Sebastian cheerfully, though he really hoped it wouldn't come to that. They were hard to light and gave off a dreadful stench when they finally got going.

"Burning dung," said Max quietly. "Oh goody. I can hardly wait."

THREE

DINNER IS SERVED

Sebastian had the fire burning by nightfall and was soon sitting on his bedroll, toasting a hunk of black bread over the flames in the vain hope of making it a bit more palatable. Max lay slumped nearby, staring gloomily into the fire, the reflection of the flames dancing like tiny devils in his large brown eyes. Every so often he arched his back slightly and let out a prodigious gust of wind.

"Excuse me," he said, each time it happened. "It's the mulch."

"No, it's *you*," Sebastian corrected him. "Can't you try and exercise a bit of control?"

"Well, we'll see how you fare after you've downed that bread. Honestly, are you sure it's safe to eat?"

"No, I'm not, but the only alternative is to eat nothing, so if I can force it down without choking on it, I shall do so."

Max sighed. "Look at us," he said. "Reduced to this! Why, I remember when your father would bring me out a bucket of Sargan grain drenched in wild bee's gold. And if I'd been working particularly hard, there'd be a couple of ripe pommers on the side . . . maybe even a yellow sweet fruit."

"That's all history now," said Sebastian.

"And what about you? Many's the time I've looked through the window of the house and seen you and your parents dining on succulent roast swamp fowl, with heaps of fried taties and thick, black mushrungers—"

"Could we talk about something else?" snapped Sebastian. "You're making my stomach rumble." He could wait no longer, so he lifted the steaming hunk of black bread to his mouth and took an exploratory bite. It was like eating hot sawdust. He forced his jaws to munch, having to work very hard to swallow down mouthfuls of the stuff. He was happy to wash it down with elvish coffee, one of the few luxuries they had brought with them, and by this method, he somehow managed to consume the rest of it. He found that the paltry meal had taken some of the dull ache out of his stomach but had done absolutely nothing to pacify his hunger. He gazed hopelessly around, but the moon was obscured by tumbled banks of rolling clouds and he couldn't see very far beyond the flickering light of the fire. Not that there was much to see anyway, just the endless plain rolling onward to some unknown world. "What I wouldn't give for a hunk of hot meat right now," he said.

"Well, you needn't look at me," Max chastised him. "Actually, we buffalopes make very poor eating."

"That's not what I've heard," said Sebastian, casting a sly look at him. "As I understand it, buffalope meat is one of the favorite ingredients on any Brigand's menu."

"Really?" Max cast a nervous glance over his shoulder. "I

19

suppose I shouldn't be surprised. From what I've heard, they're little more than animals. I've been told that when times are hard, they've even been known to resort to cannibalism."

Now it was Sebastian's turn to be nervous. "We . . . er . . . probably won't encounter any this far north," he said. "Still— just in case." He stroked the scabbard of the big curved sword that lay beside him. That too had been his father's. Alexander had been a fine swordsman and had spent many an afternoon trying to pass on his skills to his son. Sebastian remembered the long hours spent sparring with him, until the sweat spilled from every pore. Alexander had been a stern teacher and thought nothing of making Sebastian go over every move again and again, until his hands were blistered.

Max looked down at the sword doubtfully. "What do you suppose you'll do with that if some villain comes calling?"

"Well, I'll . . brandish it and . . . I know how to use a sword!" he said. "My father taught me well."

"That I do not doubt. But knowing how to swing a sword and being ready to smite somebody's head from their shoulders, without a moment's hesitation—that's a different matter."

Sebastian flung a broken branch into the fire, sending up a great shower of sparks into the night sky. "You're always getting at me," he complained. "If it's not my jokes, it's my complete inability to measure up to my father in anything I do. I wish you—"

Sebastian broke off abruptly as a distant sound rose and fell on the air—a long, drawn-out howl that seemed to echo eerily in the night.

"What was that?" asked Max fearfully.

"Oh, just a luper," said Sebastian, trying to sound casual. "They aren't a problem unless they're hunting in a pack."

As if in answer to his statement, more howls sounded in response to the first. Sebastian counted at least six or seven different tones.

"Probably miles away," he added, attempting to keep the note of desperation out of his voice. He tried to smile encouragingly at Max, but he could see a familiar expression in the buffalope's eyes. A look of apprehension.

"I've heard stories about lupers," said Max uneasily. "A pack of those things can strip a fully grown buffalope down to the bones in just a few moments."

"You shouldn't believe everything you hear," Sebastian chided him. "It would take half the night to do that."

"Oh, now I feel better," said Max.

"And besides, you can tell by listening to them—they're not hungry."

"Really?"

"Really. A hungry luper makes a particular sound. Sort of like a—"

Sebastian stopped talking. He had just heard something different. A rustling sound. His stomach seemed to fill suddenly with cold water.

"There's something behind us!" whispered Max. "In the bushes!"

"I know!" Sebastian mouthed back at him. He reached out a hand to the hilt of his sword and began to slide it gently out of its scabbard. Now he could distinguish another sound mingled with the rustling: the dull, metallic clanking of armor.

21

"Oh, mercy!" whimpered Max. "It's Brigands! They'll murder you and have me for dinner!" He thought for a moment. "From what you've been saying, they might even have *you* for dinner!"

"Quiet!" hissed Sebastian. "I'm trying to—"

"*Who goes there?*" bellowed a deep voice from the midst of the thicket.

Sebastian gave up all thoughts of delicacy and slid the curved sword clear of its scabbard. He got to his feet and stood crouched, ready to meet any attacker that came at him from out of the undergrowth.

"J-just a traveler," answered Sebastian, settling both hands around the leather grip and noting with a hint of dismay how the blade seemed to be quivering uncontrollably.

"*Two* travelers," Max corrected him.

"A traveler and his beast of burden," ventured Sebastian.

"Oh, that's nice! A little while ago I was a partner; suddenly I'm downgraded to a beast of burden."

"Will you shut up?" snarled Sebastian. He returned his attention to the bushes, trying to remember the advice his father had given him all those years ago. But nothing seemed to come to him. "We mean no harm," he said. "We're just passing through."

"Please don't eat us!" whimpered Max.

There was a long silence, during which Sebastian became aware of a rhythmic thudding sound in his ears. It was a few moments before he realized it was the sound of his own heart.

"Would you be willing to share your campfire with a fellow traveler?" boomed the deep voice.

"Er . . . possibly," said Sebastian.

"It's some kind of trick," whispered Max. "He'll get you off guard and then stick a knife in your ribs!"

"Shush!" Sebastian took a deep breath and tried to gather his courage. "Step forward and show yourself," he demanded.

Another silence. He licked his dry lips and waited, for what seemed an age. He was abruptly aware of how small and vulnerable he was, camped out here in the midst of this great, featureless plain. And how could he be sure that there was just one person out there? It could be a band of rogues, one of them trying to get him off guard, while his friends sneaked round behind him. He turned his head to take a quick peek over his shoulder, then snapped his gaze back as the bushes parted.

Somebody stepped out into the open—but at first Sebastian saw nothing. Then he realized that he needed to lower his gaze considerably.

A man was walking toward him out of the bushes, a thickset fellow wearing a battered-looking breastplate over a chain-mail singlet. He also wore a crested iron helmet, with elaborate nose and cheek protectors that covered his face entirely. In one hand he held a vicious-looking straight sword, and slung across his left shoulder was what looked like the carcass of a javralat, the fleet-footed quadruped that inhabited this part of the country.

The newcomer was undoubtedly a fierce warrior and a force to be reckoned with. But unlike most warriors, he was no higher than Sebastian's hip.

FOUR

LITTLE BIG MAN

The stranger came to a halt a few steps from the fire, sheathed his sword and reached up a hand to remove his helmet. The hand seemed surprisingly big for one so small, and the action revealed a face that was strangely babylike, with big blue eyes, jug ears and no sign of any hair whatsoever.

"Greetings, pilgrims," said the manling, in that deep, resonant voice, which really didn't suit the face at all. "I am Captain Cornelius Drummel, killer of Brigands, formally of the army of Queen Annisett." He paused for a moment as though allowing this information to sink in; but getting no response, he continued, "I see by the writing on your caravan that I am in the presence of Sebastian Darke, Prince of Fools."

"Correct," said Sebastian, making a formal bow.

"And Max," added Max. "His partner!"

Cornelius gave the buffalope a slightly perturbed look. "You have a fine fire," he observed. "Visible at quite a distance. Not

the most advisable thing in a remote spot like this, but a man must take his chances." He reached back a hand and threw the plump body of the javralat to the ground at Sebastian's feet. "I wonder if you'd allow me to cook my dinner over your fire? I've supped on raw meat these last few nights and I'm longing for something hot."

Sebastian frowned. "Well . . ."

"Of course, I'd be happy to share the food with you."

Sebastian's eyes nearly popped out of his head. "Then you . . . you would be most welcome!" he replied. "And I would be more than willing to accept your generous offer." He sheathed his sword and extended a hand to shake. The stranger took it in a powerful grip that made Sebastian wince and pumped it vigorously up and down.

"Watch him," murmured Max under his breath. "It's some kind of trick. . . ."

Sebastian waved a dismissive hand at Max. "Please, er . . . Captain Drummel. Make yourself comfortable."

"Call me Cornelius. We're not on the parade ground now."

"No, of course not. I—I've a metal spit in the caravan, it won't take but a moment to find it—"

"Don't turn your back on him!" hissed Max, then shut up as he noticed the newcomer glaring at him.

"He's a talkative one, your buffalope," observed Cornelius as he unbuckled his breastplate. "Most of them can barely string a sentence together but this one is quite eloquent."

"Umm . . . yes, he's been in our family for years. My father taught him to speak." Sebastian shot Max a withering look.

"Unfortunately." He hurried across to the caravan and rummaged amongst the piles of junk that were heaped in the back. "I don't pay him much attention. He likes to prattle on, you know, but he's harmless enough."

The manling didn't seem convinced by this and Max looked positively disgusted.

"Oh, please, do continue to talk about me as though I'm not here," he said. He glared at Sebastian. "And don't say I didn't warn you." He lowered his huge head onto his front legs and looked away, as though absolving himself of any responsibility.

"Aha!" Sebastian had finally found what he was looking for— an iron frame that slotted together to make a sturdy revolving spit that would roast the meat evenly over the flames. He hauled it out of the caravan, brought it across to the fire and, crouching down, started assembling it. "This should do the job," he said. He was so excited at the thought of eating hot meat that his hands were shaking.

"Excellent," said Cornelius. He set his breastplate aside and flexed his arms and shoulders with a sigh of relief. "Ah, that's better. I've been walking since first light. Well, let's get down to business." He pulled a fearsome-looking knife from his belt and Sebastian froze in terror.

"What did I tell you?" hissed Max. "I said he wasn't to be trusted!"

Cornelius gave the buffalope another strange look, then turned to the carcass of the javralat. "I'll prepare this fellow for cooking, shall I?" he said.

Sebastian let out a sigh of relief. As he watched, Cornelius expertly skinned and gutted the javralat with a few flicks of the finely honed blade. He flung the entrails into the bushes, wiped the knife on his trousers, then handed the skinned carcass to Sebastian.

"These are the only things worth eating that I've found on these blasted flatlands," he said. "They're damned hard to catch, though. You have to sit stock-still by the entrance to one of their burrows, and when they finally stick their heads out . . ." He made a brief chopping gesture with the flat of one hand.

Max winced. "What a world," he said. "One minute you're running happily across the plains, the next you're on somebody's dinner plate."

"This is a lawless place," growled Cornelius. "It's kill or be killed out here—and there are plenty of creatures stalking the night that would think nothing of putting *us* on the menu."

"Yes, we were just discussing lupers when you arrived," said Sebastian.

"I'm not talking about *them,* although they can be bad enough." He sat himself cross-legged beside the fire and held out his hands to warm them. "No, I speak of the grundersnat."

"The . . . what?"

"The grundersnat. Oh, a fearsome beast by all accounts. A huge leathery-winged creature with row upon row of razor-sharp teeth and vicious claws that can tear their way through just about anything."

Max looked terrified. "You . . . haven't *seen* one, have you?"

"No, but I've heard it in the night. A hellish bellowing sound that could turn the blood in your veins to ice. They say if the

28

grundersnat sets eyes on you, it will not give up until it has you in its belly."

Max's eyes got very big and round. "Oh, that's marvelous!" he said. "And to think we were nice and safe back there in our old homestead. But no, the young master said we were to go to Keladon and that was that. Nobody mentioned lupers and cannibals and flesh-eating monsters with razor-sharp teeth!"

Sebastian occupied himself with getting the javralat onto the spit. Within a few moments he had the creature impaled and was turning it around over the crackling flames. Almost instantly, an appetizing aroma began to fill the air. "Smells good," he observed brightly.

"It certainly does," agreed Max. "And as a lifelong vegetarian, I can hardly believe I'm saying that! But . . . supposing the grundersnat smells it and comes looking for some supper?"

"We'll just have to take our chances," said Cornelius; and he gave Sebastian a sly wink.

Sebastian resumed his seat by the fire, opposite Cornelius. "You'll take a cup of elvish coffee?" he suggested.

"By Shadlog's beard, I will! My tongue is near cleaved to my mouth with thirst. They told me that I'd encounter streams out here but I haven't found one in three days of walking."

"Is that so?" murmured Max. "Well, well—no water, eh?"

Sebastian ignored him. "We are without milk, I'm afraid. But I can offer you a little bee's gold to sweeten the cup."

"You are most kind, sir. I am in your debt." Cornelius clasped the proffered mug in his big hands and took a sip. He smacked his lips in appreciation.

29

"Well, this is a most welcome meeting," he said. "There was I, thinking that I would cross this plain without encountering a single person. Now here I sit, sipping coffee and enjoying good conversation. And I have no doubt that I am in for an evening of fine jest and merriment."

Sebastian stared at him blankly. "I'm sorry?"

"You *are* a jester, are you not? So I can surely anticipate some hilarity."

"He's obviously never heard your jokes," murmured Max.

"Or is it perhaps a double act I've found?" ventured Cornelius.

"Oh, Max never misses an opportunity to have his say," agreed Sebastian. "But no, I work alone." He attempted to steer the conversation in another direction. "So, Captain, where are you headed?"

"My destination is the city of Keladon."

"Ours too! I go to offer my services as jester to King Septimus."

Cornelius nodded approvingly. "And I go to enlist in his army! Well, well, we have much in common. Perhaps we would do well to travel together. My sword would come in handy should Brigands attack. And I would pay my way by keeping the larder well stocked. Nobody is better than I at catching javralats."

"That sounds like a great idea," enthused Sebastian.

"Easy for you to say," snorted Max. "You won't be the one pulling the extra weight!"

"Max!" Sebastian smiled apologetically at Cornelius. "He

30

doesn't mean that—he's just feeling a bit cranky. Where have you traveled from? You mentioned a Queen Annisett, I believe?"

"I did, sir. The proud and beautiful Queen Annisett of the kingdom of Golmira, jeweled city of the North. Have you ever had the opportunity to visit it?"

"We've never heard of it," said Max bluntly.

Cornelius chose to ignore the remark. He sat back and smiled. "Oh, it is a fine and prosperous place. I enlisted in the army there as a young man of eighteen summers and steadily worked my way through the ranks to the post of captain. I had a fine regiment of men under me and together we fought many epic battles against the neighboring kingdom of Tannis. My men were willing to put their lives at my command and I was ready to give mine for them. I don't believe there was a happier man in all of Golmira."

There was a long silence, during which Sebastian became aware of the chirruping of insects in the bushes behind them.

Then Max said, "So what went wrong?"

"Who said anything did?" snarled Cornelius.

"Well, nobody. But if everything was so wonderful in Golmira, why are you headed for Keladon?"

Cornelius's face darkened and he glared into his mug of coffee. "Because something happened," he said. "Something . . . stupid."

Sebastian and Max waited patiently to hear what it was. Finally Max had to prompt Cornelius.

"Please feel free to share it with us."

31

"Some . . . meddling pen-pusher . . . some blithering jumped-up idiot . . . pushed through a proclamation stating that every enlisted man in the queen's army had to be . . ."

"Yes?" said Sebastian.

". . . had to be . . . well, of a certain height."

"Oh," said Max and Sebastian together.

Cornelius sat there staring into his coffee mug as though he might find an answer to his troubles in those dark brown depths. It was clear to Sebastian that the little man was fighting a conflict within himself. Clearly he didn't really want to talk about this; at the same time, he quite obviously needed to discuss it with someone.

"I mean, it was ridiculous! My exploits spoke for themselves. I had slain more of the enemy than my entire detachment put together. Nobody was a better fighter, nobody had the skill with a sword that I had. But I was confounded! I even appealed to the queen in person, asking her to exempt me from this ridiculous ruling." Cornelius sighed. "It was to no avail. She spoke to me in private and told me that since she had signed the papers that made the ruling law, then there was nothing she could do. She could not rescind the order. I simply had to leave. But where would I go?"

Max opened his mouth to say, "Keladon," but Sebastian gave him a look which made him abandon the idea.

"Where indeed?" agreed Sebastian, in a sympathetic tone.

"And then one of my men told me about Keladon. He said it had the most powerful army in history, including a special unit called the Crimson Cloak—bodyguards to King Septimus himself! This most celebrated of units is made up of volunteer soldiers from all over the known world. A unit with its own rules, its own laws—and, so far as this man was aware, no height restrictions. I resolved that I would be a part of it. So I set off from Golmira four moons ago, and now here I am, sitting at a campfire and about to have dinner with you two."

"Small world," said Sebastian. Then he winced. "Sorry," he said. "No offense."

"None taken, my friend." Cornelius seemed to make an effort to shrug off his bad memories. "Anyway, that's enough about me. I see that javralat is still a long way from being cooked, so why not give me a sample of your jester's skills? I could certainly use a good laugh after my recent experiences!"

Sebastian and Max exchanged worried glances.

"A good laugh," said Max quietly. "Yes, well, that would be a novelty."

"Hmm. Let me see now . . ." Sebastian thought for a moment, leafing through the imaginary book of jests that he kept stored in his head. Finally he made a selection.

"A man is standing by a river eating a pie. Another man comes along with a little mutt on a lead and the mutt starts to jump up at the first man, after a bit of pie. So the first man says, 'Excuse me, do you mind if I throw your mutt a bit?' The second man says, 'No, not at all!' So the first man picks up the mutt and throws him into the river." Sebastian smiled and waited for a reaction but Cornelius just looked at him blankly.

"That's one of the better ones," Max told him.

"Could the mutt swim?" asked Cornelius.

"Well, I . . . I don't know," said Sebastian, somewhat confused by the question.

"You don't know? Well, you *should* know—you're the one telling the story."

"But . . . it's a joke. Whether the mutt can swim or not has no relevance."

"I beg to differ, sir. If the mutt can swim, it's an amusing tale. If not, it's a tragedy. The mutt will drown and his owner will be heartbroken. Hardly a laughing matter."

"I hadn't really thought of it like that," admitted Sebastian. He considered for a moment. "Very well. The mutt can swim."

Cornelius looked relieved and his baby face split into a grin. "Ha ha, yes, very droll!"

"You think so?"

"Oh yes, once we'd cleared up the business about the mutt. Do you have any other stories?"

Some time passed as Sebastian fired off a series of jokes at Cornelius, but it was hard work. Cornelius always questioned some small detail, which held up the flow of the story. He laughed dutifully when they finally got to the end of each one, but it felt a bit like walking uphill in a gale, and Sebastian was relieved when the javralat was finally cooked. Cornelius split the sizzling carcass down the middle with his knife and the two of them fell to with a vengeance, tearing ravenously into the succulent flesh. After a little while Sebastian became aware of Max gazing at him hopefully.

"What?" he demanded.

"Let's have a bit," pleaded Max.

"You? You can't eat this—you're a vegetarian!"

"I know, but I'm starving!"

"I can get you a bit more mulch if you like."

Max shook his head. "A delightful prospect, but nonetheless, I think I'll settle for a bit of javralat."

Sebastian shrugged. He broke off a large hunk of hot meat and set it down in front of Max.

"I've seen everything now," exclaimed Cornelius. "A buffalope eating meat! Who'd have thought it?"

"Please don't tell anyone," pleaded Max as he tore strips of flesh from the bone with his blunt teeth. "It's probably a hanging offense in Keladon!"

Sebastian and Cornelius threw back their heads and laughed at the guilty expression on his shaggy face.

FIVE

MYSTERIES

With the unfamiliar sensation of having a full stomach, Sebastian settled contentedly back to enjoy the warmth of the fire and the conversation. The clouds had rolled back and the moon rose steadily in the sky like a great ripe cheese veined with blue. Now Sebastian was even more aware of the great stretches of plain that lay all around them. When he turned his head to look, he could see across it for miles and he felt very small and insignificant camped out here in the midst of this unfamiliar landscape.

Cornelius had produced a clay pipe and he sat there, puffing out great clouds of fragrant smoke as he regaled them with stories of his adventures in the army—how he had fought his way across the known world and back again. If his stories were to be believed—and Sebastian was surprised to find that he was already beginning to trust the manling implicitly—then he had led an eventful life indeed.

"There's a whole world out there," he told his two listeners, "more than you would have dreamed possible. Travel in one direction for a long, long distance and eventually you come to a great stretch of water called 'the ocean,' which is further across than you can see even on a clear day. Cross that ocean on a ship and after many moons of traveling you will come to another land on the far side of the water, where the people look different and speak a language you cannot understand. And if you keep going in a straight line, do you know what happens?"

Cornelius and Max both shook their heads.

"Why, you arrive back where you started, of course! Because I have come to understand that the world is shaped like a great ball. We move across its surface like flies on a giant fruit."

"How come we don't fall off when we go too far?" asked Max.

"The same reason flies don't fall off," said Cornelius. "Sticky feet."

Sebastian and Max looked at each other.

"Sticky feet?" echoed Max. "That can't be right. What about when you are in one of those big boats you spoke of. Or are you saying that the bottoms of the boats stick to the surface of the water?"

Cornelius shrugged. "Well, it's a complicated subject, I'll grant you. But nobody yet has offered me a better explanation."

"I've heard one," said Sebastian. "There's an old fellow who hangs around the market in Jerabim—fancies himself as a bit of a seer—"

"Not old Bartimus?" interrupted Max.

Sebastian gave him an indignant look. "Well, yes, actually, but—"

"He's a raving lunatic!"

"I wasn't aware that you knew Bartimus."

"Everyone knows him! He goes around talking to himself."

"That may well be, but he swears that he was told by one of the most learned men in the land that the world is flat and slightly curved, like the surface of a big shield. In fact, it is a big shield, held by a giant warrior called Mungus."

"A giant warrior?" echoed Max.

"Yes. He stands in space with his feet on the back of a huge carpet. This stops him from falling through space—"

"Oh, naturally," said Max. "I can see that would work."

"The waters of the world are pools of rain that have fallen on the shield and as he moves, they slosh about, causing waves and floods and so forth. According to Bartimus, if you were to travel to the very edges of the shield, you would be able to look across a great distance and see Mungus staring down at you. Bartimus reckons that one day Mungus will get tired of holding the shield and will simply fling it into space as hard as he can. When that happens, everyone in the world will perish."

There was a long silence while Max and Cornelius considered this information.

"That's the most ridiculous story I've ever heard," said Cornelius. "How does this Bartimus character explain how I've managed to sail clear around the world and come right back to where I started?"

Sebastian shrugged. "Bartimus says that the very edge of the giant shield has an enchantment upon it that stops you from falling off. So he would probably suggest that you must simply have just gone around the edge of the shield."

"Nonsense! The man's an idiot," said Cornelius. "We sailed straight ahead the whole time, using the stars to guide us. And the captain of our ship was one of the best men in the Golmiran navy. I'm pretty sure he'd have noticed if we'd started deviating from our course."

"Quite right," said Max dismissively. "Old Bartimus hasn't got a clue. Now *I* have heard a theory that's much more interesting than either of yours. The way I heard it, the world is actually a big steel ring through the nose of a gigantic buffalope called Colin. His warm breath gives us the air we breathe, and when he sneezes, we get rain. And—"

"I take it back," Cornelius told Sebastian. "Yours is only the *second* most ridiculous story I've ever heard!"

"I didn't say I believed it," protested Max. "But a lot of buffalopes do, you know—there's a huge following for Colin. They say that when the world ends we'll all go to a wonderful pasture in the sky to be with him."

"I don't believe any of that nonsense," said Cornelius. "I go by what I have seen with my own eyes, what I have heard with my own ears, what I have touched with my own hands. And you mark my words, this world of ours is round. I'd stake my very life on it." He yawned, stretched, gave a long sigh. "By Shadlog's beard, I'm tired," he announced. "I think, gentlemen, that I'm ready for sleep. But first I must answer a call of nature." He got up and strode off into the bushes, where he quickly disappeared from sight.

Max waited a few moments and then spoke in a whisper. "I didn't hear anything calling."

"It's just an expression," said Sebastian.

"Hmm?"

"He's gone for a wee!"

"Oh. Well, why didn't he say so? Listen, are you sure we should be encouraging him to travel with us?"

"Yes, why not? He'll be useful—and he's just provided us with the best meal we've had since we left Jerabim!"

"There are more important things than a full stomach, you know."

"Oh, I'm surprised to hear you say that. You carnivore, you!"

"I'd really rather you didn't go mentioning that to people." Max frowned. "Some of my more zealous brothers and sisters might not understand. They maintain that the eating of flesh is a sin." He thought for a moment. "But seriously, young master, this Cornelius—I don't know. There's just something about him I don't trust."

"You don't trust anybody," said Sebastian as he untied his bedroll.

"We don't know anything about him. He wanders in out of the night with a javralat over his shoulder, offers to share it with us, and we're supposed to believe that makes him a nice chap."

"He *is* a nice chap. You know we elvish people pride ourselves on being able to judge a man's character at a glance."

"Oh yes, like that Berundian who charged us a small fortune for lamp oil and lied to us about finding water. According to you, he was a nice fellow too. You can't always—"

"Shush. He's coming back!"

Cornelius emerged from the bushes, strolled over to the fire and laid himself down on the other side of it. He slid his sword from its scabbard and set it down on the ground beside him.

"Well, my friends, I'll bid you good night," he said. "And I'm sorry you don't trust me, Max, but there's not really very much I can do about that, is there?"

Max winced. "Trust you? Who said I didn't?"

"Voices carry a long way at night, my friend."

There was a particularly awkward silence.

"I think there's a spare blanket in the caravan," ventured Sebastian. "It gets quite chilly at night."

"No need," Cornelius assured him. "After all my years in the army, I could fall asleep naked on a block of ice. In fact, come to think of it, I have, several times!" And with that, Cornelius turned onto his side and, after a few moments, began to snore gently. Sebastian noticed that he slept with one hand on the handle of his sword; and when he looked closer he saw that the manling was quite literally sleeping with one eye open.

"Amazing," he murmured. He glanced at Max and saw that he was lying there with a peeved expression on his face.

"What's wrong now?" he asked.

"You've never offered *me* the spare blanket!" said Max huffily, and he turned his back on Sebastian. The movement caused a big blast of wind to emerge from his rear end.

Sebastian shook his head and the bells on his hat jingled. He took it off and set it to one side, laying it down carefully as though it was some precious relic. He wriggled into his bedroll and lay for a moment, gazing up at the millions of stars glittering in the night sky. Somewhere, far off, a luper howled, a remote and lonely sound.

Sebastian sighed contentedly, relishing the feeling of having a full stomach for the first time in ages. Then he closed his eyes and was fast asleep in moments.

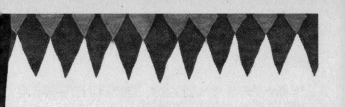

SIX

SKIRMISH

Sebastian opened his eyes and lay blinking up at the morning sky. A moment earlier he had been dreaming that he was performing his act for the court of King Septimus. His audience had sat there dressed in their finery, staring at him expressionlessly as his attempts to elicit a response became ever more frantic. All in all, it was a relief to be awake.

He sat up, stretched, yawned and then turned to look across the still-smoldering embers of the fire, where Cornelius had slept. But he wasn't there.

"Not a sign of him," said Max's voice in his ear. "He was gone when I woke up, *ages* ago. He's probably run off with all our valuables."

"What valuables?" muttered Sebastian, scratching at his side. He turned his head to see that Max was standing by the edge of the bushes, questing hopefully among them for something edible. "Perhaps he changed his mind about traveling with us."

He gave Max an accusatory look. "Probably something to do with the wind last night," he added.

"I don't remember it being windy," said Max.

"You weren't sleeping where I was." Sebastian climbed out of his bedroll, put on his hat and stood up. He scanned the horizon in a full circle but could see no sign of the diminutive warrior. "That's a pity," he said. "I was looking forward to a hearty breakfast."

"And you shall have one!" said Cornelius, popping up out of the bushes with a suddenness that made Max choke on a mouthful of grass. "I've had the good fortune to find a nest full of gallock eggs." He strode forward, showing Sebastian his upturned helmet, which was full to the brim with round blue spheres. "I trust you have a pan we may fry these beauties in?"

"Er . . . yes, of course." Sebastian hurried to the back of the caravan, hoping that he hadn't sounded like he was already taking Cornelius for granted. "What a pleasant surprise," he said. "You must have been searching all morning." He grabbed some kindling and a battered old pan.

"It's just a case of knowing where to look," said Cornelius, sitting beside the fire.

"What kind of bird is a gallock?" asked Max suspiciously.

"No kind of bird at all," replied Cornelius. "Since it's a serpent."

"Serpent's eggs?" cried Max, pulling a face. "Oh, that really is going too far!"

"I can assure you, they are delicious," said Cornelius, taking the kindling from Sebastian and adding it to the fire. "But of course, if you'd prefer mulch, I won't be offended."

Max looked thoughtful. "I suppose one *should* try unfamiliar foods once in a while," he said. "Just for the experience."

In the end Max ate four of the eggs and would have had more if there'd been any left. "They're really rather nice," he exclaimed, licking the last traces from around his mouth. "Considering where they came from."

"Javralat meat, serpent's eggs—let's just hope the unfamiliar diet doesn't have its usual effect on you," said Sebastian as he harnessed Max to the caravan. "Don't forget I'll be sitting right behind you."

"I can't imagine what you mean," said Max primly.

Then it was time to pack up camp and resume their journey.

They set off at a good pace. Cornelius opted to walk alongside the wagon rather than listen to Max's incessant moaning about the extra weight he had to pull. Cornelius thought they were still a good day and a half away from their destination. Somebody had told him that the towers of King Septimus's grand palace were visible from a good distance off, but as yet the horizon was an unbroken horizontal line of pale brown against the clear blue of the sky.

They trudged on for hour after hour and eventually the flat ground gave way to gently rolling hills of grassland that seemed to sway rhythmically in the breeze. Around midday they crested a ridge and noticed something below them in the distance—a thick column of gray smoke rising into the sky—and as they moved steadily nearer, they could just discern what looked like a line of wagons. There was some kind of

45

commotion going on around them that was raising a thick cloud of dust. Cornelius pulled an ancient-looking telescope from his belt and lifted it to his eye. He studied the scene for a moment, then drew in a short, sharp breath.

"Shadlog's teeth!" he exclaimed. He thrust the telescope back, pulled down the visor of his helmet and drew his sword.

"Come on, Sebastian," he said. "Somebody's in trouble!"

"But . . . the caravan . . ."

"It will follow on by itself quite happily. Grab your sword and follow me!"

And he set off at a run, moving at incredible speed for one so small. Sebastian stared after him for a moment, then unsheathed his own sword. He jumped down from the caravan.

"I hope you don't think you're leaving me on my own," protested Max.

"You'll be fine. I can't let Cornelius go into danger unaided, can I?"

"Why not? He's trained at that kind of thing. You, on the other hand . . ."

But Sebastian didn't hear the rest of Max's sentence as he took off after Cornelius, his long thin legs covering the ground at a sprinter's pace. Within a few moments he had caught up with the manling and could have easily overtaken him—but he slowed a little to stay alongside. Now he could clearly see the line of wagons he was running toward; and that they were being attacked by a troop of ragged men riding equines.

"Brigands!" roared Cornelius. "Attacking what looks like a respectable supply column. They'll take no prisoners!"

Sebastian put his head down and concentrated on running. They had quite a distance to cover and part of him didn't really want to get there, because that would mean fighting. He remembered what Max had said about how being able to use a sword was quite a different matter to lopping someone's head off. But it was too late to back down. The next time he looked up, he seemed to be uncomfortably close to the action. Now he could see everything.

The soldiers who had been accompanying the supply column—handsomely equipped men wearing red plumed helmets and bronzed breastplates—had gathered themselves into a protective circle around one rather opulent carriage and were selling their lives dearly to defend it. The two fine equines that had pulled the carriage lay dead, pin-cushioned with arrows, and many of the guards were suffering a similar fate, the ground already littered with their dead. As Sebastian watched, more of them fell victim to the rain of arrows that the Brigands kept firing into them as they rode round and round their victims, yelling like madmen.

"That's not very fair!" yelled Sebastian.

"Welcome to the real world," Cornelius shouted back at him. "Don't worry, we'll soon even up the score."

As the two newcomers approached the action, one of the Brigands, a huge bearded man sitting astride a gray equine, noticed their approach and broke away from his companions to attack Cornelius. He came thundering toward the little warrior at high speed, a huge battle-axe raised to slice him in two. Sebastian felt like shutting his eyes but somehow couldn't. Just

47

as he was thinking that it had been nice knowing Cornelius, the manling performed an extraordinary maneuver, rolling forward and slipping beneath the flying hooves of the equine. Then he launched himself upward, slashing with the blade of his sword into the creature's exposed belly. The equine lost its footing and went tumbling headlong into the dirt, flinging its rider head over heels.

Cornelius didn't hesitate but plunged onward with a blood-curdling cry as more riders broke away from the fight to approach him. Sebastian couldn't watch anymore because he saw that one rider had spotted him and was racing to the attack. Sebastian swallowed hard and tightened his two-handed grip on his father's sword, telling himself that if he must die here, then he should do it well and not show fear, even though he was quaking inside.

The Brigand came galloping toward him, his ugly face painted with stripes of what looked suspiciously like blood. He was laughing and swinging a huge sword above his head. The equine's hooves seemed to shake the very ground that Sebastian was standing on. He desperately tried to remember the advice his father had given him about situations like this:

Let your opponent make the first move but anticipate it. Once you have evaded his blow, make your move and don't hesitate for a second!

The Brigand came alongside him and leaned over in the saddle to take a swipe. As he lashed out, Sebastian swayed sideways and the tip of the sword hissed a deadly arc a few inches from his right ear; then he swung back and slashed with his own blade, feeling it bite clean through the rider's chain-mail

vest at his waist. The equine raced on, but as Sebastian turned to look, the rider tipped sideways in his saddle and went crashing heavily into the dirt. He lay there, writhing in agony, blood seeping through his vest.

Sebastian felt a sudden rush of exhilaration go through him. He'd done it! He'd faced a Brigand in mortal combat and emerged victorious! He opened his mouth to give a shout of triumph, but in that instant something heavy slammed into his back, driving the breath out of his lungs. He went sprawling to the ground, in total confusion, rolled over several times and came to rest lying on his back, his sword no longer in his hand. He looked up and saw a huge, barrel-chested Brigand approaching him, giving him a gap-toothed grin. He was brandishing the heavy club with which he had just struck Sebastian, and it was clear from the way he swaggered closer that he had every intention of using it again.

Sebastian looked desperately around for his sword and saw it lying a short distance away. If he could just clear his thoughts enough to make a dive for it—but the Brigand was shaking his ugly, bearded head.

"Forget it, Elf-man. It's not going to happen," he said. He came closer, the club raised to strike.

Sebastian lay there, only vaguely aware of a strange thundering that seemed to shake the very ground beneath him. He steeled himself for the killing blow and offered up a quick prayer that his father would be there to meet him in the next world. But the blow never came.

Instead, a huge horned head lurched into view, striking the

Brigand full in his chest and sending him tumbling across the ground like a broken doll.

"Max!" Sebastian looked up delightedly, but such was the impetus of the caravan that the buffalope could not stop, and he went racing crazily past, the wheels missing Sebastian by inches. The stunned Brigand was just struggling back to his feet when Max and the caravan trampled him flat and thundered on into the thick of the battle, leaving a cloud of dust in their wake. Sebastian shook his head and got back to his feet. He retrieved his sword and ran after the caravan into the dust cloud.

Suddenly he was immersed in a strange half-lit chaos of fighting, struggling men. A Brigand with a huge horned helmet came lurching at him out of the dust and Sebastian reacted instinctively, slashing at the man's helmet with his sword. He felt the impact of the blow all along the length of his arm and the man dropped backward out of sight. Sebastian stood there, staring at his sword in amazement.

"Ha, ha, that's the spirit, lad!" roared a voice down by his hip, and he saw Cornelius go running past. He was spattered with blood and dirt, but looked as though he was having the time of his life. "I think I've dealt with all their archers. Now, come with me. Must be something pretty valuable in that carriage!"

Sebastian followed the little warrior without question and found himself a short distance away from the opulent carriage. The last of the guards had just fallen to the swords of the Brigands and now one of them, a huge, barechested, shavenheaded man with a goatee beard, was triumphantly reaching out to pull aside the satin curtains that covered the doorway. As

51

he did so, a large clay pot came flying out of the gloom and hit him full in the face, knocking him backward to the floor. He lay there stunned for a moment, then grunted in surprise as first Cornelius and then Sebastian used his chest as a convenient springboard to launch themselves up onto the wooden steps of the carriage. They turned at bay, their swords raised to defend the curtained doorway, and found themselves confronted by a half-circle of scowling, armed-to-the-teeth warriors.

There was a long and terrible silence as the Brigands gathered themselves for the onslaught.

This is it, thought Sebastian. *We can't fight them all. We're done for.*

SEVEN

SOME STUPID GIRL

The silence continued for what seemed an age.

Cornelius looked slowly around at the half-circle of savages, letting them see the determination in his eyes. Then he spoke in a commanding tone.

"Brigands, hear my words! I, Captain Cornelius Drummel, have killed many of your number today, and be sure that I will kill every one of you who tries to put a foot upon this step."

"Archers!" shouted one of the Brigands. "Come forward and shoot these two idiots!"

There was another silence while everyone waited for an archer to appear, but it quickly became apparent that one wasn't going to show up.

"I took the precaution of killing all your archers," Cornelius told them. "I find them such a nuisance in a situation like this. And before you waste time looking for a bow, let me assure you that I always cut through the strings. I don't believe in unfair advantages."

There were worried murmurs at this news. The Brigands were looking this way and that, assuring themselves that it was true. They really didn't have a single archer left.

"My advice to you gentlemen," said Cornelius, "would be to take what booty you can salvage from the rest of these wagons and leave, while your heads still sit firmly upon your shoulders."

Now there was a murmur of conversation amongst the Brigands. Then one of them, a squat, red-bearded man with plaited hair and crudely executed body tattoos, shouted back.

"Those are big words from such a little, little man!"

There was some laughter at this remark but it faded quickly when Cornelius made his reply.

"Little I may be, but by Shadlog's bones, I'm man enough to cut off your ugly head without raising a sweat."

"Cut it off? You couldn't even reach it!"

More laughter from the mob, but Cornelius simply smiled. "Don't take my word for it!" he shouted. "Please, step up here and find out for yourself."

There were shouts of encouragement from Red Beard's companions and he looked around at them for moral support, before shrugging his powerful shoulders, hefting his huge double-handed sword and stepping forward to meet Cornelius.

"Take a step back, Sebastian," said Cornelius calmly; and Sebastian did as he was told.

Watching the scene, Sebastian would have sworn that Cornelius barely moved. The manling gave an almost imperceptible flick of his wrist, the silver blade blurred into motion and the big man grunted in surprise, clutching at his stomach. He dropped to his knees, bringing his head into range of Cornelius's sword. Cornelius whirled round, the blade flashed a second time and the man's body crumpled slowly to the ground, while his head bounced down the steps and rolled back toward his comrades, a surprised expression on its face. The Brigands all stood there staring down at it in stunned amazement.

"Does anybody else fancy their chances?" roared Cornelius. But evidently nobody did. Muttering and cursing, the Brigands turned away and began to trudge toward the other wagons.

"Cowards!" snapped Cornelius, spitting in their general direction. "Come on, supposing I tie one hand behind my back, how about that?"

There were still no takers.

"Never did come across a Brigand who had much aptitude for hand-to-hand combat," growled Cornelius. "A pity—I was just getting warmed up." He glanced at Sebastian and winked. "You acquitted yourself well, lad. We may make a soldier of you yet. Now, I'll stay here just in case any of those barbarians decide to come back for another try. You nip inside and see what it was that those guards sacrificed their lives to defend."

Sebastian nodded.

He turned, pulled back the curtains and stepped into the gloomy interior, remembering as he did so that the last person who had tried to enter had been treated rather harshly. In the same instant, something hard crashed down on his head with terrible force, knocking him to the floor. He crouched for a moment on his hands and knees, a myriad of multicolored lights dancing around inside his skull, glad that he'd still been wearing his jester's hat, which had absorbed some of the impact. He was vaguely aware that somebody was approaching, doubtless intent on making another attack. Without hesitation he launched himself headlong at the dimly perceived figure, knocking it backward into the depths of the carriage. His arms closed around somebody's shoulders, there was a sudden clatter as a heavy object struck the floor, and then the figure was tipping backward onto what felt like a feather bed and struggling to escape his grasp.

He lifted a fist to strike but it suddenly occurred to him that this adversary was a good deal more fragrant than the Brigands he had encountered outside. His upraised hand brushed against a velvet drape, so he grabbed at it and tore it down, allowing a sudden flush of light to enter the interior.

He found he was crouched on top of a girl—a beautiful one at that. She lay there glaring up at him, her green eyes narrowed to slits of anger, her full red mouth arranged into a disapproving scowl.

"Take your hands off me, imbecile!" she shrieked. "How dare you touch me?"

Sebastian frowned, but released his hold and moved back off what he could now see was a silken couch.

"Sorry," he said. "I thought—"

"I don't care what you thought!"

"Are you all right in there, lad?" he heard Cornelius shout.

"Uh . . . yes, I'm fine. It's just some stupid girl who tried to brain me with a"—he looked around a moment and found the culprit lying on the ground—"a chamber pot." Thankfully, it appeared that the rather fancy porcelain pot had been empty when she had used it.

"*Some stupid girl!*" she cried, looking absolutely horrified. "How dare you? When my uncle hears of this outrage, he'll have you and those other Brigands hunted down like—"

"Hey, whoa, just a minute!" Sebastian glared at her. "I'm no Brigand! In case you weren't listening, my friend Cornelius and I just saved you from that rabble. We . . . we rescued you." His own words surprised him. He had not until this moment realized that this was what they had actually done.

"Really?" She looked far from impressed. "And where are my guards?"

Sebastian frowned. "All dead, I'm afraid."

"Oh. I see." The girl looked aside for a moment as though she could hardly believe her own ears. "What? Every last one of them?"

"I believe so. We haven't really had time to look properly. We were just trying to work out what it was the soldiers were guarding so tenaciously. Have you got treasure in here?"

The girl stared at him. "They were guarding *me*, you cretin. Have you any idea who I am?"

"Umm—somebody with a pretty high opinion of herself, judging by the fuss you're making."

The girl stood up, her hands on her hips. She glowered at him. "I am Princess Kerin of Keladon."

"Keladon! Oh, that's a coincidence, that's where we . . ."

Sebastian's voice trailed off as he registered fully what she'd said. "I'm sorry, did you say, er . . . *Princess*?"

"Yes, you oaf. Princess Kerin. King Septimus is my uncle."

It took a while, but Princess Kerin eventually calmed down enough to accompany Sebastian outside, where they found Cornelius still guarding the doorway. It was clear from the sheepish expression on his baby face that he had heard every word. He immediately turned to face her.

"I am your humble servant, Your Highness," he said, and bowed his head in reverence.

"There's no need for that," she told him irritably. "You can stand up."

"I *am* standing up," said Cornelius humbly.

"Oh yes, so you are! Gosh, you're really rather small, aren't you?"

"Small of stature, but with the heart of a giant, Princess. I am from Golmira, the kingdom of the—"

"Whatever." Princess Kerin clapped her immaculately manicured hands together. "So—what's happening out here, then?"

"The Brigands are looting the supply wagons, Your Highness. I thought it best to allow them that in exchange for sparing this carriage. And just here, I'm afraid, is where your noble Royal Guard made their final stand."

He indicated the litter of dead men sprawled around the entrance to the carriage. Princess Kerin looked down at them and her eyes widened in shock. She looked for all the world like somebody who had just awakened from a terrible nightmare.

"Dead?" she whispered, as though unfamiliar with the word. "How could they be dead? They . . . they . . ."

"They gave their lives to protect you," said Sebastian.

She nodded. "They were brave men. I would ask you to collect up the insignia of each of them. When I get back to Keladon, I shall write to each of their families and—"

Her voice choked up and for an instant tears filled her eyes; but she seemed to make a conscious effort to pull herself together. She lifted her gaze from the dead men to a couple of hairy villains who were rifling through a large trunk that they'd pulled from a nearby caravan. One of them had found a frilly gown and was holding it up against his hairy chest, as though considering trying it on. She seemed to steel herself and a hard expression came into her eyes. She seemed, once again, cool and imperious.

"If you hadn't come along when you did, I'd probably be a captive by now," she murmured. "Nasty, filthy brutes! Probably haven't bathed for weeks, and I bet they never clean their teeth." She turned back to look at Sebastian and Cornelius and the tears were quite gone. Sebastian was astonished by this sudden transformation. "It seems I'm in your debt," she said calmly. She glared at Sebastian. "So I'll overlook the fact that you jumped on me."

"It was self-defense," retorted Sebastian. "You hit me with a—"

"Your Highness, may I ask how you came to be out here in this desolate place?" interrupted Cornelius, trying to head off a potential row.

"Oh, that was my uncle's idea. He sent me off as part of a deputation to meet Queen Helena of Bodengen, which borders our lands. She has this supposedly handsome son, Rolf, who she's anxious to get married off. Uncle Septimus seemed to think it would be useful if I got to know him. Has his mind on some kind of alliance, I think." The princess rolled her eyes as though it was all too much effort to even talk about. "*Anyway*, I'd seen a painting of Rolf and he *did* look quite hunky, so I agreed to go."

"Well, *naturally*," said Sebastian, but she didn't seem to notice his sarcasm.

"When I got there, I discovered that the court painter had made Rolf look considerably more attractive than he actually was. He'd neglected to record the missing teeth and the sloping forehead. So I insisted that we come straight back, and that's when those awful Brigands ambushed us." She sighed. "I suppose I should have listened to the captain."

"The captain?" echoed Cornelius.

"Of the Royal Guard. A lot of his men had fallen ill and were unable to accompany us. He said we should wait a few days, until they were back up to strength—but I insisted on leaving straightaway. I'd promised Uncle Septimus that I'd be back for my birthday."

"Your birthday?" Sebastian raised his eyebrows.

"Yes. My seventeenth. It's tomorrow."

Sebastian could scarcely believe his ears. "So, let me get this straight. All these men died . . . because you wanted to get back for your birthday?"

"Uncle Septimus was quite insistent," said Princess Kerin. "And how was I to know that we would encounter Brigands? Uncle Septimus said that he had a special surprise for me and urged me not to delay."

"Very nice, I'm sure," snarled Sebastian. "And I hope worth the lives of—"

"We shall of course accompany you back to Keladon," interrupted Cornelius hastily. "To ensure your safekeeping. But we have a few preparations to make. Please bear with us while we get things organized."

"But Cornelius!" Sebastian was indignant. "She—"

"We'll, er . . . go and see what needs to be done! Why don't you return to your quarters, Your Highness, and leave this rough work to us?"

Princess Kerin frowned, then shrugged. "Very well," she said. "But don't be long. I get bored very easily."

She turned and slipped back in through the curtained doorway. Sebastian made to follow her, his mouth open to say something else, but Cornelius clutched the hem of his singlet and dragged him down the stairs.

"Cornelius! What are you—?"

The manling said nothing but continued to pull him across the plain, stepping carefully in and out of the fallen soldiers. When they were a decent distance away, he stopped and looked up at Sebastian.

"You need to cool down a bit," he observed in hushed tones.

"But didn't you hear her? She said—"

"I *know* what she said," hissed Cornelius fiercely. "And yes, she's decidedly spoiled and quite annoying. But don't forget, she's a princess."

"A spoiled brat, more like," growled Sebastian. "Why, for two pins I'd put her across my knee and—"

"—and she'd have you hanged in the market square in

61

Keladon for the amusement of the population. The likes of us don't go criticizing the likes of her and you'd do well to remember that. From here on in, we just say, 'Yes, Your Highness, at your service, Your Highness!' and do as we're told. The last thing we need is for her to take offense at us."

Sebastian scowled. "It isn't going to be easy," he observed.

"No, but it'll be worth it. Let's face it, if we can return her safe and sound to her uncle, he's sure to be grateful. That could do us a lot of good, considering we're both seeking employment at his court. And don't forget, he won't be king for much longer. In a short while, when Kerin comes of age, she will ascend to the throne."

"Kerin? Queen of Keladon? But how—?"

"Because her parents are both dead. Her uncle is merely minding the throne until she is of age. I assumed you knew all this."

Sebastian shook his head. "My father never mentioned it. I doubt that he knew any more than the fact that there was a rich king who needed a jester." He thought for a moment. "So she's an orphan?"

"Yes; and soon to become the most powerful woman in the land. So let's forget about your personal opinion of her and see if we can round up a couple of equines to harness to that fancy carriage of hers."

The mention of the word "harness" reminded Sebastian of something.

"Max . . . ," he murmured. "Have you seen him lately?"

"Not since he went racing past me, dragging your caravan behind him. He was going like the wind!"

Sebastian lifted his head and gazed hopefully left and right across the plain, but at first he could see no trace of his old friend. A wave of apprehension swept over him. Supposing he had been taken by Brigands? He remembered about their liking for buffalope meat. But after a few moments of frantic searching he spotted Max plodding slowly back toward him, pulling the caravan, which appeared to be largely undamaged after its rough handling.

"There he is," he said, relieved.

"But there's something wrong," said Cornelius quietly.

Sebastian noticed that Max was moving slowly, lifting his feet with apparent difficulty, his head lowered until his nose skimmed the ground. As he drew closer, Sebastian saw with a jolt of horror that an arrow was sticking out of the buffalope's left flank.

"Max!" he cried. Horrified, he ran across the intervening distance and flung his arms around the buffalope's shaggy neck. "You've been hurt!"

Max looked at Sebastian with mournful eyes. "They shot me!" he murmured. "Those ignorant savages fired an arrow into me. I . . . I'm done for. It's all over for me, young master. I can feel my life blood draining away."

"No," gasped Sebastian. "No, you'll be all right. You're strong . . ."

But Max shook his horned head. "It is not to be, my young friend." He gasped as though a sudden pain had washed over him. "My race is run and I . . . I feel my ancestors calling to me." He stared up at the blue sky. "They call me now to the eternal

63

pasture. After a life of toil, who can deny me a little rest?" He looked into Sebastian's eyes, which were filling with tears. "No, don't cry for me, young master. This is not a time for grief! Dry your eyes and look to the future. When I finally meet your father, I shall tell him he has a son to be proud of. And my spirit will watch over you on the remainder of your journey."

"Max, please don't speak like this." Now Sebastian was weeping openly. "We'll get you fixed up. I'll find herbs and make a poultice. With a few days' rest you'll be all right. You've still got years ahead of you."

"If only that were so." Max gave a little sigh and his eyelids fluttered. "But I feel the darkness creeping over me."

Sebastian shook his head. "Please, old friend. Please don't leave me!"

"I . . . I must. Speak well of me when I am gone. Tell everyone you meet that you once knew a buffalope who was a fine and noble—Oww!"

He broke off suddenly as Cornelius reached up on tiptoe and wrenched the arrow out of his side. "Do you mind?" he protested. "I was just making my dying speech."

"You're not dying," Cornelius told him flatly. "This thing barely broke the skin. It'd take more than that to get through your tough old hide."

"But—it's a mortal wound," protested Max.

"Mortal wound, my backside," said Cornelius bluntly. "It's a scratch. I've never heard such a fuss in all my born days." He tossed the arrow aside and moved away in search of some equines to pull the royal carriage.

Sebastian gave Max a withering look. "A mortal wound," he said, through gritted teeth. "Life blood draining away. Honestly!" He turned and began to walk after Cornelius.

"Well, it *felt* like a mortal wound!" shouted Max indignantly. "It was quite deep, actually."

"Cornelius said it was nothing."

"That . . . that's easy for him to say. He's not the one with an arrow sticking out of him. It . . . it could have been poisoned! You didn't think about that, did you? Even now, I could be doomed. Doomed!"

Sebastian caught up with Cornelius, who was having a quiet chuckle.

"He's got some imagination, that one," he observed.

Sebastian dashed the tears from his eyes with his sleeve. "That is absolutely the last time I listen to him," he said. "I really thought for a minute he was—" He shook his head. Somehow he couldn't bring himself to say the word "dying," as though saying it might somehow make it happen. "He saved my life back there, you know. Charged down a Brigand who was moving in for the kill. I . . . I don't know what I'd do without Max. He's always been there, ever since I was a baby."

Cornelius slapped him heartily on the hip. "Come on," he said. "Let's round up those equines and get this show back on the road. We've still got quite a journey ahead of us."

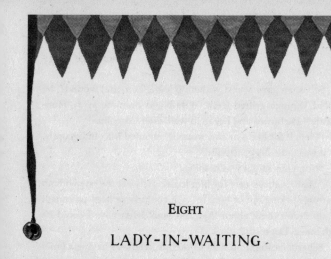

EIGHT

LADY-IN-WAITING

It took them quite some time to hunt down the equines. They were warriors' mounts, unused to the arduous task of pulling a heavy wagon, but they would have to do. Max, meanwhile, seemed to have accepted that his recent wound was not life threatening and announced himself ready to continue.

Sebastian and Cornelius were just making a few last-minute repairs to Max's harness, which had been damaged in the skirmish, when Princess Kerin came stalking over, looking decidedly impatient.

"Aren't we ready to go yet?" she demanded tetchily. "I'm bored!"

Cornelius bowed his head and elbowed Sebastian's leg to make him do likewise. "Very nearly, Your Highness," he assured her. "Just a few final preparations to make and we'll be on our way. I am, however, somewhat concerned—"

"Concerned, little man? About what?"

"Well . . . the equines we've managed to find, they're very

skittish and unused to heavy work. I worry that they might bolt or, worse still, overturn the carriage. It would be ironic, would it not, to have saved you from the Brigands, only to put your life in danger again?"

"Hmm." Princess Kerin considered for a moment, studying the colorful design on the side of Sebastian's wagon as she did so. Then she brightened a little. "No matter, I will ride with the elfling," she said.

Sebastian glared at her. "What?" he said, horrified. Then, after another nudge from Cornelius, he attempted to moderate his tone. "But . . . Your Highness, my humble caravan is not really suitable for somebody of breeding. . . ."

"I realize that," she assured him. "But I'm sick and tired of silence and would have some conversation." She gestured at the title on the caravan. "Besides, a self-proclaimed Prince of Fools should at least be good for a little entertainment. I'll just get my travel cloak." She turned and walked back toward her carriage.

Sebastian stared after her glumly. "Oh, that's just perfect," he said. "Now I'll be stuck with her for the rest of the journey."

"Don't tell her any of your own jokes," said Max. "If you absolutely must tell one, stick to your father's material. It's safer."

"And keep a civil tongue in your head," Cornelius reminded him. "We need to stay in her good books."

"Yes, all right, all right! Honestly, you two act as though I don't know how to talk to people. I'm a jester, don't forget. I have the gift of the gab!"

Max and Cornelius exchanged worried glances.

"We're doomed," muttered Max wearily. "We are most definitely doomed."

*   *   *

They were on the move again, but Sebastian was somewhat perturbed. Why had Princess Kerin forsaken the comfort of her own carriage to ride alongside him? And why did she insist on asking so many stupid questions?

She sat beside him now, chattering on about various bits of nonsense like some gossiping shepherd girl—not at all regal as he'd always imagined a princess should be, but noisy and irritating. Oh, she was pretty enough, perhaps more than just pretty. But so spoiled! If she hadn't been who she was, Sebastian would gladly have pushed her off the caravan into the dust.

The landscape was changing, the lush rolling grasslands occasionally dotted with small copses of tall slender trees. The higher branches were thickly hung with clusters of dark red fruit, and flocks of big black birds were competing noisily for it, their cawing a hideous shriek overhead.

Sebastian leaned out from his seat and glanced back at Cornelius, hunched in the driver's seat of the carriage, trying to keep the two frisky equines under control as he followed in Sebastian's tracks. Even at this distance the manling's face held a certain expression, as though silently reminding Sebastian to watch what he said. Meanwhile, Princess Kerin kept right on yapping.

". . . so I said to her, the color of a dress may be of no importance to you, my dear, but when it comes to matters of the court, I like to think I know what I'm talking about. She soon quietened down, I can tell you!"

Sensing a pause, Sebastian swung back into an upright position. "I'm sorry?" he said. "Your Highness," he added, as an afterthought.

"I do believe you weren't even listening to me!" said Princess Kerin crossly.

"I . . . I was just . . . I thought those equines were going to start playing up. Please, do go on, Princess, it's . . . fascinating. It's not every day a simple man like myself has the opportunity to learn about a royal court."

But the princess was glowering at him like a spoiled child. "You're not really a man at all, are you?" she observed flatly. "Not in the usual sense of the word. I believe you're what people call a 'breed.'"

Sebastian felt his face color a little but he made a heroic effort to remain courteous. "My mother is elvish," he told her. "So I have some of her features. And also some from my father, a human."

"I wonder what made him want to marry an elf," she said.

"I imagine he was in love with her," suggested Sebastian, a little more coldly than he had intended.

"Was? Isn't he in love with her anymore?"

"My father's dead, Princess. He died a little while ago."

She looked rather uncomfortable at this news. She gazed off into the middle distance for a moment, where a large flock of the black birds were flapping noisily in the branches of a tree.

"I'm sorry to hear that," she said. "I know what it's like to lose a parent. In my case, it was both of them, and I was so young. . . ." A disturbed look flickered briefly across her face, as though she was remembering bad times, but then she seemed to shrug the thoughts away. "What did your father do?" she asked.

"He was a jester, like me. Or rather, I'm like him. At least, I'm trying to be."

"And are *you* in love, Mr. Darke?"

He laughed nervously. Now it was his turn to feel uncomfortable. "No," he said. "Not yet, anyway." He smiled. "But one day, I'm sure I shall feel as my father did about my mother."

"Love!" She rolled her eyes. "The poets at court are always prattling on about that. I sometimes wonder if there's any such thing. I think poets invented it just to have something to write about." She frowned. "And is she lovely, this mother of yours?"

"I think so," said Sebastian. "But what boy would not say that of his own mother?"

"She's given you some interesting features, though," the princess observed. "You have quite handsome eyes. And I rather like those pointed ears."

Now Sebastian didn't know what to say. He could feel his face reddening even more and he pretended to be occupied with the reins he was holding. After a few moments he stole a glance at her but looked quickly away when he saw she was still studying him with her vivid green eyes. He had to admit to himself that she was extraordinarily beautiful. A pity that she was so silly and shallow.

"So . . . ," she said, after a rather uncomfortable pause. "You're hoping to find employment with my uncle. As a jester."

Sebastian nodded. "Yes. Is he . . . the humorous sort, your uncle?"

"Not so you'd notice. He's rather fond of sarcasm, but I doubt if that counts. He's . . ." The princess seemed to search for the right words for a moment. "He's an enigma, my uncle

71

Septimus. It's not always easy to get into his head. He is very fond of me, of course, very protective. I imagine if I put in a word for you, it would carry a lot of weight with him."

Sebastian glanced at her hopefully. "And would you be prepared to do that?" he asked her.

She shrugged. "Well, I don't know. That would depend on whether you're funny or not. You haven't exactly been a load of laughs so far, have you? Why don't you give me a few samples of your, er . . . art?"

Sebastian was uncomfortably aware that Max had just thrown a mournful look over his shoulder, but did his best to ignore it.

"Well," he said. "Let me see now. . . ." He searched his mental store for something he thought might possibly appeal to her. Finally he happened on a story that he thought might have some chance of making her smile. "Did you hear the one about the man who was walking along the street and his hat blew off? And he was about to pick it up, but this other fellow came along with a mutt walking beside him, and the mutt ran over and tore the hat to shreds. So the man went to the mutt's owner and he says, 'Look what your mutt has done to my hat!' So the other fellow shrugs and says, 'Well, what do I care? Clear off!' The man is disgusted. He says, 'Now look here, I don't like your attitude.' And the other fellow says, 'Well, it's not my hat he chewed!'"

There was the customary long silence that usually followed one of his stories and he began to resign himself to yet another failure—but then suddenly, unexpectedly, something quite extraordinary happened. Princess Kerin tilted back her head and laughed. And it wasn't a feeble chuckle, or a halfhearted snigger. No, it was a genuine laugh, full of merriment.

"That's very good," she said, when her laughter had subsided a little. And she seemed to mean every word of it.

Sebastian was so taken aback, he nearly fell out of his seat. He looked over at Max, who was staring back again, this time with a bewildered expression on his face.

"You . . . you really thought it was funny?" ventured Sebastian.

"Of course! 'Attitude.' 'Hat he chewed!' That's brilliant. Tell me some more."

Scarcely believing his luck, Sebastian tried her with some more jokes. Each one was rewarded with a more enthusiastic response, until by the fifth one she was virtually helpless with laughter, tears streaming down her lovely face.

"Stop," she cried. "I'll wee myself!"

This was such an unprincesslike thing to say that Sebastian felt quite shocked but, in a strange way, delighted. He found that he was warming to Princess Kerin in a way he could never have imagined possible. He smiled and gave Max an enthusiastic flick on the rump with the reins.

"Let's not get carried away," he heard the buffalope say—but Sebastian was too pleased to care.

"So . . . how do you remember them all?" asked Princess Kerin, once she had got herself under control.

"I just memorize them," he told her.

"I'm useless at telling jokes," she said. "I always get the details wrong. It'll be nice to have somebody at court who can liven things up a bit. It can be terribly stuffy being a princess."

"You'll be queen soon," Sebastian reminded her.

"Yes." Her good humor seemed to evaporate and she looked suddenly very serious. "I can't say I'm looking forward to it.

73

I've known since I was a little girl that I'd have to do it sooner or later, but it always seemed so far away. Now, all of a sudden, it's crept up on me. Tomorrow's my birthday and then it's just one short year away."

"A lot can happen in a year," said Sebastian.

"I suppose it can. But still, it seems too close for comfort. I hope I'll be a good queen." She gave him a curious sidelong look. "What do you think?" she asked.

Tricky one, that.

"I . . . wouldn't have the first idea," he said. "I don't really know what's involved." He felt slightly emboldened by the fact that she had liked his jokes and made an uncharacteristically forthright remark. "I suppose it always helps if a queen is beautiful. And . . . you're certainly that."

She gave him a questioning look and then shook her head. "You're just saying that because you think it will get you a job," she said.

"No, I mean it . . . you are. Really." His face was burning again, and he found it very difficult to look at her.

"Gosh," she said. "Nobody's ever said I'm beautiful before."

"I find that hard to believe," he said.

"Oh, people have said I'm regal and full of majesty and other piffle like that. But nobody's used that word." She looked at him thoughtfully. "What about my nose?" she asked him.

"Your . . . nose?"

"Yes. It has a bit of a twist to it. See?"

He was obliged to look her directly in the face and was aware of her eyes boring into his own. "Umm . . . I . . . I can't see anything wrong with it. Your nose. It's . . . proud."

"That's just a nice way of saying it's too big!" she protested.

"No, it's perfect. On your face, no other nose would sit as well. It's . . . really a very, very nice nose."

There was a long silence while they sat there staring at each other, a moment that was rudely interrupted by the sound of Max breaking wind.

" 'Scuse me," he said. But the spell was shattered. Sebastian and Princess Kerin turned away from each other and fixed their gazes on the way ahead.

"Well, I'm sure that there's a lot more to being a queen than having a proud nose," she said at last. "I understand you need certain qualities."

"Honesty," said Sebastian, and immediately regretted it.

"What do you mean?" she demanded, rather sharply.

"Er . . . well, I think that's probably something that a queen might need, to . . . rule wisely. And, er . . . I was thinking . . ." His voice trailed off as he realized he was overstepping the mark. "It's . . . none of my business really."

"No, go on with what you were about to say. I insist."

Sebastian felt as though he were growing steadily smaller in his seat but it was too late to evade the issue. "It was the way you behaved when you discovered that your guards had been killed. For a moment it looked like you were genuinely upset— there were real tears in your eyes—but then you did something to make yourself all hard, like you didn't really care."

Princess Kerin glared at him. "What if I did?" she protested.

"Well, Your Highness . . . I'm only saying. There's no shame in shedding tears for those who have died. We wouldn't have thought any the less of you."

"I see." All the warmth had gone out of Princess Kerin's voice now. "So you're saying I'm dishonest. That I show a false image to the world."

"It wasn't really my place to say anything," said Sebastian glumly.

"Too right it wasn't! You realize, of course, that I could have you executed on the spot when we arrive at our destination."

"But . . . I . . . Princess, we saved your life!"

"You needn't think that counts for anything. Of all the presumptuous—" Her temper seemed to suddenly tip over a precipice into a chasm of spite. "Who are you, anyway, to be criticizing somebody like me? A jumped-up jester in an ill-fitting outfit who tells pathetic stories for a living."

"You seemed to think they were quite funny!" muttered Sebastian.

"It was sympathy. I just felt sorry for you!"

"Please, Your Highness, I didn't mean—"

"I don't care what you meant! Well, I'm not staying here to be insulted." She turned aside and jumped down from her seat.

"Princess, please! Where are you going?"

"To my own carriage," she snarled, and began to march away, her hands on her hips.

"But it's not safe! The equines . . ."

She ignored him. Leaning out, he saw that she was approaching Cornelius, who was looking at her with a baffled expression on his face. He was about to rein in the equines, but she simply made a leap for it, clambered up the swaying steps of the carriage and disappeared inside.

Sebastian dropped back down into his seat with a groan and buried his face in his hands.

There was a long silence as the caravan moved on across the hillside. Then Max said: "Well. That could have gone better."

Sebastian looked down at the buffalope's swaying rump. "Please," he said. "This is not a good time—"

"I mean, it was all going so well! You had her eating out of your hand. Unbelievable as it may seem, she was even laughing at your jokes! And then, just when everything was looking perfect, when all you had to do was butter her up a bit, what did you do? You criticized her! You said she wasn't fit to be queen."

"I know! I can't think what came over me. But, you know, deep down inside, she probably knows I'm right."

Max looked back over his shoulder, a long, pitying look. "We'll try to draw comfort from that when we're being executed in the town square," he said grimly.

"Oh, it won't come to that," Sebastian assured him. "After all, we rescued her, didn't we?"

But Max made no reply and they plodded on in stony silence.

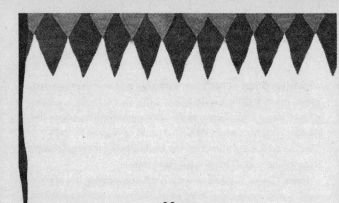

NINE

TEARS BEFORE BEDTIME

The sun was setting once again, and above the treetops to the west, the sky was piled with great columns of bloodred cloud. There was something else too: the tip of a spire rising sheer into the air. To be visible at such a distance it must surely have been the highest building in all creation.

They were tantalizingly close and yet, Cornelius decided, not close enough. He shouted that they should make camp for one more night and finish their journey the following morning.

The copses of trees had grown steadily more widespread as they'd journeyed through the day, until now they were following a path that led through what was little short of woodland. They came to a large clearing and saw what had to be the most welcome sight of all. A stream was meandering through it, the first water they'd seen since they'd started across the plains. Sebastian brought the caravan to a halt and Cornelius pulled up alongside him, an accusatory expression on his baby face.

"What did you say to her?" he hissed angrily, but Sebastian ignored him. He jumped down from the caravan and un-hitched Max, who made a beeline for the stream and began to drink deeply.

"Now who says you can't trust Berundians?" asked Sebastian, slapping him playfully on the rump.

Max lifted his head briefly, water dripping from his mouth. "Yes, but we didn't find it till we were nearly in Keladon," he retorted. "And stop trying to divert attention from the fact that you have made a blunder."

"Thanks for the sympathy," muttered Sebastian.

Cornelius appeared from around the back of the carriage. He was slotting together a series of jointed metal pieces, which fitted into a set of leather compartments in his belt. As Sebastian watched, he assembled a beautiful miniature crossbow.

"Had this made for me by a master craftsman in Golmira," he said. "No good for hunting javralats but great for food on the wing." He pointed up at the restless black shapes moving in the trees.

"Supper," he announced. "You get a fire going, I'll pick off a couple of those beauties. They look like they should make good eating. We might try tasting some of that fruit too. It would make a welcome change from meat." He looked up at Sebastian again. "The princess seemed very upset," he whispered. "I tried calling in to her several times along the way but she didn't even deign to answer me."

"Look. Forget about it," snapped Sebastian. "I really don't want to talk about this."

"Suit yourself." Cornelius wandered off into the trees, looking

79

up at the branches above him, which were silhouetted by the red light of dusk. Sebastian, meanwhile, inspected the wound in Max's flank, which looked sore but not infected.

"No need for mulch tonight," he said, with forced jollity. "The grass here looks pretty tasty."

Max sighed. "The condemned beast ate a hearty meal," he muttered, and moved away from the stream to browse on the lush grass beside it.

"Oh, come on," said Sebastian. "It might not be as bad as all that." He looked thoughtfully toward Princess Kerin's carriage, where a dull wash of yellow light glowed from under the curtained doorway.

Up in the trees there was a sudden swish of air and a black shape plummeted from the topmost branches to hit the ground with a thud.

"Looks like your supper's sorted out," observed Max.

Sebastian hurried to the wagon to fetch some kindling. He was hungry again and the big birds would take some time cooking.

A short while later Sebastian and Cornelius were sitting at the campfire, watching the carcasses of two plump birds turning on the spit and dripping fat into the flames. They had tried a couple of pieces of the crimson fruit as an appetizer but it tasted rather sour and they had quickly abandoned the idea of a healthy alternative to meat. There was still no sign of Princess Kerin, and Cornelius was beginning to worry about her. He kept throwing nervous glances toward her carriage, then looking accusingly at Sebastian.

"She must be starving in there," he said. "One of us should at least try and persuade her to come out for some supper."

"Be my guest," said Sebastian quickly. "I've already felt the sharp edge of her tongue, thank you very much."

"Yes, but look, it's your fault she's in there."

"Oh? How do you figure that out?"

"Because you questioned her ability to be queen."

Sebastian glared at him. "I . . . How did you . . . ?" He turned to look at Max, who was suddenly very occupied with munching grass. "Oh, thanks very much . . . big-mouth!"

Max lifted his head and gave Sebastian an innocent look. "Oh dear, did I say something out of place?"

"Turncoat!" Sebastian stared gloomily into the fire. "I didn't mean it to go as far as it did," he said. "I think she overreacted."

Cornelius seemed to consider for a moment. "Whatever your reasons for saying it, it's up to you to try and make amends. We only have tonight. If we arrive in Keladon with her in that kind of mood, the chances are we'll all be in big trouble. Now, I suggest that you go over to her carriage and apologize to her."

Sebastian scowled. "Do I have to?" he said. "It'll mean tremendous loss of face."

"Perhaps. Rather preferable to tremendous loss of head, though, wouldn't you agree?"

Sebastian sighed. "Oh, very well," he said. He got reluctantly to his feet. "She'll probably just tell me to clear off."

"Well, if she does, at least we can't say you didn't give it a try," reasoned Cornelius. "Now, just make sure you keep your temper. . . ."

"And don't say anything else you might regret," added Max, talking through a mouthful of grass.

"Yes, yes!" Sebastian stalked away across the campsite, leaving the warmth of the fire behind him. It was very quiet and the moon was full and bright. The flocks of black birds were all asleep up in the branches of the trees, which cast long angular shadows across the clearing. Somewhere not so far off something howled, a long, low, mournful tone.

Sebastian approached the steps of the carriage where, not so long ago, Cornelius had made a valiant stand against a rabble of armed Brigands. He stood for a moment, listening, but no sound came from within. He climbed the steps and then politely rapped his knuckles against the door frame.

"Your Highness?" he ventured. "We were wondering if you would honor us with your company for supper."

There was a long silence. Then her voice came softly from within.

"Please go away," she said.

He was about to follow the instruction, but something within him rebelled. "No," he said. "I will not. Princess, you may punish me for disobeying you, but I refuse to go until we have discussed this like two adults."

Silence.

"Listen. I . . . want to apologize to you. I overstepped the mark. I know that. But . . . I still stand by what I said. And anyway, what's worse? Being left in ignorance of your own faults, or being told, so that you can make changes?"

More silence. But no, not quite. Sebastian moved his head

closer to the curtains because he thought he had picked up a muffled sound from within. He listened very carefully for a moment. Yes, he had been right. It was the sound of crying.

"Princess?" Emboldened by the sound, he climbed the last step and pushed through the curtain, instinctively lifting one hand to guard his head, just in case she was in a vengeful mood. But no, she was not waiting for him with a chamber pot this time. In the subtle glow of an oil lamp, he saw that she was sitting cross-legged on her silken bed, her head bowed, her shoulders moving rhythmically up and down. She looked up at him and he saw that her lovely face was wet with tears.

"You're right," she gasped. "I'm a terrible person. I'm selfish, shallow and self-opinionated. And I'll never be a good queen, never!"

Sebastian stood there staring at her in astonishment, realizing that this was his doing. He felt terrible.

"Your Highness," he whispered. "No. You mustn't say such things." He hurried over to the bed and, without thinking, sat down beside her and threw an arm round her slender shoulders. She didn't push him away. Instead, she turned toward him and buried her face against his chest, until he could feel her hot tears seeping through the fabric of his singlet. Suddenly it was all coming out of her in a rush. She sounded not like a princess, but a little girl, lost and afraid.

"You have to understand, I've been spoiled all my life. Everything I wanted was there for me on a plate, I only had to snap my fingers! So little wonder that I grew up believing that I was something special. And then I lost my parents when I was still so young and I had to make myself hard and not show my feelings. The people at court were watching me, waiting for me to break down, but I would not give them that satisfaction. I had to hide my true self behind the image I show to the world. . . ."

"Hush," whispered Sebastian, lifting a hand to stroke her hair. "It's all right, really." But she didn't seem to hear him.

"I . . . I know I say things sometimes . . . stupid selfish things . . . but it's like there's a little voice inside me, buzzing inside my head, telling me that I can do what I want, I can say what I want, because one day soon I will be *queen*! And I *want* to be queen, but at the same time I don't, because that's such a terrible responsibility, and what happens if I make some stupid mistake and I'm too proud to say I was wrong?" Now her voice dissolved into a flurry of frantic sobs and it was no longer possible to understand what she was saying; so Sebastian just held her until her tears subsided and she was able to control her breathing enough to speak.

"You were right," she whispered. "I have much to learn."

"Princess," he said, "you have no idea how much I wish I had held my tongue. I didn't mean to upset you. That was the last thing I wanted."

She pulled back from him a little and gazed up at him, her lovely eyes catching the light of the oil lamp. He had a sudden irrational desire to kiss her, but managed to suppress it. That was a complication he really couldn't afford.

"You are worried about your future employment," she said. "You needn't be. I won't hold your words against you."

"It's not that," he assured her. "That doesn't matter. Well, it *does* matter . . . but not as much as other things." He looked at her for a moment. "Princess Kerin, may I speak frankly?"

She smiled, dashing the tears from her eyes with the sleeve of her sumptuous gown. "I fear you already have," she said.

"Well, I intend to say more," he said fearlessly. He took a deep breath. "When I first met you, I confess that I didn't like you."

"Oh." She looked crestfallen. "I hope this gets better," she said.

"It does. You know, my mother always told me that beauty . . . *true* beauty, lies within a person. It's not what you see. It's what you *sense* about them. The elvish people have an ability to detect it. I may have inherited a little of that skill from my mother, but my powers are not as acute as hers. So it takes a while for me to get a clear picture. A while ago I told you that the outer princess was beautiful; and indeed she is, as any fool can see. But now I have realized that there is another person inside the one that I first met. And I can tell that this inner princess has everything that a queen needs. She has compassion enough for ten people. She is sensitive and intelligent and caring and she has a lot of love to give. She only needs to learn how to free her inner self and then everyone will know what I know now. That she is a very special person indeed."

There was a long silence. Princess Kerin sat there looking at him, her expression doubtful. Then she smiled.

"It did get better," she said. "And I see that as well as a jester, you are something of a poet, Mr. Darke." She reached out and took his hands in hers. "We will be friends, you and I. I have spoken to you of things I have never told anyone."

"I'm glad," he told her. "I feel privileged to have heard them."

She smiled bewitchingly. "Now," she told him, "there is one more question that I must ask."

"Ask it," he told her.

"What's for supper? I'm absolutely starving!"

He laughed at that. "Well, Your Highness, we can offer you roast fowl, which even now is sizzling over the fire. It won't be very grand, I'm afraid, but—"

"Lead me to it," she said. "My belly thinks my throat's been cut!" She got up off the couch and they moved to the curtained doorway.

As they stepped through it, they could smell the mouthwatering aroma of meat roasting over the fire. They descended the stairs and walked side by side toward the campfire, where Cornelius and Max were waiting for them. Sebastian almost laughed out loud at the look of relief on Cornelius's face as they approached.

"Everything is well?" he asked anxiously.

"Yes, indeed. The princess has agreed to join us for supper," announced Sebastian and, for an instant, the little warrior's face split into a delighted grin; but then suddenly his expression changed. A hard look came into his eyes and his mouth compressed into a thin, tight line. He was staring toward Sebastian and Princess Kerin with a look of cold hatred.

Sebastian was perturbed enough to stop in his tracks. "Cornelius?" he whispered. "What's wrong?"

The little man made no reply. Instead, he came to his feet and, in one lithe movement, snatched the big-bladed knife from his belt. He grasped the tip of the blade between thumb and forefinger and flung it with all his strength, straight at Sebastian's head.

Ten

THE VISITORS

Sebastian froze, stunned by the suddenness of the transformation. Why was Cornelius trying to kill him?

He had a brief glimpse of the deadly knife, spinning end over end as it flashed toward him. Then, in an instant, the glittering arc of steel whooshed past his left ear and buried itself with a thud in something that was approaching from behind. There was an eerie, high-pitched yelp and something crashed heavily to the ground at Sebastian's feet, nearly knocking him over. He looked down in dull surprise to see a huge, furry creature lying dead at his feet, the handle of the knife standing out from its chest. Its mouth was open and a huge purple tongue lolled out from between rows of yellow, razor-sharp teeth.

Sebastian glanced at Princess Kerin. She was staring down at the beast, wide-eyed and openmouthed in terror. It wasn't necessary to say the word, but Sebastian said it anyway.

"Lupers!"

He heard the howls from behind him and, spinning round, he saw their lithe shapes flitting silently through the trees. He counted six or seven of them, sinewy gray creatures that ran upright on their powerful back legs, their heads improbably large on their long, lithe bodies. Their front legs were extended in front of them, displaying the huge, curved claws that could do so much damage to their prey, and their mouths were open, powerful jaws dripping saliva. The smell of the roasting fowl had drawn them to the clearing but now they were intent on bigger game.

"To the fire!" roared Cornelius, jolting Sebastian out of his daze. He willed his limbs to work, but his muscles were jittering and he was weak with terror. "The knife!" he heard Cornelius yell. "Get the knife!"

Sebastian dropped instinctively into a crouch and, grabbing the handle of the knife protruding from the luper's chest, gave it a powerful tug. As the blade slid free of its fleshy sheath, suddenly, shockingly, the creature moved, lashing out with its paws and snarling like something insane. Sebastian felt razor-sharp claws tear through the fabric of his sleeve, even as he scrambled away from what must have been the creature's death throes. He sprang upright and pulled Princess Kerin across the clearing toward the fire, aware as he did so that the nearest lupers were almost on his heels. As he came to the fire, Cornelius threw his sword to him. He caught it one-handed, flung the knife into the ground at Cornelius's feet and, turning back, unsheathed his weapon.

A terrifying sight filled his vision. The nearest luper was springing straight at him, claws extended to rend and tear.

Sebastian only just had time to get the point of the blade between himself and his assailant. He felt the powerful jolt in the muscles of his arm as the ravening beast connected with the tip of the blade; then a heavier impact as the beast's body slid down the sword and came crashing into him.

He was thrown backward with the creature sprawled on top of him, and the thud of his shoulders against the ground drove the breath from his lungs. He found himself lying on his back, looking up into the luper's snapping jaws, which were inches from his face. He lay there, dimly aware of the creature's warm blood spurting over his hands, which still held the handle of the sword. The luper's jaws inched closer, closer, and saliva splashed onto Sebastian's face. Then its eyes bulged horribly and a shudder rippled through its body. The great jaws snapped shut as death came sweeping in on dark wings and, quite suddenly, the creature's muscles went slack. Sebastian was able to push it aside.

He kneeled to pull the sword out of the luper's chest, then got back to his feet, looking desperately around at a vision of chaos lit by the flickering light of the campfire. Cornelius was fending off two of the beasts, sword in one hand, knife in the other. The creatures were trying to drive the manling away from the fire, which they obviously feared, but he made sure that he kept stepping back toward it, the twin blades slashing deadly arcs at his assailants.

A short distance from him, Princess Kerin was waving a burning branch she had snatched from the fire at another luper. It was doing its best to lash the weapon out of her hand.

And further away still, Sebastian caught a glimpse of Max,

bucking and kicking frantically beneath the onslaught of two more lupers, which were attempting to drag him to the ground.

There was no time to think. Sebastian ran to Princess Kerin's side, telling himself that she was the most vulnerable one here. He stepped between her and the luper and brought the curved sword down in a tight arc, slicing one of the beast's front paws clean off. The creature threw back its head and howled in agony. A moment later the howl was cut short as Sebastian's blade slashed across its throat and it span aside, to fall writhing and shuddering on the ground.

Sebastian pushed Princess Kerin behind him. "Stay with me," he told her. He began to edge toward Cornelius and she moved with him; but in that same instant the manling dispatched another of the creatures, a great brute of a beast. Mortally wounded, the luper pitched sideways and slammed into Sebastian, knocking him backward into Princess Kerin. All three of them went down in a tangle of limbs and Sebastian found himself pinned beneath the weight of the dead luper, unable to move the arm that held his sword. He struggled to push the carcass off himself, then froze at a deep rumbling growl inches from his head.

He saw to his horror that another luper was crouched low to the ground, ready to lunge at him. Sebastian was afforded a grandstand view between the dripping fringes of the creature's jagged teeth and deep into the dark maw of its throat. It was not a pretty sight. He renewed his efforts to struggle free but could not release his arm, and the luper was tensing its muscles to spring—

And then Princess Kerin stepped in front of Sebastian and plunged the burning branch straight into the luper's open jaws. It jolted in its tracks and reared up on its hind legs, snapping the branch in two and flinging burning embers from its open mouth. It turned its attention to Princess Kerin, its eyes blazing with feral rage. She stood her ground, holding the broken branch in front of her as though it was still a useful weapon. Sebastian thought that he had never seen a braver act but was sure that she was about to die.

"Run!" he screamed, but she ignored him. She waited calmly for the attack that would claim her young life.

And then there was a sudden bellowing sound, so loud that everything seemed to stop for an instant. A thing came somersaulting through the air above the luper's head; something small that was spinning around in a blur of motion. And it was making this unearthly racket. The noise was so strange that the luper grunted and lifted its head to stare up at the strange thing wheeling in the air above it. A thing that held two points of razor-sharp steel in its fists.

One moment the luper's head was still attached to its body. The next, the head was falling through the air toward Princess Kerin, who made an expression of disgust and fended it away with the broken branch. The head went tumbling toward the campfire, where it came to rest, the blank eyes gazing sullenly into the flames. The spinning thing dropped to the ground and landed on its short legs. It was only then that Sebastian realized it was Cornelius.

"What on earth . . . ?" he gasped.

The manling bowed. "Golmiran death leap," he said. "Only to be used in extreme circumstances." He gestured at the severed head. "I think that just about qualifies." He moved across to Sebastian, and he and Princess Kerin helped lift the dead luper off him. Sebastian struggled free and got back to his feet. The three of them looked anxiously toward Max and saw to their relief that one of his attackers lay crushed and broken in the grass while the other was limping away though the trees, howling in pain.

"And don't come back!" shouted Max emphatically. "Not until you've learned some manners."

In the following silence, the crackling of the fire seemed unreal. The four survivors stood for a moment, looking anxiously around to ensure that there were no lupers left to attack them. Then they turned to face each other, grinning and nodding and generally celebrating the fact that they had survived.

"We made a pretty good team there," said Cornelius at last. He sheathed his sword and moved back to the fire, where the carcasses of the birds were just on the point of burning. He sniffed at them appreciatively.

"Well, I don't know about you," he said, "but that little dustup has given me quite an appetite." He sat cross-legged beside the fire and started to maneuver the first bird off the spit.

Sebastian stared down at him for a moment and then gestured at the dead lupers strewn all around them. "Cornelius!" he protested. "You cannot seriously intend to go on with your supper in the midst of all this carnage?"

Cornelius glanced around, then shrugged. "Why not?" he

said. "I've eaten in worse circumstances. Why, once, trying to evade capture at the battle of Gerinosis, I consumed a four-course meal while lying at the bottom of a heap of dead soldiers." He extended one foot and kicked the head of a luper away from the fire. "As long as they're not close enough to steal a bite, I'm happy enough."

"That's positively barbaric," said Max. "I mean to say . . . we came close to dying just then."

Cornelius grinned. "All the more reason to celebrate the things that make life enjoyable," he said. He tore off a large drumstick and took a big bite of the succulent meat. "Umm. Absolutely delicious," he said.

Sebastian and Princess Kerin exchanged inquiring looks.

"Well, it does smell good," admitted Princess Kerin.

"Be a shame to waste it," added Sebastian.

Then they too shrugged and went to join the little warrior, while Max looked on in absolute revulsion.

All three of them had to admit that it was the tastiest, most downright delicious meal they'd ever eaten.

ELEVEN

ALMOST THERE

The following morning was Princess Kerin's birthday. Cornelius provided her with a fine breakfast of roast fowl and promised her that they would be in Keladon in time for her celebrations. They were just finishing their meal when several mounted soldiers rode into camp. Sebastian recognized their bronzed breastplates and red cloaks as the same uniform that had been worn by Princess Kerin's guards. The troop was led by a tall, stern-faced officer, who wore a purple cloak, an obvious sign of his rank.

Sebastian reached instinctively for his sword at the first sign of the newcomers but Cornelius stayed his hand.

"Relax," he said. "I think they are King Septimus's men."

The captain of the troop reined his equine to a halt and sat for a moment gazing sternly down at the people around the fire.

"What is your business here?" he demanded. "This land belongs to King Septimus. Anyone wishing to travel across it must first pay a tax of— Good grief!" It had taken him a few moments to recognize Princess Kerin, but when he did, he reacted with evident shock. He jumped down off his mount and went down on one knee before her.

"Your Highness!" he gasped. "What are you doing out here with these ruffians? If they have harmed or frightened you in any way, by my oath, I swear they shall live to regret it!"

Princess Kerin stood up and did her best to look regal—not easy, when her face was dirty and her fine dress was caked with dust and blood.

"Fear not, Captain Tench," she said. "These men are heroes: they saved me from an attack by Brigands."

"Brigands?" Captain Tench looked across the clearing at the heap of luper bodies, which Sebastian and Cornelius had stacked up the previous night. "They are the hairiest Brigands I've ever seen."

Cornelius laughed. "Oh, the Brigands were the other day, back on the plains." He pointed to the lupers. "Those fellows dropped by for supper last night. But there wasn't enough to go round so we had to be robust with them."

Captain Tench stared at the little warrior for a moment, as though he didn't much like what he saw. But he bowed politely. "The kingdom of Keladon is clearly in your debt, sir," he said. He stood up and pointed to one of his men. "You! Ride with all speed to the city and let King Septimus know the joyful news! Speak to nobody else on your way there. Tell the king that his niece was attacked but has been saved."

"Yes, sir!" The soldier whipped up his mount and galloped away through the trees.

"We shall act as escort to take you safely into the city," announced Captain Tench.

"Excellent news," said Cornelius. "And I wonder, Captain, could you spare a man to drive the princess's carriage? I've had more than my fill of those frisky Brigandian equines and would like to ride alongside my good friend, Mr. Darke."

Again, Captain Tench bowed respectfully. "As you wish." He turned back to face Princess Kerin. "Your Highness, if you will allow me, I will escort you back to your carriage, where you may prepare yourself to greet King Septimus."

"Yes, of course." Princess Kerin looked rather regretfully at Sebastian, as though she sensed that something was over between them. "It's been quite an adventure," she said, and he knew that she was telling him that it was now time for her to go back to being a princess again. Sebastian could almost feel an invisible barrier coming down between them. He thought how he had held her in his arms as she cried, and felt sad that they would probably never share such intimacy again.

"Perhaps it isn't over yet," he ventured hopefully; and she rewarded him with a fleeting smile.

"Perhaps." She turned away and allowed Captain Tench to take her arm and lead her back to her caravan.

"So," said Sebastian, trying to sound positive. "It looks as though our troubles are over."

"Oh, I hope so," murmured Cornelius, gazing thoughtfully across the fire at Captain Tench, who was shouting orders to his soldiers. "I do hope so."

*   *   *

A few hours later Sebastian's caravan emerged from the cover of the last few trees and he and Cornelius finally had a clear view of the city of Keladon.

It nestled against the side of a hill, within the shelter of the high stone walls that encircled it. A tight cluster of white painted houses, temples and villas seemed to huddle close together for security, rising in irregular steps on the steep incline that rose to the base of the king's palace. This magnificent edifice, hewn from glistening white marble, rose stark and austere from the midst of the surrounding habitation. Most imposing of all was the spire, which thrust sheer upward from the very center of the building, until it seemed to touch the clouds. From its very top fluttered the royal flag, a huge silk pennant featuring the royal insignia of two prowling lizards.

The scale of it all was quite unnerving. Sebastian swallowed and told himself that very soon he would be attempting to earn a living in Keladon by telling jokes. There was part of him that wanted to turn the caravan round and head back home, but he knew he couldn't do that. This was his, and his mother's, last hope.

He glanced at Cornelius and saw that the little man was gazing up at him thoughtfully.

"You seem troubled," he observed.

Sebastian nodded. "It's a big place," he said. "Jerabim is a sleepy little market town, nothing like this. I suppose it's just nerves."

"You have every right to be nervous," said Max mournfully, plodding slowly onward. "I've heard your routine."

"Oh, thank you, that's certainly boosted my confidence," said Sebastian.

Cornelius chuckled. "Take no notice of him," he said. "He's just a prophet of doom."

"He's got a point, though. Nobody seems to like my jokes. Apart from Princess Kerin, of course."

"Well, that's not a bad start," said Cornelius. "If you only ever have one fan, it's best to have one who has good connections. Use her as a starting point and see if it will grow from there."

"But what if it doesn't?"

"It will if you believe in yourself."

Sebastian frowned. "But . . . how is it done, Cornelius? Take you, for example. You never let anything get the better of you. You're brave and courageous, and yet you're so . . . so . . ."

"Small?" suggested Cornelius.

"Well . . . I wasn't going to say that but . . . now you mention it . . ."

Cornelius laughed. "Self-belief is such an important thing," he said, "particularly in your line of work. If you don't think a joke is funny, how can you expect anybody else to?"

Sebastian shrugged. "I don't know," he admitted miserably.

"But think of it this way. You set off from your hometown and found your way through hills and forests. You fought a bunch of Brigands and, though badly outnumbered, you drove them away. Only last night you faced up to an attack by a pack of bloodthirsty lupers and emerged victorious—"

"Yes, but Cornelius, that was because *you* were there!"

The little warrior shook his head. "Yes, I was there, but I

didn't see you standing idle, Sebastian. You were in the thick of it. You gave as good as you got." Cornelius paused and gave Sebastian a sly look. "And a decent fighter I may be, but I don't have what it takes to stir the heart of a princess."

"What?" Sebastian stared at him. "Oh no, that's . . . we just . . ."

"Believe me, I saw the way she looked at you back there. I don't have much experience of that kind of thing, but I think I know a smitten woman when I see one."

"That's ridiculous," murmured Sebastian. "Me . . . and Princess Kerin? I don't think so." He laughed, but Cornelius just sat there with a knowing look on his baby face.

"We'll see," he said; and left it at that.

They continued on their way in silence, each lost in his own thoughts as they covered the last few miles to the city of Keladon.

PART TWO

TWELVE

TO BE A KING

Septimus studied his expression in the gilt-framed mirror. He was practicing a look of profound sorrow but it kept coming out all wrong. On his thin, mournful face, framed by two long waves of lank black hair, the result was more like a look of severe constipation.

"Bother!" he snapped, and tried it again, screwing up his eyes and turning his thin lips down at the edges. Any time now he expected a messenger at the gates to tell him of the awful tragedy that had befallen his niece. He knew that the entire court would be watching him as he received word and he couldn't allow a single person to suspect that the news was rather less of a surprise to him than it might have been.

That was if they *had* murdered her, of course. Septimus was worried that they might have taken her hostage and would be demanding a massive ransom for her safe return: that would complicate matters considerably. But Magda, who had cooked up the whole scheme, had assured him that Brigands were far too thick to think of anything like that. They would certainly kill her; possibly even cook and eat her; but putting together a ransom demand would require somebody who could actually write—not a likely occurrence in Brigandia.

Out in the courtyard, trumpets sounded, announcing the arrival of a messenger. Right on cue! Septimus had one last attempt at a sad look in the mirror and then told himself that if all else failed, he could just cover his face with his hands and pretend to be weeping.

A high-pitched voice sounded out in the corridor. It was his personal assistant, Malthus.

"Your Majesty! An urgent message from Captain Tench!"

Septimus smiled triumphantly.

Good! He had spoken to Tench that morning, in front of plenty of witnesses, voicing his concern at the lateness of Princess Kerin's return. Evidently Tench must have discovered something: hopefully the scene of a massacre. Septimus turned away from the mirror and swept imperiously to the door of his private chambers.

"Open," he said; and the two minions who stood guard outside the door swung it open for him, to reveal Malthus, standing there looking pale and concerned in a crimson jerkin and a pair of pale green tights.

"Your Majesty," simpered Malthus, in that familiar irritating whine. "A messenger from—"

"Yes, yes, I heard! Lead on, Malthus. Oh, I do hope nothing has befallen that sweet child, particularly on this day of all days. Her seventeenth birthday . . . I've even bought her that special present and everything. I trust you've been looking after it, Malthus?"

"Yes, Your Majesty, I've just given it some fresh nuts." Malthus turned and scurried down the huge curve of the marble staircase. Septimus followed, ignoring the rows of uniformed men who lined each side. He descended to the huge marble-floored forum, where the messenger waited patiently on one knee, surrounded by the various lords and ladies of the royal court, all of whom were studying the king as he descended the stairs.

That was the problem with this place. Hardly anything ever happened in private; and Septimus knew that ever since the death of his brother and his wife, there were many who had their suspicions about his involvement in that little misadventure. Not that any of them had proof, of course. All the coconspirators who had helped bring the former king's reign to an early end had been silenced forever.

Septimus frowned. It was hard work being evil but the rewards were high. He enjoyed being king immensely and had no intention of allowing that situation to change, not while there was still breath in his body. He reached the bottom of the staircase and looked down at the soldier who had been entrusted with the bad news, a big, handsome lout of a man whose name Septimus didn't know, but who looked none too bright.

"Speak up, man," said Septimus. "What news have you?"

"Your Majesty, I come from Captain Tench with an important message."

"Yes, I know that. Get on with it."

"He urged me to come straight to you and to speak to no other."

"Yes, well, very good, you have done exactly that."

"No, sire, I have failed in that matter." The soldier looked rather crestfallen. "On my way in through the gates, a merchant asked me what time of day it was and, without thinking, I replied."

Septimus glared at the man. "Yes, well, that hardly matters, you idiot! What exactly is the *news*?"

"Oh yes." The soldier cleared his throat. "Your Majesty, just a short distance outside the camp, I . . . that is, we . . . that is, the troop commanded by Captain Tench, of which I am a member—"

"Oh, for pity's sake! Could you please get to the point?"

"Of course, Your Majesty. I was attempting to do so." He cleared his throat again. "Just a short distance outside the palace, we came upon the scene of a massacre. . . ."

Yes! Septimus had to restrain himself from punching a celebratory fist into the air, but managed to keep his expression grim.

"A massacre, you say. Oh no, please tell me that my beloved niece was not present."

"She *was* there, Your Majesty. I saw her with my own eyes."

"Oh, woe!" cried Septimus. He slapped a hand against his forehead and rolled his eyes heavenward. "Oh, that such a young and fragile beauty should have been snuffed out so prematurely!"

"Er . . . Your Majesty, she was—"

"No, don't tell me! Spare me the awful details of her untimely demise."

"It was more the demise of the lupers, Your Majesty."

"The lupers?" Septimus glared at the man. "What lupers?"

"The ones that attacked the caravan."

"Lupers attacked the caravan? But . . . what of the Brigands?"

"Brigands, Your Majesty?"

"Yes. Didn't you say that she had been attacked by—?" Septimus checked himself with a jolt of alarm. No, nobody had actually mentioned Brigands. Bad move. He was aware of the eyes of the courtiers burning into him. "Oh, *lupers*! You know, I could have sworn you said Brigands. They, er . . . they have a similar sound, do they not?"

The soldier was staring up at him blankly. He clearly didn't think so. But Septimus pressed on regardless.

"Now then, let me get this straight. You're telling me that Princess Kerin . . . my poor beloved niece . . . has been killed by lupers?"

"No, Your Majesty."

Septimus winced. He glared down at the man. "Then what the blue blazes *are* you telling me, you imbecile?"

The soldier flinched. "Your Majesty, I am telling you that Princess Kerin was *attacked* by a pack of lupers—"

"Yes, yes, so she was ripped to shreds! That's terrible, terrible!"

"My lord, she wasn't harmed. She has survived and is alive and well."

"Oh, the tragedy, the . . . the . . ." Septimus's face went through a whole series of contortions as he tried to find an appropriate expression for the news. He initially went for the look of sadness that he had been practicing upstairs. Then, realizing

107

it was totally wrong, he tried for one of relieved delight, baring his teeth and popping his eyes; but judging by the way the soldier flinched away from him, what he had actually managed was an expression of total insanity.

"Alive?" he screamed. "Alive! I . . . I can hardly believe it!" He looked around at the courtiers, aware now that his eyes were filling with tears of frustration. "Look at me!" he cried. "I'm so pleased I'm actually weeping tears of joy!"

He returned his attention to the messenger. "So how did the . . . how did my beloved niece come to survive?"

"She was rescued, Your Majesty. By two travelers. The self-same men who rescued her from the Brigands you spoke of."

Septimus felt like kicking the man in the teeth, but this really wasn't the time or place. "I spoke of no Brigands. That was you!"

"Er . . . no, Your Majesty. I spoke of lupers; you—"

"So where is my niece now?" bellowed Septimus, drowning out the irritating whine of the man's voice.

"She approaches the palace, Your Majesty, under armed escort. And, of course, bringing her saviors with her."

"Oh, then I . . . I must make ready to . . ." He clenched his fists and made an effort to control himself. "To receive them," he hissed. He walked past the messenger, taking the opportunity as he did so to "accidentally" stand on the fingers of the man's hand, feeling a satisfying crunching sensation under his foot. He addressed the court. "Make ready for a celebration!" he announced. "My niece, your future queen, is shortly to be returned to us, safe and well, on this most special of days . . . her birthday. We will meet them in the courtyard with all due pomp and ceremony. Now I must away to my chambers to, er . . . umm . . . dress for the occasion!"

He strode back, stepping on the messenger's other hand as he passed. He swept up the marble staircase and was aware of Malthus trailing along in his wake. He turned and glared at the man. "What do you want?" he snapped.

"Umm . . . I come to attend Your Royal Highness," said Malthus. "To prepare you for—"

"I'm a big boy now, Malthus. I'll see to myself." He started away, but then paused as a thought occurred to him. "The soldier who just brought the message . . ."

"Yes, sire?"

"I think he should be rewarded for bearing such good tidings, don't you? See that he's promoted to the rank of captain. With immediate effect."

"Very well, sire."

"And send him to join our expeditionary forces in the swamps of Dysenterium."

"Er . . . but, Your Majesty, that's hardly . . ."

"Hmm?"

Malthus swallowed hard. He knew well enough that King Septimus was not a person who tolerated having his decisions questioned.

"That's actually very convenient," said Malthus brightly. "I understand that the last captain just died of some festering infection in his guts." He turned away and went back down the stairs to break the good news to the messenger, who was kneeling below, whimpering in pain as he inspected the crushed and broken fingers of his hands.

Septimus meanwhile had a pressing engagement. He reached the top landing, and instead of turning right for his chambers, he headed left into a rarely used part of the palace. He strode along a dimly lit corridor looking for Magda.

He found her in her chamber, leaning over a table, pouring some foul mixture into a receptacle made from an upturned human skull. She was intent on her work and Septimus was in no mood for niceties, so by way of greeting he launched a kick at her skinny backside, sending her tumbling across the table and scattering her latest experiment all over the floor.

She turned like a beast at bay, an expression of anger on her wizened old face, her one good eye glittering with malice as she bared the few brown stumps of teeth left in her mouth. She lifted a gnarled, liver-spotted hand to make a hex sign at her assailant. Then she recognized who had just kicked her and all the malice went out of her in an instant. She attempted an unconvincing smile. "Your Majesty," she croaked. "This is an . . . unexpected pleasure."

"The pleasure is all yours," he assured her, leaning across the table and fixing her with a look of profound anger. "You stupid malodorous old hag! I've just spoken with a messenger. Princess Kerin lives!"

"Ah." Magda could not conceal a look of dismay. "He is sure?"

"Positive. It seems she survived the attack by Brigands and a later one by a pack of lupers, all thanks to the intervention of two travelers."

"Travelers?" Magda sniffed suspiciously. "What travelers?"

"How should I know? Two superwarriors, by the sound of it. Two interfering nitwits." He paced around for a moment in silent agitation. "I take it you had no hand in the business with the lupers?"

"No. Not a bad idea, though. Wish I'd thought of it."

"Well, it would have been to no avail, thanks to these two meddling do-gooders, who no doubt I will now have to welcome with open arms. Oh, it makes me want to vomit! All that time in preparation! *Trust me*, you said. *It can't fail, Your Majesty!* Well, it *did* fail, and I'm no closer to getting rid of my one rival for the throne! I should have followed my instincts and had her killed here in the palace."

"But, my lord, that would have been a terrible mistake. Never forget that she is the people's princess. They love her. The slightest indication of anything nefarious and they would rise against you!"

Septimus sighed. She was right, of course. One of the really annoying things about Magda was that she was generally right. It was the main reason he hadn't had her boiled in oil years ago. It was she who had pointed out that anything that befell Princess Kerin must happen away from the palace, when Septimus was not present to invite suspicion.

It was she who had persuaded him to send Kerin off to visit Queen Helena of Bodengen, under the pretext of marrying her off to her son Rolf. It was Magda who had sent one of her

111

minions into Brigandia to spread word of a vulnerable carriage that would soon be crossing the plains, carrying rich pickings. And it was Magda who had arranged for a fiendish potion to be given to the guard of honor in their nightly ration of wine; one that would incapacitate more than half of them, meaning that the caravan would have to head for home with its troop of guards well under fighting strength. And the lure that would ensure she would risk a quick return? Her seventeenth birthday party. There was no way such a spoiled brat would risk missing that.

The whole scheme had taken months to prepare and weeks to execute and now, because of the interference of two unknown warriors, it had all come to nothing. King Septimus felt like spitting; and indeed, he did just that, right in the corner of Magda's room.

"Oh!" he said. "Is there nothing I can do? Can nobody rid me of that accursed child?"

Magda was rubbing her gnarled old hands together, as though trying to clean them. "Perhaps, sire, if you would allow me another chance—"

"I think you've had quite enough chances, you malignant old boiler! You remember what I said when you undertook this task? That if you failed, your miserable life would be forfeit."

Magda's good eye had turned the color of panic, but she never faltered in her reply.

"I . . . do remember, Your Majesty, of course. But you see, I think perhaps now the tide is finally turning in our favor."

He gave her an irritated look. "Meaning . . . ?"

"Two strangers, sire, soon to arrive here in Keladon. Strangers can be a useful commodity."

"I haven't the faintest idea what you're on about," he growled.

She gave him a twisted smile. "Strangers can be blamed for certain things. Since there is nobody who knows them and can vouch for them, people are often willing to believe the very worst about them—if you catch my drift . . . ?"

"Magda, if this is an attempt to play for time—"

"Oh no, Your Majesty! But please, let me get the measure of these two great warriors. I think I will be able to find a solution to our little problem soon enough." She began to pace around the room as she warmed to her theme. "You, for your part, must welcome them as conquering heroes. Spoil them, let them want for nothing, indulge them in their every desire!"

"And why would I do that, exactly?"

"Because then it will be all the more shocking when they turn and bite the hand that has fed them!" She cackled as only a hag can cackle.

"Oh, very well," said Septimus wearily. "We'll try it your way. But I mean it this time. No more chances. If you don't deliver on your promises, I swear you will feel the edge of the executioner's axe. And not with your thumb."

Magda fluttered her eyelid and tried to keep the relief out of her voice. "Of course, sire. Your humble servant, as ever." She bowed low and stayed in that position until Septimus got bored with standing there and swept out of the room. Only then did she straighten up, placing a hand on her aching backside, where the king's boot had undoubtedly left quite a bruise.

She was all too aware of the vulnerability of her position. She would have to conclude this matter once and for all if she wanted to live. She had been threatened by King Septimus several times before; but this time, she felt sure, he really meant it. She started at the sound of a mighty trumpet fanfare from out in the courtyard and limped to the window to watch the arrival of the two heroic strangers and the rescued princess.

Even before the caravan had entered the gates, her devious mind was drawing up a plan of action. . . .

THIRTEEN

IN KELADON

The mighty iron gates of the city swung silently open and Max hesitated for a moment before a slap of the reins against his haunches urged him forward.

The caravan moved slowly inside, passing the fierce-looking, heavily armed warriors who guarded the gates. Some of them stood at floor level, others were ranged at intervals on a wooden platform that jutted out from the top of the encircling walls, ready to repel any attack that might be launched against the city. Off to one side stood the mighty timber mechanism that opened and closed the gates. This was operated by two massive buffalopes, chained into leather harnesses. Max snorted at the sight of them and gave the creatures a friendly toss of his head.

"Lovely day!" he observed, but they either didn't hear him or were in no mood to make conversation, so he moved on.

Ahead lay a broad avenue, flanked by long rows of merchants' stalls selling fabrics, spices, cooking utensils, tools, weapons—everything you could possibly think of. Crowds of people milled back and forth around the stalls, many of them throwing suspicious looks at Sebastian's caravan, some yelling out jocular greetings at the prospect of some entertainment. Prosperous-looking businessmen in richly jeweled cloaks strolled around trying to look important. Women in full-length dresses, many of them modestly veiled, walked a respectful distance behind their menfolk. And children—great gangs of ragged, dirty-faced urchins—were running here and there as they tried to beg coins from the populace.

Princess Kerin's carriage came into view and everything seemed to freeze. The people stopped what they were doing and bowed their heads in a gesture of silent respect. Many of them even went down on one knee as she passed by. It was clear that she was held in very high esteem. Once the carriage had moved past them, they fell into step behind it and followed, curious to see what this was all about.

Sebastian had never seen so many people together in one place before. Jerabim was a sizeable market town, but nothing like this. As he looked left and right, beyond the merchants' stalls, he saw that scores of labyrinthine alleyways led off between the ranks of tightly clustered buildings and he glimpsed shadowy figures moving in there; dark shambling creatures that seemed to hide from the glare of the sun. Sebastian had an impression that there were two parts to the city—the grand, gleaming aspect that was presented to the world; and a darker, more sinister part that hid in the shadows and waited for the unwary.

Strange discordant music spilled from a café as they passed by, and he saw many prosperous-looking men sitting under a roof of vines, smoking huge pipes which passed into gleaming metal bowls. A small orchestra was playing and a woman was dancing on a stage, her lithe, sinewy body gleaming beneath a shimmering layer of oil. She moved with a strange, hypnotic allure and Sebastian noticed that the eyes of every man in the café were riveted to her as though they were under some kind of spell.

The caravan moved on, leaving the café behind, and they rounded a slow curve in the road. Now a really awesome sight lay directly ahead of them at the far end of the avenue. The road inclined steadily upward to the marble palace of King Septimus. Even at this distance it looked impressive, its marble columns shimmering in the sunlight, its massive curved archways and gold minarets like something out of a fever dream.

"It's even more beautiful than I had supposed," murmured Cornelius. "Imagine how rich the king must be to have a palace like that!"

Sebastian nodded, but made no reply. He was feeling very small and insignificant at this moment. What had he been thinking of, coming here? What hope did he have of gaining the patronage of such a mighty king? The best thing for him to do right now would be to turn the caravan round and head for home.

Cornelius must have sensed his terror. "Cheer up," he said. "You'll be fine! Just remember, believe in yourself."

Sebastian forced a smile and nodded; but he didn't have any faith in his own abilities, not one shred.

117

As they drew closer to the palace, an unseen bell started tolling, and Sebastian could now see the fine green lawns that surrounded the building and the huge stone fountains, from which water cascaded in a magical, unending supply. He had never seen their like before. In Jerabim, where water was regarded as a precious commodity, such a thing would have been unthinkable.

Finally, after what seemed an age, they pulled to a halt at the bottom of a short flight of stone steps, which led up to a broad sweep of gleaming courtyard. As they did so, a group of armed soldiers wearing deep red cloaks came marching through the palace doors and ranged themselves in a line across the doorway. They pulled out their swords and held them crossed over their breastplates, ready to use them at the slightest provocation.

"The Crimson Cloak," whispered Cornelius. "The king's bodyguard."

Then, through the palace entrance filed a whole crowd of illustrious-looking people: men and women, the lords and ladies of the royal court, dressed in rich brocade and soft, brightly colored velvet. Many of the men wore turbans and the women were veiled with fine, translucent fabric. Everyone wore jewels at their necks and on their fingers. The large group divided itself in two with practiced ease and moved left and right, where they stood inspecting the new arrivals with disapproving looks on their faces. Sitting up in the caravan, Sebastian remembered that his jester's outfit was torn and dirty and spattered with blood. He wished he'd thought to change into something more presentable before entering the city.

Now a shrill fanfare echoed through the still air and six bearded warriors came out through the doors, blowing on golden trumpets. They also split into two groups and ranged themselves left and right behind the lords and ladies.

"What a performance!" said Sebastian.

"Quiet!" snapped a voice, and he glanced up to see Captain Tench, still sitting astride his equine a short distance away and looking at him in a very surly manner. "Climb down from there," he added, and Sebastian and Cornelius did as they were told. As Sebastian turned back to face the palace, he saw that one more figure was moving out through the open doorway.

It was a tall, lean man dressed in a splendid purple gown, over which, despite the heat, he was wearing a thick fur robe. At the sight of him, every one of the lords and ladies went down on one knee, and he strolled between them with all the arrogance of a man who is well used to such subservience. He came forward to the edge of the steps, and his bodyguards parted and shuffled to either side to allow him to pass. He stood there, his hands on his hips, looking down at Sebastian and Cornelius, a questioning look on his thin, pale face.

Sebastian felt an instant twinge of dislike. Perhaps it was his elf intuition working overtime, but he thought that King Septimus had one of the most untrustworthy faces he had ever seen.

Cornelius immediately dropped to one knee and slammed a chain-mail-clad elbow into Sebastian's leg, prompting him to do the same. The king seemed happier with this state of affairs. He gazed left and right, as though looking for somebody.

"Where is my niece?" he asked.

"Here, Uncle!" Princess Kerin appeared in the doorway of her

119

carriage, and Sebastian saw that she had taken the opportunity to change her clothes. She wore a beautiful red velvet gown and a fine jeweled tiara that glittered in the sunlight. She stepped down from the carriage and walked across to climb the steps that led up to the courtyard. As she passed Sebastian, she glanced down at him and he could have sworn that she slipped him a sly wink, but it was so fleeting, he might simply have imagined it. She walked over to her uncle and gave him an elegant curtsy.

"Your Majesty," she said.

"My dear niece! How wonderful to see you safe and well on this most special of days." The king came forward and embraced Princess Kerin, holding her to him for a moment and then releasing her. He turned to face the crowd that was gathering around the edges of the steps and raised his voice to speak to them.

"People of Keladon," he cried. "May providence be praised! Our much-loved princess has been safely returned to us on the very day that she reaches seventeen summers. Just one more year and she will be your queen!"

This announcement was met by a huge roar of approval from the rapidly expanding crowd. The king turned back to Princess Kerin and spoke in a quieter tone. "After hearing of your misfortune, I have done nothing but chastise myself. How could I have been so stupid as to allow you to be placed in such a dangerous situation? Can you ever find it in your heart to forgive me?"

"Uncle, it wasn't your fault," said Princess Kerin.

"Well, no, obviously!" snapped King Septimus. Then he laughed—rather nervously, Sebastian thought. "Er . . . but that doesn't make me feel any better about the situation." He did a double take and glanced back toward the few soldiers who had escorted the princess back into the city. "Where is your Royal Guard?" he asked.

"All dead, sire," said Cornelius. "They died bravely to the last man, fighting to defend the princess."

The king glared down at Cornelius, as though astounded that he had dared to speak without permission. "Dead?" he cried.

"Yes, sire, they were badly outnumbered."

"But . . . I sent a detachment of twenty men with her."

"Many of them were unable to accompany us back," explained Princess Kerin. "We had but six with us, because—"

"—they were all taken ill," said Septimus. "I know."

The princess looked puzzled. "How did you know?" she asked.

"Hmm?" He gazed at her blankly for a moment. "Well, because I am the king, it's my business to know." He seemed to consider for a moment. "That messenger from Captain Tench, he told me."

"Really? I didn't realize he had that information."

"Well, of course he did! He told me everything—the Brigands, the lupers . . . all in all it's a miracle you survived."

Princess Kerin nodded. "I wouldn't have," she assured him, "if it hadn't been for my two champions."

"Ah yes, now I'm really looking forward to meeting *them*!" said King Septimus. "Where are they?"

Princess Kerin stared at him. "Why, they're right there in front of you," she said.

King Septimus looked down at Sebastian and Cornelius and looked away again, as if expecting to see somebody else. But there was nobody else. "These two?" he said in disbelief. "These are your champions?"

"Actually, there's *three* of us," said Max. "I helped too!"

The king's eyes bulged in astonishment. He pointed at Max. "It spoke!" he said. "That great hairy brute just spoke!"

Princess Kerin smiled. "Yes, I'm sorry—of course I should have said *three* champions, not two. So, Uncle . . . may I introduce to you . . . Sebastian Darke, from the town of Jerabim. . . ."

Sebastian stood up and made a bow.

"Captain Cornelius Drummel from the great northern city of Golmira . . ."

Cornelius did likewise.

"And, er . . . Max, the talking buffalope, also from Jerabim."

King Septimus seemed to be having trouble accepting what he had just been told. "And these . . . *people* are the mighty warriors—the ones who fought off an army of Brigands . . . and a pack of lupers?"

"The very same," Princess Kerin assured him. "If it were not for them, I would almost certainly be dead by now."

"Dead," murmured King Septimus. There was a strangely unsettling tone in the way he said it, Sebastian thought. He sounded almost wistful. Then he seemed to recover himself. "Well then, it would seem that I am in the debt of these, er . . . gentlemen." He approached them. "You must tell me, good sirs, how best I may reward you."

There was a brief silence. Then Sebastian spoke.

"Your Majesty . . . my intention in coming to Keladon was to seek employment as a jester to your court."

"A jester?" King Septimus looked uncertain. "It's some time since we had one of those," he murmured. "I'm not sure that I . . ."

"He's a very good one," said Princess Kerin. "In fact, on our journey here, Mr. Darke has kept me entertained with many excellent jokes and stories and I can vouch for the fact that he is quite hilarious."

King Septimus considered for a moment. Then he smiled. "If he is to your taste, Princess, then he is to mine also. Of course I shall employ him! Shall we say . . . three golden crowns a month?"

Sebastian almost shouted with delight. This was more money than he had ever dreamed of. But Princess Kerin hadn't finished yet.

"Uncle, I think a man of his experience is worth five crowns," she said. "That's certainly what he was used to receiving in the royal court of Jerabim."

Sebastian stared at her. He had never been anywhere near the court of Jerabim and she knew it. But she had said it with such absolute conviction, nobody would have suspected the invention for a moment.

"Well, then we must go one better!" announced Septimus. "We'll call it six crowns. And of course you will receive board and lodging here at the palace. Well, what do you say, Mr. Darke? Do we have an agreement?"

"We certainly do, Your Majesty." Sebastian tried and failed to wipe the grin off his face. He looked down at Cornelius, who was smiling up at him, as if to say, "See, I said you could do it!"

"And we will sample your talents after Princess Kerin's birthday feast tonight," added King Septimus, which got rid of the grin in an instant. The king turned his attention to Cornelius. "Now, little man, what can I do for you?" he asked.

Cornelius bowed again. "Your Majesty, I came to Keladon with but one purpose in mind. To join the Crimson Cloak."

King Septimus stared at Cornelius for a moment. Then he laughed. "The Crimson Cloak!" he said. "You? Forgive me, Captain, but . . . you are such a little fellow, I hardly think the position would suit you."

"On the contrary, Your Majesty, I believe it would suit me down to the ground. I only ask an opportunity to prove my worth to you."

King Septimus smiled, but there was no real mirth in his eyes. Sebastian, who now had every excuse in the world to like the man, still found that something in the king's demeanor troubled him.

"Well, Captain Drummel, I must tell you that any man in the land is free to apply for a position in the Crimson Cloak. And to gain entry, he has only to achieve one thing. He must first beat my champion in unarmed combat."

Cornelius rubbed his hands together. "I would be more than happy to undertake such a contest," he said.

King Septimus looked decidedly smug. "Perhaps you should wait until you've actually *seen* my champion," he said. He lifted a hand and clicked his fingers. "Send out Klart," he shouted. There was a long pause and they could dimly hear a series of people shouting out the name somewhere in the depths of the palace.

"Klart is a native of the island of Mavelia," said the king, inspecting the perfectly manicured fingernails of one hand. "I don't suppose either of you have visited it?"

Sebastian and Cornelius shook their heads.

The king smiled sweetly. "Let's just say that they are a . . . rugged people," he said. "And I will quite understand if you wish to reconsider facing him in a fight."

After what seemed an age, a figure came shambling out from the open doorway of the palace. Sebastian took a sharp breath. The man was so big, he had to stoop to avoid bashing his shaggy head against the arch of stone above him. He was a veritable giant, a great big muscular brute, with dirty shoulder-length red hair and a wild beard. He was dressed in what looked like the furry hide of a buffalope, and as he came striding forward across the courtyard, the ground seemed to shake under the impact of his heavily booted feet. He raised his mighty arms to wave to the crowd and they cheered him gleefully. Obviously this was not the first time they had seen him fight.

"Cornelius, this is ridiculous!" said Sebastian. "You can't fight *him*, he's as big as a house."

The little warrior shrugged and cracked his knuckles together. "There's a very old saying around Golmira," he said. "One that I have lived by for years. 'The bigger they come, the harder they fall.'"

King Septimus chuckled at that. "Bravely spoken, little man!" he said. "Well then, if you're intent on doing this, step up here and try your luck. But I can take no responsibility for the outcome. Klart tends to play rough."

"So do I," said Cornelius quietly. He unbuckled his sword and knife and dropped them to the ground. Then he climbed the steps to the courtyard. The king gestured to the others present and they all moved back to give the two warriors space to fight.

FOURTEEN

MAKING THE GRADE

"Now," said the king, "let's have a good clean fight, boys. No biting, no gouging—and, Klart, this time, absolutely no eating your opponent." He stepped back to give them more room.

The two men stared at each other in silence for a few moments and then began to circle, both of them crouched in fighting stances. Sebastian didn't know what to think. With his own eyes he had seen Cornelius defeat powerful foes, but Klart was so big and so strong, it seemed an impossible contest.

It was Klart who made the first move, swinging down with a right fist, but Cornelius simply dodged the blow and danced back again. He resumed his fighter's stance and went back to his circling. The crowd cheered appreciatively. Klart tried several more times to hit his little opponent but to no avail: Cornelius was simply too fast for him. The third time that Klart tried it, Cornelius danced quickly in, jabbed a punch into one of

the giant's knees and danced out again. Klart bellowed with anger and tried lashing out with one foot, hoping, no doubt, to kick Cornelius clear off the courtyard; but the little man nimbly stepped aside and caught the heel of Klart's extended foot in his hands. He pulled sharply upward, effortlessly tipping the giant off balance.

Klart fell backward and hit the marble floor with such an impact that he cracked a couple of tiles. He gave a grunt of dull surprise and was about to get back up when Cornelius performed an agile somersault, leaping up into the air and coming down hard on Klart's stomach, driving all the air out of him. The big man doubled up with a grunt and, as his head came forward, Cornelius took two fingers and rammed them up Klart's nostrils, as far as they would go. Then he began to twist the fingers around.

A bellow of agony came out of Klart, so loud that Sebastian had to cover his ears, for fear of them bursting. The giant was trying to pull away from Cornelius, but the little warrior had hooked his fingers in tightly and the big man simply could not shake free of his grasp.

"Now," said Cornelius calmly, "just say mercy and I shall release you."

Klart did say something but it sounded like "Arrrrrggggg-hhhhhh!" He increased his attempts to get free, even swatting at Cornelius with his huge hands, but Cornelius hung grimly on and twisted even more. The crowd was going wild now, shouting and cheering for Cornelius.

"Doh!" roared Klart. "Pleeeese, dopppit!"

"Not till you ask for mercy," insisted Cornelius.

There was a long moment while the big man tried to resist saying anything; but Cornelius gave an extra hard twist until his two fingers were arranged vertically. Finally, clearly in agony, Klart had to yield.

"Merzy!" he bellowed. "Merzy!"

Cornelius relinquished his hold, wiped his fingers on Klart's robe and hopped down off his chest. He strolled back to an astonished King Septimus and made a formal bow as the crowd broke into wild applause.

"Your Majesty," he said, "it will be an honor to serve you."

The king looked like somebody who had just awoken from a dream to discover that he had sleepwalked naked into a crowded marketplace. He gazed around at the cheering, applauding crowd and then down at the smiling face of Cornelius, and he shrugged his shoulders.

"Very well," he said. "It would seem that you are now a member of the Crimson Cloak." He threw a disgusted look at Klart, who had got back to his feet and was standing rubbing his throbbing nose. "And as for you, you big oaf, get out of my sight!"

Klart looked crestfallen. He turned and shambled dejectedly back to whichever dark corner he had emerged from. Sebastian felt quite sorry for him. He was not the first warrior to learn the hard way that Cornelius was a gifted fighter. As he slunk away, he received a chorus of jeers and boos from the very crowd that had been applauding him when he arrived. It made Sebastian appreciate how fickle an audience could be.

"And now," said King Septimus, "let us go in and—"

"Ahem!" said Max. "Excuse me, Your Majesty . . ."

The king paused and looked back at him in surprise.

"I hope you weren't forgetting me," said Max. "After all, I *did* play a very big part in the rescue."

"A buffalope?" said King Septimus in disbelief. "A beast of burden?"

"He doesn't much care for that description," said Sebastian anxiously. "He thinks of himself more as my—"

"Partner," prompted Max.

"Well, he did take on the Brigands," admitted Cornelius.

"And two huge lupers," added Princess Kerin.

The king looked at each of them in turn, as though hardly believing the situation he had found himself in. His face turned a deep shade of purple, and for a moment it seemed as though he was going to start yelling at people. But then he managed to get control of himself. He sighed and spread out his hands in a gesture of defeat.

"Oh . . . very well," he said. "Supposing I have him installed in the royal stables alongside my best equines? They eat the finest food and lead a pampered existence. I hardly see that there could be a more appropriate reward for a . . . a buffalope."

"That sounds most agreeable," said Max, after some consideration. "And if Your Majesty could see his way to sending me a few fresh pommers, to go with my dinner, that would be a wonderful bonus!"

Sebastian glared at Max. "Don't push it!" he warned him.

For an instant King Septimus seemed somewhat flustered.

But then he looked at his niece and gazed around at the crowd of onlookers, who were hanging on his every word, and he managed to force a smile. "Of . . . course," he said. "For the ones who saved the life of Princess Kerin, nothing is too much trouble." He beckoned to someone in the crowd and a man stepped forward, a stocky, brutish-looking fellow in a leather jerkin. "Ostler, take this . . . this fine animal to the royal stables. See that he has everything he needs to make him comfortable. And please ensure that Mr. Darke's caravan is safely stored away until he has need of it."

The ostler gazed at Max, nonplussed for a moment. Clearly it would be the first time that a buffalope had enjoyed the luxury of the royal stables. But he knew better than to question the king. He bowed his head. "As you command, sire," he said, and, reaching up to Max's halter, he began to lead the buffalope and caravan away across the square, the crowd shuffling aside to let him through.

"I'll see you later," Max called over his shoulder. "After I've rested."

Sebastian and Cornelius exchanged amused glances.

"I pity that poor ostler," murmured Sebastian. "I would say his patience is about to be tested to the very limit."

Now King Septimus turned his attention to Captain Tench. "Captain, I have a task for you."

"Of course, sire." Captain Tench dismounted and handed the reins of his equine to one of his other men. He walked quickly across to the steps and went down on one knee. "What is your pleasure, Your Majesty?"

"I wish you to see to it that Captain Drummel is installed in the quarters assigned to the Crimson Cloak. He is to be treated with the respect due to all members of my personal bodyguard. Have I made myself clear?"

"Yes, sire." Tench got back to his feet and gazed down at the little warrior, then gestured for him to follow. Though he was obeying his orders without hesitation, the expression on Captain Tench's face suggested that he would rather be throwing himself into a pit of excrement than doing this.

The little warrior grinned up at Sebastian. "No doubt I'll see you at the feast later on," he said. And he followed Captain Tench across the courtyard toward the palace entrance.

The king turned to look at Sebastian. "Now, Mr. Darke, that only leaves you to take care of. Let me see now—who would be the best person? Ah, yes. Malthus!"

The king's skinny little personal assistant jumped forward as though he had been prodded in the buttocks with a hot knife. "Yes, Your Majesty?"

"Take Mr. Darke to our most opulent guest room and ensure that he wants for nothing. You will personally see to his every wish."

"Of course, Your Majesty." Malthus turned to Sebastian and bowed his head in reverence. "If you would care to follow me, Mr. Darke?"

Sebastian was thrilled. He just wished his mother were here to see him, standing in this fabulous place and being treated like a lord. He glanced at Princess Kerin and saw that she was smiling at him once again.

"What do you think of Keladon so far?" she asked mischievously.

"Your Royal Highness, it's beyond my wildest dreams!" he told her. "I never expected to be treated so grandly."

"It is only what you are worth," she assured him. "I'll let you get settled into your chambers and I'll look forward to your performance tonight."

"Umm . . . yes, tonight." Sebastian had temporarily forgotten about his impending debut and her words seemed to unleash a whole flock of butterflies in his stomach. He bowed once more to King Septimus, and as he did so, he noticed that the king was gazing at his niece, his face quite expressionless—and yet once again Sebastian's elvish sixth sense seemed to tingle. He was now quite convinced that although King Septimus pretended to care for Princess Kerin, he actually despised her.

"Now, Princess," he heard him say, "you'll be wanting to see the special birthday present I have for you. . . ."

But there was no time to dwell on it. Malthus was leading the way toward the magnificent open doors of the palace and Sebastian had to follow. Hopefully, he would have the opportunity to talk to Princess Kerin later.

The huge crowd behind him cheered with enthusiasm, and as he followed Malthus, he had a wild urge to skip like a happy child. It was only by an exceptional effort that he managed to stop himself.

FIFTEEN

PALACE OF DREAMS

Sebastian had never seen anything like it. From the cool marble-clad floors to the high, gold-embellished ceilings, this was opulence on a scale that made him want to walk around with his mouth hanging open. The walls were adorned with massive paintings and richly embroidered textiles. Huge stone pillars rose from floor to ceiling, each of them carved with a multitude of faces, figures and fantastical creatures. Every surface was encrusted with ornaments of gold and silver, decorated with precious jewels. And every doorway was flanked by armed soldiers in full uniform, brandishing swords or spears.

Sebastian was beginning to see that the stories he had heard about King Septimus's wealth were no exaggeration. He truly must be the richest man in the known world. And who would be surprised to learn that he was not eager to hand that wealth on to somebody else?

Malthus led Sebastian up a huge curving staircase, hewn

from pure white marble. At intervals along the staircase, life-size paintings of austere-looking men and women, dressed in their finery, glowered down at whoever passed by.

"The kings and queens of Keladon," announced Malthus, waving one hand at the portraits, as though he had done this so many times, he didn't even have to think about it. "From days of antiquity right up to the present. The royal lineage stretches back to the earliest times."

Sebastian thought that they looked a stern and fearsome bunch, the kind of people you wouldn't like to bump into on a dark night. But Malthus, who seemed to have settled happily into the role of tour guide, just rattled out a line or two about each of them with practiced ease.

"That's Balthazar the Baleful," he said, indicating a fierce-looking man with a spiky gray beard. "He was the king who instigated the custom of the populace giving half their earnings toward the upkeep of the palace, a practice that still continues today." He gestured around at the grandeur that surrounded them. "As you can see, we do quite well out of it."

Now he pointed at a portrait of a short, stooped woman with a fearful squint and an expression that suggested somebody was holding a goblet of sour milk under her nose.

"Queen Wendolyn the Woeful. Her husband died three days after the wedding and she spent the entire fifteen years of her reign in floods of tears. She had to continually change her clothes because they kept shrinking. Hence the nickname."

They climbed a few more steps and Malthus gestured at a painting of a short, rather fat little man with a red face.

136

"King Ferdinand the Flatulent; a good and noble ruler whose short reign was somewhat disrupted by an unfortunate habit. No doubt you can guess what that was."

"Umm . . . flatulence? That's wind, isn't it?"

"Hmm. They say that on a good night he was able to blow out the candles without getting out of bed—if you catch my drift?"

"Right."

"Unfortunately, one night the gas ignited and blew his bedchamber to smithereens. A ghastly end to his reign."

Sebastian tried to look solemn but felt a powerful urge to laugh. "They . . . they all seem to have nicknames, don't they? How come King Septimus doesn't have one?"

Malthus glanced around quickly and lowered his voice to reply. "He does," he murmured. "But nobody would ever dare use it in his hearing." He looked around again, and now his voice was little more than a whisper. "It's Septimus the Slaphead."

Sebastian frowned. "Why Slaphead?" he asked.

"Shush! Keep your voice down!" Malthus moved closer. "It's because he's completely bald."

"Bald? But—"

"Shush! He suffered from a nervous disorder as a child and all his hair fell out over a period of a few days. It never grew back. That's a wig he wears, and nobody's ever allowed to see him without it."

"Then how . . . ?"

Malthus was now so close to Sebastian that he was literally whispering in his ear: "I accidentally walked in on him once

137

when he wasn't wearing it." Malthus's face wore an expression of absolute terror at the memory. "Luckily, I caught sight of him in a mirror before he saw me and I was able to slip back out of the room unnoticed." Malthus rolled his eyes. "Believe me, if he'd known, I'd have had an appointment with the executioner's axe."

"Oh, surely not!"

"I mean it! He can be absolutely ruthless when he puts his mind to it. I sometimes think that Septimus the Severe would be a more appropriate name for him. I've heard that years ago he commissioned a wigmaker to prepare hundreds of wigs, enough to last him three lifetimes—and then he had the man put to death so he couldn't tell anybody else." Malthus thought for a moment. "And listen," he added, "you didn't hear that from me. If you suggest to anyone that I told you, I will deny it and I can assure you, it will be I who am believed, not some stranger from Jerabim."

"Oh, have no fear, I won't breathe a word." Sebastian couldn't help feeling that a gossip like Malthus was not the best man for a king to have as an assistant. They had reached the first-floor landing now. Malthus turned to his right and led Sebastian along a corridor, with rooms opening off at intervals.

"A word of advice," said Malthus. "I would go through your store of jokes and assiduously remove anything that has a reference to hair in it. Just in case. You don't want to end up like Hengist the Hirsute, do you?"

Sebastian frowned. "Who's Hengist . . . ?"

"The Hirsute. He was a nobleman from Berundia. Very hairy fellow. Hair everywhere. Head, shoulders, arms, teeth—"

"Hairy teeth?"

"Well, maybe not the teeth, but you get the picture. Septimus took an instant dislike to him. Put it like this . . ." Once again, Malthus cast a secretive glance around. "The two of them went out hunting javralats together and only one of them came back." He waggled his eyebrows at Sebastian. "Draw your own conclusions."

Sebastian smiled but found himself going through his mental store of jokes looking for anything that could be problematic. He couldn't think of any jokes he used that mentioned hair or wigs.

"Now," said Malthus brightly, "I've selected something really special for you. It's what we call the Slaughter Suite—"

"I beg your pardon?"

"Oh, relax, it's nicer than it sounds," Malthus assured him. "The 'slaughter' bit just refers to the murals." He opened a heavy wooden door and Sebastian found himself looking into a large, luxuriously appointed chamber, which would have been delightful were it not for the painting of an extremely bloody battle that occupied the whole of the back wall. It depicted a troop of foot soldiers being trampled into the mud by a battalion of Keladonian cavalry, mounted on vicious-looking armored equines. Malthus led Sebastian into the room.

"That painting commemorates the magnificent victory of King Septimus over the forces of King Rabnat of Delaton. Over three thousand men hacked to pieces in one charge!"

"Lovely," said Sebastian weakly. He tried to put the painting out of his mind and went instead to the magnificent four-poster bed in the very center of the room. He sat on the mattress and bounced up and down a bit and had to admit it was an incredibly comfortable bed; but turning had drawn his gaze to another painting on the far wall, which seemed to depict a series of horrific tortures. Luckless individuals tied to chairs were having their fingernails pulled out, their kneecaps smashed by hammers and their tongues pierced with red-hot metal spikes. "Oh dear," he said.

Malthus shrugged. "Well, I'll admit the décor leaves something to be desired. But it was a toss-up between this and the rooms commemorating the Rodent Infestation and the Plague of Boils."

"I'm sure it will be . . . very comfortable," said Sebastian, thinking that he could always use some sheets to conceal the awful pictures. He didn't want to appear ungrateful, and after bedding down on the hard ground for several weeks, anything would be an improvement.

Malthus pulled back some heavy velvet drapes and revealed a tall casement window. "You've got a lovely view of the palace grounds," he said encouragingly. "And next door you've got your very own en-suite cess bucket."

"That's . . . lovely," said Sebastian, trying to sound delighted.

Malthus indicated an embroidered cord dangling from the ceiling. "If you need anything at all, just pull that and a servant will attend you." He looked around the room with an air of satisfaction. "I'm sure you'll be most comfortable here, Mr. Darke."

"I'm sure I will too."

"Is there anything else you need, before I take my leave?"

"Well, there is *one* thing . . . but I'm sure it wouldn't be possible."

"Oh please, just ask!"

"It's my mother back in Jerabim."

Malthus frowned. "You want your mummy?" he asked.

"No! Not exactly. But I'd love to let her know that I've arrived here safely and that I've been employed by King Septimus."

"No problem!" Malthus indicated a writing desk with a quill pen and some sheets of parchment. "Just scribble down a note for her and I'll have one of our express riders deliver it. Hmm . . . Jerabim . . ." He thought for a few moments. "If we get the note off tonight and he rides flat out, it could be there in—oh, five or six days."

"That soon? Incredible!" Sebastian moved over to the desk and sat down.

"Just ring the bell when you're ready," concluded Malthus. "The servant will take it straight down to the post room. I'll see you later," he added. "At the performance."

"Oh yes. Later . . ."

Sebastian tried not to think about the performance. He dipped the quill into the inkpot, thought for a moment and then wrote a quick note.

Dear Mother,

> *Have arrived safely in Keladon. Everyone here very welcoming and King Septimus has engaged my services for six gold crowns a month! My first performance is tonight at a grand banquet.*

> *On the way, Max and I met a really nice fellow called Cornelius. He's a captain from Golmira—only a little chap but he*

has the heart of a giant. We also rescued a princess from an attack by Brigands! It turns out she is King Septimus's niece and will be Queen of Keladon one day. She is really nice and we are great friends. I think you would approve.

We had a bit of a bad time with some lupers on the way, but I am glad to say we are here now and everything is going as planned. I will send money just as soon as I can.

I hope you are well and not too lonely.

Max sends his regards—he's staying in the royal stables, where he's no doubt being spoiled rotten!

Your loving son,
Sebastian

Reading the note through, Sebastian couldn't help remarking to himself that it sounded like the ramblings of some deranged idiot, and he was worried that his mother would think that he was simply making it up or, worse still, had gone quite mad. He rolled up the parchment and secured it with a piece of string. He was about to ring the bell to summon the servant when there was a knock at his door.

"Come in," he said, expecting it to be Malthus with another snippet of gossip to share. But it was Princess Kerin.

SIXTEEN

THE PLOT THICKENS

The princess stepped into the room.

"Hello!" said Sebastian. He stood up so quickly that his lanky knees caught under the writing desk and nearly overturned it. He regained his balance and made a clumsy attempt at a bow, but she waved a hand at him as if to say that it wasn't necessary to be so formal.

"I thought I'd drop by and see how you're settling in," she told him. He saw that she had a small, furry creature sitting on her shoulder.

"What on earth is that?" asked Sebastian.

"It's a boobah. They live in the jungles to the far south. He's my birthday present from Uncle Septimus. I thought you might like to see him." As she spoke, the creature jumped from her shoulder, clambered up one of the bedposts and crouched up on the roof of the four-poster, making strange chattering sounds. "I'm going to call him Tiddles," she said.

"Why, he's almost like a little man!" observed Sebastian. He smiled mischievously. "Perhaps you should have called him Cornelius."

"I wouldn't let *him* hear you say that," she said. Then she looked sad. "You were right, of course. He's a lovely present but he wasn't worth the lives of my Royal Guard. Next time I will think before I act, I promise." She walked over and then froze, looking at the mural on the wall behind him. "Oh my goodness," she said. "I'd forgotten about that hideous painting!"

He smiled. "You get used to it after a while. It's not as bad as the one behind you." He pointed to the torture scenes and she turned to look, then winced.

"Honestly," she said. "Uncle's taste in art leaves something to be desired. One of the first things I'll do when I'm queen is redecorate the guest rooms. I mean, something more understated. A nice soft magnolia, perhaps." She turned back to look at him. "So . . . are you all set for tonight's performance?"

He shrugged. "I suppose so. I'll need to clean myself up a bit—and I'd better get a new outfit from the caravan before I go on. This one still has luper blood on it."

She laughed. "That was quite an adventure," she said. She moved across to his bed and sat down on the end of it. "Well, at least this seems comfortable enough," she observed, bouncing up and down. She patted the coverlet with one hand. "Come and sit beside me," she suggested.

He did as he was told, lowering himself rather uncomfortably onto the bed. He wasn't at all sure that he should be sitting on a bed with a young woman who would soon be queen.

"You seem nervous," she observed.

"No!" he replied, rather too quickly. "Not—not at all. I'm per-fectly relaxed."

She seemed unconvinced by this. "Perhaps you're worried about tonight," she said.

"Well . . . yes, you know how it is. New venue, new audience. You never really know what to expect."

"I suppose you've appeared in lots of grand places."

"Oh . . . a few," he agreed; and hoped that she wouldn't ask him to name any of them.

"Are all jesters like you?" she asked.

"I don't know. I've never met any. Apart from my father, of course. And he was human." They sat there in an uneasy si-lence for a moment, staring at a painting on the end wall, which appeared to depict a group of jubilant soldiers setting fire to a temple, while in the background a line of priests were being lined up for execution. Princess Kerin seemed to be waiting for something, and once again Sebastian experienced an irrational desire to kiss her; but he told himself that it was hardly his place to be kissing princesses. He turned to look at her.

"Princess, may I ask you a question?"

"Of course."

"You promise you won't get angry?"

"I can't say until I've heard the question, can I?"

"No . . ." Sebastian looked down at his feet for a while, noticing how scuffed and worn his boots were. Then he took a deep breath. "Your uncle . . . King Septimus. Do you . . . Well, do you trust him?"

"Of course I do!" She stared at him. "Why do you ask?"

"Well, only because . . . some people would say that he might enjoy being king of Keladon and . . . he might not want to hand power over to somebody else. Even his own niece."

She grimaced. "Yes, but Uncle Septimus has always known that he would rule only for a time, just until I was old enough. There was never any question. And after my parents died he was so kind to me, so thoughtful . . ."

"Umm . . . yes. That was the other thing. I hope you don't mind me asking, but how did your parents die?"

The princess stared at him for a moment as though she was shocked by his question. Perhaps nobody had ever dared to touch on the subject before. Sebastian realized he was once again in danger of upsetting her, but it was too late to withdraw the question. Princess Kerin seemed to think about it for a long time before she answered.

"They were murdered," she said in a very small voice. "They were given poisoned wine to drink."

"And it never occurred to you that perhaps your uncle—?"

"It didn't even happen here," she interrupted him. "But in Bodengen. They were guests of King Valshak, who was the ruler at that time; they were there to approve an alliance between our two countries. At the feast somebody gave them poisoned wine and they were dead in moments. Uncle Septimus wasn't even with them—he was back here at the palace and learned of their death at the same time as I did."

"I see." Sebastian felt quite wretched now for having voiced his suspicions.

146

"My parents came home in two coffins. I was thirteen years old at the time. We mourned them and buried them, and Uncle Septimus was declared king until I was of age. His first act as monarch was to declare war against Bodengen; a war that lasted until recently, when Queen Helena came to the throne. Now Uncle Septimus is keen to revive the alliance that was planned all those years ago. Which is why my first act as monarch will be to marry Queen Helena's son, Rolf."

Sebastian stared at her. "What?" he said. "Rolf? Rolf with the missing teeth and the sloping forehead?"

She nodded, not looking him in the eyes. "Yes," she said. "*That* Rolf."

"But . . . you aren't going to go through with that, are you? I mean, you said yourself that you didn't *like* him."

"What has that got to do with anything?" she asked him crossly. "Do you think I have any say in the matter? Marrying him will be my duty, performed for the good of my country."

"But that's terrible!" Sebastian got up from the bed and paced around the room in agitation, hardly believing what she had just told him. "My mother always says that there's only one reason to marry somebody and that's because you are in love with them."

Princess Kerin sighed. "That's all well and good for ordinary people," she said. "But for ones like myself, nothing is ever as straightforward. Besides, as I told you the other day, I don't *believe* in love. The only people I ever cared for were taken from me when I was a child. There's nobody else in the picture."

Sebastian frowned. "Maybe you haven't looked properly," he said.

She sat there for a long time in silence, regarding him with those deep green eyes. Then she got up from the bed, came over to him and kissed him gently on the cheek. "For luck," she said.

There was a silence and they stood there gazing at each other, as something unspoken passed between them. Sebastian knew in that moment that she did feel something for him, but that it would almost certainly never come to anything.

"I'd better go now," she said. "Here, Tiddles, good boy!" The boobah climbed obediently back down the bedpost and jumped onto her shoulder. She started for the door, then hesitated for a moment and looked back at him.

"You know," she added, "I prefer it when you are telling your jokes and stories. It's so much less complicated." She smiled sadly. "I'll see you tonight." She went out of the room, closing the door behind her. Sebastian stayed where he was for a moment, gazing at the door, hoping . . . perhaps expecting that she would come back again.

But time passed and she didn't return. So he walked over to the desk, remembering the message for his mother. He reached for the pull-cord and rang the bell to summon the servant.

Magda was still peering out of her chamber window when the king came storming back in and kicked her up the backside a second time. She turned with a yelp, terrified to see that the anger he had displayed previously had been just the beginning. Now he was absolutely livid.

"My face hurts!" he growled, staring down at her.

"I beg your pardon, Your Majesty? I'm afraid I don't—"

The king lifted two fingers to point at the corners of his own mouth. "It's where I've been grinning like an imbecile," he said. "Being nice to that brat of a princess. Giving her a very expensive gift, which I had intended to keep for myself; and worse, welcoming those three . . . filthy tramps down there. One of them was a jester. You know my history with jesters, Magda. But no, I had to greet him with open arms!" He began to pace up and down, his face set in an expression of total revulsion.

"Your Majesty, I think I—"

"And if that wasn't bad enough, I had to watch my champion being knocked down by some short-arsed warrior who doesn't look big enough to be let out of sight of his mother!"

"If you would just—"

"And finally . . . finally . . ." The king was now so incensed that Magda half expected to see steam coming out his ears. "Finally, I have to stand there like a fool, while demands are made upon me by a . . . a"—he could hardly bring himself to say the word—"a *buffalope*! A stinking, filthy fleabag of a beast which thinks it can treat me as some kind of servant. I mean, what is the world coming to? Have I gone mad?"

He was leaning forward over Magda now, his face purple, his teeth bared, his eyes bulging. He had never looked angrier or more terrifying. She was almost too afraid to say anything, but was more fearful of the consequences of not convincing him that she could rescue the situation.

"Your Majesty, if you would just allow me to speak . . . ," she ventured.

He folded his arms across his chest and stood there waiting. "Well?" he asked her.

150

"I . . . I realize how much it must have cost you to be agreeable to those people. But you managed it very well. And now everyone in your court has *seen* you welcome them." She lifted a skinny finger and waved it in the air. "So the foundation of our little deception is in place." She began to edge toward the door. "And it simply remains for me to find the weak spot; the opening we shall exploit to make the people think that the strangers are evil."

King Septimus scowled. "And how exactly will we achieve that?" he asked her.

"Er . . . well . . . at this precise moment, Your Majesty, I'm not too sure of that final element."

"You what?"

The anger was bubbling back to the surface and Magda very wisely decided to make herself scarce. "But I *will* be sure just as soon as I have spoken to the jester!" She was going out of the door now, moving with surprising speed for one so ancient. The king glanced around quickly and noticed a heavy bronze drinking goblet on a nearby table. In one swift movement, he scooped it up and flung it after her, through the open doorway. He was rewarded with a dull clunk and a gasp of pain. The goblet clattered unseen onto the stone floor, but after a slight pause he heard the old woman hobbling away down the staircase.

Septimus scowled and prowled over to look out of the window. The people had moved away from the palace steps now and were drifting back toward the marketplace. With some satisfaction, he saw that the messenger who had brought him the news of Princess Kerin's survival was sitting on the steps, cradling his head in his injured fingers. No doubt news of his "promotion" had just reached him. King Septimus couldn't be sure, but from up here he got the distinct impression that the man was weeping like a child.

It wasn't much but it lightened the king's mood considerably. . . .

SEVENTEEN

THE ROYAL STABLES

After the servant girl had collected his letter, Sebastian found that he couldn't relax and he began to feel more and more nervous about the evening's performance. So he made his way downstairs and asked one of the guards to direct him to the royal stables.

It was behind the palace, set in the midst of some beautiful lush gardens, where more of those incredible fountains splashed their never-ending supplies of water into stone basins.

The stable gates were open and Sebastian went in. On either side of a broad, straw-covered avenue, rows of spacious stalls held some of the most splendid-looking equines he had ever seen: proud, spirited creatures with finely arched necks and flared nostrils. He was just thinking that they made odd stable partners for Max when he heard the familiar doleful voice droning away from a stall down at the far end of the building. It was merely a matter of following the sound, which got progressively louder as he approached.

". . . so there I was, facing down two huge lupers, both of them slavering at the jaws and ready to tear me to pieces. But they had reckoned without my inbred courage and determination. A twist of my horns and a kick of my back legs and they ran whimpering through the forest, completely vanquished."

Sebastian ducked his head round the entrance of the final stall and saw Max, lounging on a bed of deep clean straw. His words were directed at a small and rather fat mule, who just stood there looking at him blankly.

"I don't like to boast," continued Max, "but we buffalopes are known for our tenacity; and my family more than most. Why, it's said that even at a young age, I was able to—"

Max broke off as he registered the sound of a polite cough from behind him. "Ah, here's my young master now!" he said. "Osbert, may I introduce Sebastian Darke, Prince of Fools and King of Jesters?"

The mule looked over at Sebastian and bared his teeth in a goofy grin. " 'Allo!" he said. "Osbert much pleased to meet jester man!"

Max gave Sebastian a knowing look. "Osbert's not the most erudite of companions, but he's the only one here who's actually deigned to talk to me." He nodded his horned head at the stalls further along the building. "That lot are all far too stuck up to give me the time of day." He huffed. "It's their loss," he added.

"Their loss," echoed Osbert. "Posh twerps."

Sebastian smiled at Max. "So how have you settled in?" he asked. "I trust your dinner was up to scratch?"

154

"Can't complain," admitted Max, sounding almost disappointed at the fact. "They serve a very nice oatmeal with bee's-gold sweetening; and plenty of fresh fruit. Mind you, after that journey, I deserve a bit of feeding up." He glanced at his companion. "Osbert has been showing me how things are done around here. He's the army mascot, apparently."

"Me army good-luck charm," said Osbert, with evident pride. "When soldiers march on parade, Osbert go too. It bad luck if anything happen to Osbert. So me well looked after!" Saying so much seemed to have momentarily exhausted him. "I go lie down," he concluded, and strolled out of the stall.

Max gazed after him for a moment, then lowered his voice considerably. "A nice enough fellow but not much going on in the old noggin. Doesn't have a lot to say for himself."

"Unlike you," observed Sebastian. "I think that as I came in, I heard the unmistakable sound of you blowing your own trumpet."

"Well, you have to make your own entertainment here. It would be a long day indeed without any conversation."

"Perhaps." Sebastian gazed around the interior of the stables. "I must say, this is rather grand. Better appointed than our house back in Jerabim. I don't suppose you know where they stored the caravan, do you? I need some fresh clothes for this evening's performance."

"It's along here." Max got back to his feet. "I'll go with you."

"Oh, don't disturb yourself," said Sebastian mockingly. "I wouldn't want you to *strain* anything."

"You're developing a sarcastic streak," said Max disdainfully.

"It is ill-becoming in one of such tender years." He led the way out of the stalls and Sebastian followed. "Feeling confident, are we?" asked Max. "Only I rather like being here—I wouldn't want anything to happen that might change it—"

"I'm sure I'll be fine," said Sebastian grimly. "But thanks for your vote of confidence."

"Now stop taking everything as a personal affront. I was only saying . . ."

They had reached a large storage bay at the far end of the stables, and there stood Sebastian's caravan.

"Here it is, safe and sound," announced Max. "It's lucky I'm so close. I've been able to keep an eye on it."

"Hmm." Sebastian wasn't convinced. He noted that the wooden tailgate was down—he was sure it hadn't been when he'd left it. Sure enough, as he came nearer, he heard the soft sounds of movement from within, and one hand went instinctively to the handle of his sword. He stepped onto the tailgate and peeped inside the jumbled interior. A short, cloaked figure was bent over a container of props, searching through its contents with two gnarled hands.

"Who are you?" demanded Sebastian angrily. "What are you doing in my caravan?"

The figure jolted round, revealing an ancient, wizened face, one eye no more than a white sightless blob. As Sebastian stared at it, the face broke into a hideous, gap-toothed grimace, which was probably intended to be a smile, but which in the gloom of the caravan's interior was absolutely terrifying. Max gave a snort of fear and shrank back from the steps. Sebastian began to pull his sword from its sheath, but paused as the creature spoke to him.

"Fear not, young master, it is only I, Magda, adviser to King Septimus."

"What do you want here?" asked Sebastian.

"The king bade me come down and, er . . . ensure that you have everything you need for tonight's performance."

Sebastian was unconvinced. "If that's the case, wouldn't you have been better off coming to my chambers?" he said.

"Oh, well, I . . . thought I'd find you down here . . . making preparations." Magda's spindly fingers gestured at the various props and costumes that hung in the crowded interior. "I must say, you have a fine collection of equipment. I couldn't help noticing this." The fingertips brushed against the side of a large upright wooden cabinet that was secured against one wall.

"Oh, the disappearing cabinet," said Sebastian without enthusiasm. "Yes, my father used that in his act, but I—"

"You are a *magician*?" Magda seemed quite excited at this news.

"I'd hardly call myself that! But I do sometimes include the odd magic trick in my performance."

"Splendid news!" Magda clapped her hands together in a show of apparent delight. "His Majesty loves magic tricks, particularly disappearing acts. He will be thrilled! Princess Kerin too!"

Sebastian came up the steps into the wagon. "I wasn't planning to include this illusion in tonight's performance."

"Oh, why not?" Magda gave him a disapproving look. "You do not wish to please His Majesty?"

"Well, er . . . of course I do! It's just that the trick isn't part of my usual routine. I generally just tell jokes."

"Jokes. Hmm." Magda looked decidedly troubled. She paced around the cramped interior of the wagon for a while. "Well, it's entirely up to you, of course, but . . ."

"What?"

"That's what our *last* jester said. *I just tell jokes*."

This was worrying news to Sebastian. He hadn't been aware that somebody had been here before him. "There was another jester?" he inquired.

"Oh yes. Percival, his name was. A merry soul. How we used to laugh at his antics!" She sighed, shook her head. "Such a pity, what happened to him."

"What do you mean, *what happened to him*?"

"Well . . . His Majesty very quickly got tired of the jokes and riddles and requested something . . . er . . . different. Alas, poor Percival could not think of anything else to amuse the king and so he got the chop."

"He lost his job?" asked Sebastian hopefully.

"He lost his *head*. You see, King Septimus is not a man to suffer fools gladly. Those who fail to entertain him in one way, generally find themselves entertaining him in another. By meeting with his executioner."

"Oh." Sebastian sat down, rather heavily, on a wicker chest. He might have known it wouldn't be as straightforward as he'd imagined. Yes, he was now employed as the king's jester, just as he had hoped to be—but if the king didn't find him *funny*, it might just be the shortest spell of employment in history.

Magda came and sat on the wicker chest alongside him. "That is why, young Master Darke, I think you should include some magic tricks as well. If poor Percival had been able to offer such diversions, the chances are he might still be with us."

Sebastian licked his lips nervously. "Perhaps you're right," he admitted. "It wouldn't harm to keep him sweet." He looked up at the old hag. "It's very good of you to help me out like this."

Magda gave a little bow. "My pleasure," she assured him. "After all, we both want the same thing, do we not? A happy king means an untroubled life . . . and when he sees the vanishing act—"

"Oh, I really don't think I can do that one."

Magda looked decidedly annoyed. "Why not?" she asked.

"Well, because it requires an assistant. And I don't have one."

"An assistant? What do you mean, an assistant?"

"Well, somebody who can vanish, obviously."

Magda appeared to be deep in thought. "Couldn't you ask for somebody from the audience?"

Sebastian shook his head. "That's no use. They'd see how the trick was done. It has to be somebody I can trust not to tell anybody how it was achieved."

Magda gave him a sly look. "You mean to tell me it's not *real* magic?"

"No, there's a secret compartment at the back of the—" He realized she was playing with him. "Oh, very good! But you see, unless I can get an accomplice, I can't—"

Suddenly the old woman snapped her bony fingers as though she'd just had a great idea. "Princess Kerin!" she croaked. "What a wonderful idea—and what a marvelous birthday treat for her! Leave it to me, young master. I'll have a quiet word with

159

her and explain that you need her help. I'm sure that after everything you've done for her, she wouldn't leave you in a fix."

Sebastian frowned. "Oh no, but really—the princess? I don't think the king would approve of her being involved."

"He'll be thrilled. Trust me." She leaned toward him and fluttered her one good eyelash like a young servant girl, a truly unnerving sight. "I'll go and speak to her right away. It will be a wonderful illusion. Imagine, Princess Kerin—*dear* Princess Kerin, disappearing in front of everyone!"

"And reappearing," Sebastian reminded her.

"Yes, yes. His Majesty will be delighted!" She hobbled toward the exit, nearly tripping over a scattering of props in her haste to depart. "I'll arrange to have the cabinet brought to the banqueting hall," she screeched. "Till tonight!" And then she was gone. He heard the sounds of her hurrying away through the stables.

He got up off the chest, opened it and started rummaging through the layers of colorful costumes within, looking for the cleanest, smartest outfit he had. When next he looked up, he saw Max's face peering apprehensively in through the doorway.

"Well, thank goodness *she's* gone," he said. "Did you ever see a more frightful creature?"

Sebastian gave the buffalope a stern look. "How many times have I told you not to judge people by the way they look?" he said. "She was actually rather helpful."

Max snorted disdainfully. "A hag like that doesn't go out of her way for anyone unless there's some kind of a trick involved," he muttered.

"There you go again!" cried Sebastian. "Hasn't anyone ever told you that beauty is only skin deep?"

"That one has thicker skin than I have," said Max. "Oh, come on, I wouldn't trust her any further than I could butt her. It's obvious to anyone that she's a *witch*."

Sebastian was starting to get angry. His nerves were already badly frayed and Max wasn't helping the situation. "She's not a witch!" he yelled. "She's just an elderly lady who's trying to be nice. Now, please, if you have nothing good to say, kindly clear off and let me prepare for my act in peace."

"Whatever happened to your famous elf intuition? Surely one look at her should tell you she—"

But Max didn't finish the sentence. Sebastian had picked up a juggling ball and flung it at his head. It bounced off one of his ears, startling rather than hurting him. But it might as well have been a knife, judging by the wounded look he gave Sebastian.

"Oh well then," he murmured. "If that's how you feel about it . . ." He turned and walked slowly away with his nose in the air.

"Max, I didn't mean that," shouted Sebastian; but the buffalope was gone, and though Sebastian waited for a few moments, expecting him to return, he didn't come back. Sebastian shook his head and went on with the task of selecting a suitable costume. He had enough on his mind, without worrying about a sulky buffalope.

Later, when he passed the stall, he saw that Max was lying on his pile of straw with his head turned resolutely away. Sebastian stood there for a moment, hoping Max would look round and see him. But he appeared to be staring straight ahead with a fierce concentration. Finally Sebastian was moved to speak. "Aren't you going to wish me luck?" he asked.

There was a long cold silence before Max answered.

"I'm sure you won't need any help from me," he said. "After all, what would I know? I'm just a stupid buffalope who thinks the worst of everyone."

Sebastian stood there for a long, silent moment, wishing that he had hung on to his temper. But time was passing too swiftly and he still had to prepare himself. "I'm sorry you feel like that," he said.

He turned and walked quickly away toward the palace.

EIGHTEEN

A SHOT OF COURAGE

Walking briskly along with his clean costume draped over one shoulder, Sebastian was stopped dead in his tracks by the sight of the figure that was strolling toward him.

It was Cornelius, dressed in the bronze breastplate and magnificent crimson cloak that befitted his new post. Under one chain-mail-clad arm he carried a plumed helmet. He was leading a tiny, dapple gray pony along by its halter. The pony was fitted out with a handsome leather saddle and bridle and was a perfect miniature of a Keladonian warrior's mount.

As he moved closer, Cornelius glanced up and saw Sebastian approaching him. He grinned with evident pride and performed a quick turn so that his friend could better appreciate his new uniform.

"You look magnificent!" said Sebastian. "That outfit could have been made for you."

Cornelius chuckled delightedly. "It was actually made for the seven-year-old nephew of one of the officers," he said. "The boy's grown out of it now but the officer thought it should fit me and it does! It's a perfect replica, right down to the last detail."

"And who's your new friend?"

Cornelius turned back and ruffled the pony's shaggy mane with affection. "This is Phantom," he said. "She was the child's mount, a dwarf species from the plains of Neruvia. She's been languishing in a stall at the royal stables for quite some time and she's positively bursting for a bit of adventure. I've ridden her around the paddock a few times and I think she'll suit me very well. She's sturdy, clever and obedient. Everything a warrior could ask for."

Sebastian grinned down at his friend. "It looks as though we've both landed on our feet," he said.

But Cornelius frowned. "Perhaps . . . but . . ."

"What?" Sebastian was puzzled. "You're not happy with the way things have turned out?"

Cornelius sighed. "Perhaps I have a suspicious nature," he said, "but I can't help feeling it's all been a bit too easy."

"I know what you mean. I keep wanting to pinch myself, make sure that I'm not dreaming. King Septimus has been very welcoming. . . ."

"Almost *too* welcoming?" ventured Cornelius.

Sebastian nodded. "The thought has occurred to me that . . . well, it seems churlish after all he's done, but I can't bring myself to trust him entirely."

Cornelius nodded. "He's a man who smiles only with his

mouth. The good humor never reaches his eyes." He waved a hand as though exasperated by his own thoughts. "As I said, I may be too suspicious. It could be that our apparent good fortune is exactly what it seems." He nodded at the costume that was slung over Sebastian's shoulder. "For your debut tonight?"

"Yes. I can't say I'm looking forward to it. I'm counting on you to laugh very loudly at every one of my jokes."

Cornelius shook his head. "I'm afraid I won't be there to hear them."

Sebastian was disappointed at this news, but tried not to let it show in his expression. "You have . . . other plans?"

"I have my first mission to undertake. I am to journey into Brigandia to deliver a very important package." He patted a large bulge in one of the saddlebags draped over Phantom's back.

"Brigandia? That's a dangerous place to venture."

Cornelius shrugged. "As a member of the Crimson Cloak, I must expect my duties to be hazardous. I didn't join up to sit around twiddling my thumbs."

"Yes, but, Cornelius, it's your first day! Couldn't they ease you into it a bit more gently?"

Cornelius laughed out loud at that. "A bodyguard follows his orders without question," he said. "It's as simple as that."

"And what's in this mysterious package?"

"I do not know. I am not permitted to look."

"But you must wonder."

"Too much curiosity can be a dangerous thing, Sebastian. And sometimes ignorance can be a blessing." Cornelius paused and glanced up at the sky, where the sun was already declining toward the horizon. "I can't stand around here talking," he said. "I have many miles to cover before nightfall." He reached up, grasped the pommel of the saddle and vaulted nimbly astride Phantom. The little pony reared up, shaking her head, eager to be off. "Good luck tonight," he added. "But I'm sure you won't need it."

And with that, he squeezed Phantom's flanks with his knees and the pony galloped away across the palace grounds, heading for the main gates. Sebastian stood and watched as the man and his mount disappeared from view round the side of a building.

He felt more nervous than ever. He had somehow imagined that Cornelius would be there to take care of him if it all went wrong. But no, he could expect no help whatsoever from anyone else. It was up to him now.

He turned and hurried on toward the palace.

Back in his chamber, he washed and put on his clean costume, a rather fetching harlequin outfit with striking multicolored diamonds all over it, and a brand-new, three-pronged hat. He regarded himself dismally in a full-length mirror, noting that this costume was even baggier on him than the previous one. He struck a few foolish poses in the mirror and pulled several idiotic faces. He had never felt more nervous in his entire life and he wished that Cornelius—and yes, even Max—could be there to watch his performance. But Cornelius would be well on his way to Brigandia by now and there wasn't the faintest chance that a buffalope would be allowed into the palace's grand banqueting hall.

He went over to the window and peered out anxiously. Darkness had already fallen and in the cloud-tumbled sky he could discern no trace of stars. He walked back to the mirror and studied his reflection again. He tried telling himself a joke, but even without an audience he couldn't seem to get the words to come out right.

"There are two merchants working to market . . . I mean, two merchants walking to market. No, that's ecological! Merchants would never walk when they can run—I mean, ride. So they were riding to market. And one of them shed—one of them said, 'How far have we troubled? Er . . . traveled!' And the other one fled . . . er . . . sped . . . er—oh, botheration!"

He wondered what his chances were of getting out of the city unseen and heading back to Jerabim. But he was sure that Max would take a very dim view of that idea. What, leave the luxury of the royal stables after just one day of taking it easy? No, there was no way out of this. He would simply have to go down there and face his fears. . . .

There was a sudden knock on the door that nearly made him jump clear out of his skin. "Yes?" he gasped.

The door creaked open and there was the hideous face of Magda peering in at him.

"The young master is ready?" she asked, in that wheedling croak that he was already beginning to dislike.

"As ready as I'll ever be," he muttered.

"I have spoken with Princess Kerin. She is more than happy

to help you with your illusion. I have had your magical apparatus set up in the banqueting hall. It is going to be quite a finale!"

"If I get that far," whispered Sebastian.

She hobbled into the room, looking concerned. "You are nervous?" she inquired.

"Nervous isn't the word," he told her. "I'm terrified. I've never performed for a king before. What if they don't think I'm funny?"

"Oh, you mustn't worry, young master. The royal court is a very receptive audience."

"Oh yes. That's probably what they told Percival just before his last show!"

Magda frowned. "I shouldn't have mentioned your predecessor."

"I'm glad you did! It pays to know where you stand. With one foot on a banana skin and your head on the executioner's block!"

Magda moved creakily across to a small table where a jug of wine and a goblet stood. "A goblet of wine will relax you," she said; and poured it out for him.

"Oh, I don't think I should drink before the show!" he protested. "I need to keep a clear head."

"Nonsense. A good stiff drink will give you confidence." She was bent forward over the table and Sebastian did not notice when she pulled a small vial of green liquid from her sleeve and upended it into the goblet. "There now," she said, lifting the goblet and giving its contents a surreptitious swirl before handing it across to him. "The wine of Keladon is famous for its special qualities. Why, just one swallow gives a man the courage and confidence to take anything in his stride. Try it."

Sebastian took the goblet and stared doubtfully at its rich, red contents. "Well, I suppose one mouthful can't hurt," he said. He lifted the goblet to his lips and took a gulp of the warm liquid. It was incredible, but he really did feel something surge through him—a rush of vitality, a jolt of confidence. He stared at Magda in amazement. "I do believe it's working," he said, astonished.

She nodded. "Of course it is," she murmured. "Trust Magda. Try some more. You will be invincible!"

He did as he was told and immediately felt a warm flush rising to his cheeks. Something in his head flickered and flared. Quite suddenly all his inhibitions seemed to have flown right out of the window. He found that he was prepared to say the first things that came into his head—things that were suspiciously like the truth. He pointed at Magda.

"I'm not saying you're ugly, but when they were handing out the looks, you must have been right at the back of the queue! I mean, no offense, but I've seen better-looking plagues! In fact I'd like to commission a painting of you. I'd put it on the mantelpiece to keep the kids away from the fire!"

Magda's face broke into that hideous gap-toothed grin. "Oh yes," she said. "Very good. I think you'll do nicely." She reached out and took his arm gently in hers. "Come, I think it's time we went down to the performance, don't you?"

"Whatever you say. . . . Whew! What's that smell? Either you haven't washed recently or the drains are backing up!" He allowed her to lead him out of the room, but somehow he just couldn't stop talking. "Listen, I don't know where you got that cloak from, but I think maybe the scarecrow wants it back!"

He kept on babbling as she led him along the corridor and down the marble staircase to the ballroom, where his royal audience was waiting for him.

Cornelius had been riding for what seemed like hours. There was little moonlight and he could not see very far in front of him; but he had done his level best to follow the directions he had been issued with and he was sure that he was on the right track.

The silence was broken only by the chirruping of unseen insects and, somewhere far away to the north, the eerie howl of a luper. Phantom gave a nervous snicker and kicked up her heels. Cornelius reached down a hand to stroke her dappled neck.

"Easy, girl," he said. "It's a long way off." But the recent attack by lupers was on his mind, and when he lifted the hand, he let it come to rest on the pommel of his sword. He kept his gaze on the way ahead.

He rode on in silence for a while and was rewarded by a sudden wash of moonlight breaking through a gap in the clouds. The silvery light picked out something on the far horizon. A lonely wooden barn stood in the midst of the plain. This was the place where he was to deliver his package.

He slowed Phantom to a walk and rode steadily closer, trying to observe everything he could. The barn was ancient, almost falling down with disrepair. It was odd that there were no equines waiting outside the barn; its doors and windows were tight shut against the night. As he came closer still, Cornelius could perceive a faint glow of lamplight issuing from under the door.

"Well, somebody's at home," he murmured thoughtfully; and Phantom blew softly through her nostrils as if in reply.

They were close now. Cornelius eased Phantom to a halt, but for the moment he did not dismount. He sat there, listening intently, hoping perhaps to hear voices from within; but there was only the faint whooshing of night breezes, gusting low over the plain and rippling the long grasses.

There was nothing for it but to dismount. Cornelius did so, taking his time. He tethered Phantom to a nearby bush and the little pony stamped a rear hoof in agitation and began to browse halfheartedly on the grass. Cornelius reached up and unstrapped the leather saddlebags. He reached in and removed the package—a small square box wrapped in cloth.

"Wait here," he told Phantom; and then felt faintly ridiculous. Of course the pony was going to wait here: she was tethered to a bush, wasn't she? He shook his head, tucked the parcel under one arm and walked slowly toward the door of the barn. He stood for a moment longer, listening, but there was no sound from within.

He lifted one hand and rapped on the wood with his knuckles. The sound seemed loud enough to send shock waves across the plains, but the door wasn't secured. Beneath the soft push of his knuckles, it swung smoothly and silently open. Cornelius immediately felt that something was wrong. An ancient, deserted barn like this, and yet somebody had oiled the hinges of this door recently. The smell of the oil was in his nostrils as he stepped inside.

He stood looking uncertainly around, his free hand still clenched around the handle of his sword. He took in the interior of the barn at a glance; saw the ancient bales of hay that rose up on every side of him; the long wooden table in the center of the room; the figure of a man sitting at the far end of the table, a bronze tankard in front of him. The man was staring expectantly at Cornelius.

"Welcome," he said. "I believe you have something for me."

Cornelius nodded but made no attempt to move.

"Come then," said the man impatiently, gesturing with one hand. He was an elderly fellow, gray bearded and balding. "Bring it to me."

Cornelius frowned, thinking that the barn held a hundred places of concealment. But he had his orders and must follow them to the letter. He walked across the hay-strewn floor until he was standing by the table. He set the package down in front of the man, who looked up at him and grinned mirthlessly. Seated, he was still a head taller than Cornelius.

"You've ridden a long way," he observed. It wasn't a question but an observation. He reached out with his big, dirty hands and began to unwrap the package. Cornelius watched with interest, wondering what could have been so important. The man's fingers unpicked the leather thongs that bound the parcel and the covers fell away, revealing that it contained money—a large mound of golden crowns, a tidy sum. Cornelius couldn't help feeling disappointed. He had expected something more interesting than mere money. But the bearded man seemed pleased. His grin deepened and he looked back at Cornelius.

"A small fortune," he said. "Would you like to know what the money is for?"

Cornelius shrugged. He wasn't particularly interested.

"It's the price a king will pay," said the bearded man, "to rid himself of a troublesome pest." And with that, he stood up and pulled a sword from his belt. "Men!" he yelled. "Take him!"

Cornelius froze for an instant in the act of unsheathing his own sword. He was aware of movement all around him, bales of hay being pushed aside as men emerged from cover; ragged, armed men with the unmistakable look of Brigands. It was an ambush, and Cornelius had walked right into it. He took the opportunity to look right around the interior of the barn. There were fifteen, maybe twenty of them, and they were advancing on him with grim determination in their eyes.

He grinned and pulled his sword free of its sheath. "Gentlemen," he said. "I see you've all arrived for your lesson in armed combat. So we'll begin, shall we?"

NINETEEN

ON WITH THE SHOW

Sebastian paced up and down behind the curtains, unable to stand still. It wasn't nerves but impatience. He just couldn't wait to get out there and show them a thing or two. Part of him knew that it wasn't natural to feel like this, that it must have been something in the wine the old woman had given him. But he didn't care about that. He was absolutely bursting with confidence, convinced in his own mind that he was the funniest man in history. Here was his opportunity to prove it.

Beyond the curtains he could hear the murmur of the courtiers as they settled themselves into their seats; up in the gallery at the back of the room, minstrels were playing some kind of oddly discordant dance music. Then suddenly the music stopped, to be replaced by a brassy fanfare of trumpets. Sebastian pulled back the curtains a little and peeped out. King Septimus had just stridden into the room with Princess Kerin on his arm. They walked down a central aisle between the ranks of kneeling lords and ladies and took their seats on two opulent thrones at the very front of the room. King Septimus waved a hand and everyone else took their seats again. They all sat looking at the stage. Then Malthus walked out onto the raised area where Sebastian was to perform his act. He bowed low before speaking.

"Your Majesty . . . Your Royal Highness . . . on this most special of days the palace of Keladon is proud to present for your delectation the number one act from royal courts throughout the world—the Lord of Laughter, the Monarch of Mirth, the King of Comedy! I give you the one and only Sebastian Darke, Prince of Fools!"

Malthus left the stage as the curtains parted and Sebastian nearly sprinted out into the light, the opening line of his carefully prepared routine ready to spill from his tongue. But the moment he was in position, the words seemed to evaporate like steam; and though he knew that it was wrong, that it was complete folly, he somehow just couldn't stop himself: he started to improvise.

He stared around at the glum-faced audience for a moment, his hands on his hips. "What?" he asked. "Did somebody die?"

Silence.

"I know *I* did. I did a summer season in Brigandia once. I'm not saying the audience was quiet, but I'd have got more reaction from a séance. One guy started eating soup and everybody got up to dance!"

Silence again . . . and then a sudden chuckle of laughter. Princess Kerin. All heads turned to look at her for a moment

and then, realizing that a royal precedent had been set, everybody else decided to follow her example. Everyone, that is, except King Septimus. His expression didn't change one little bit.
But a polite ripple of amusement passed through the crowd,
and Sebastian, encouraged, went on.

"Hey, but you know, it's great to finally play the palace! Mind
you, I heard the last guy that played this gig didn't go down
too well. He kept his head through the performance but lost it
straight afterward. Actually, the executioner broke it to him in a
nice way. He said, 'Percival, you need to lose ten pounds of
ugly fat—and I'm just the guy who can help!'"

Another laugh, stronger this time.

"So there's poor Percival, kneeling down with his head on the
block. A messenger comes running up and says he's got an urgent letter for him. Percival says, 'Throw it in the basket, I'll
read it later!'"

Again, laughter from Princess Kerin—and after a short pause
the other members of the court joined in.

"The king suddenly feels sorry for Percival and decides he'll
let him off. So he says, 'Arise, Percival.' Nothing happens. The
king says it again, a little louder this time. 'Arise, Percival!'
Still he doesn't make a move. 'What's wrong with the man?'
asks the king. Somebody in the crowd shouts out, 'Tell him
to get up, Your Majesty. He's a jester, he doesn't know what a
rise is!'"

Louder laughter now, though King Septimus was scowling
furiously. Perhaps he didn't much care for a joke that implied
that he didn't pay his jesters enough money. If Sebastian had

been more clearheaded, he might have taken heed, but he was totally out of control now.

"Hey, have we got any merchants in tonight?" A few hands went up. "I *love* merchants! But I couldn't eat a whole one! Seriously, did you hear about the merchant who was attacked by Brigands? They beat him up and stole his money. But it's not all good news! He was stranded miles from home and it was getting dark. He saw a farmer standing by his gate and he threw himself on the farmer's mercy, begged him for a place to stay for the night. So the farmer feels sorry for him and tells the merchant he can spend the night with his pigs. The merchant is horrified. 'But what about the awful smell?' he asks. 'Don't worry,' says the farmer, 'they'll soon get used to it!'"

There was some genuine laughter from the majority of the audience, but notably none from any of the people who had put their hands up. Undeterred, Sebastian continued.

"What do you call a merchant falling off a cliff? A promising start! How do you save a merchant from drowning? Take your foot off his head! How do you know when you're passing by a merchant's house? Toilet paper hanging on the washing line!"

"That's enough about merchants!" shouted a disgruntled voice in the crowd.

"Oh, can't take the heat, eh? Well, let me see now, who else is there?" He gazed slowly around the crowd and his gaze came to rest on the stern face of the king. "Of course," he said. "His Majesty King Septimus." He paused for a moment, gazing out at the ranks of horrified expressions staring back at him. He knew that it was insanity to make jokes about the king who had

177

just employed him, but he was like some reckless beast stampeding madly toward a cliff. "You know, I'd like to start by saying that the king is a kind, generous and intelligent ruler. I'd *like* to say it, but I recently took a vow of honesty!"

Princess Kerin started to laugh but stopped abruptly as she registered what Sebastian had actually said. It was suddenly very quiet in the room and Sebastian's words seemed to echo as he continued.

"You know, His Majesty is an incredibly rich man, but you have to ask yourself how he got to be so rich. It's easy—he has this special arrangement where he gets everything he needs from the people around him. The only other creature with a similar arrangement is a vampire. King Septimus has a saying: 'What's mine is mine and what's yours is mine.' They say that's why he never got married. It's not that he doesn't like the ladies; he just doesn't want anyone close enough to get their hand in his pocket!"

Again, an excruciating silence followed his words.

"Something I said?" he asked, adopting an expression of innocence. "Oh, come on, I'm only saying what you're all thinking! Of course, having no wife means that Septimus had no heir!" This was met with a gasp from the audience. "I said heir," insisted Sebastian. "As in son and heir, heir to the throne, heir apparent. I was thinking the other day that most kings have affectionate nicknames. You know, James the Just, Simon the Sincere, Michael the Magnificent—but poor old Septimus, he doesn't have one." Sebastian hesitated, then clicked his fingers. "Oh wait, that's not true. I just remembered. He's known in some circles as . . . Septimus the Slaphead."

In the terrible silence that followed you could have heard a feather fall.

The bearded man and Cornelius stood in the dimly lit barn staring at each other. When Cornelius spoke, his voice was calm.

"First," he said, "we'll learn to handle an obvious attack."

The bearded man lunged forward, his sword raised to strike; but Cornelius parried the blow with his own blade and then performed a quick somersault up onto the tabletop, a maneuver which brought him to the same height as his adversary. As his feet thudded onto the sturdy wood, he intercepted a second blow and ran the bearded man through, all in one fluid motion.

"When in the act of defeating an enemy, always keep an eye out for the unexpected," said Cornelius.

And even before the bearded man had crumpled to the floor, he sensed a movement behind him and lashed with his sword over his left shoulder. He was rewarded with the thud of a blade against a steel helmet and a bellow of agony, but he didn't turn round to see his opponent fall. Instead he moved to the center of the table, knowing that the Brigands would have to lean forward to strike at him, putting them off balance. He knew also that he was completely encircled and could not hope to evade all those swords for more than a few moments.

"When a position becomes precarious, always seek to find a better one," he announced to the room at large. A spear came flying toward him and he swayed sideways and deflected it with his left arm, feeling the wooden shaft glancing off bone. It spun aside and lodged itself in the ribs of an advancing

Brigand, who cried out in surprise and went down in an un-gainly sprawl.

"Sometimes happy accidents will occur!" said Cornelius.

He glanced quickly around at the ragged circle of flashing steel rapidly closing on him and then up to the roof beams above his head. He picked his spot, a point where a horizontal beam met an upright. Then he ran forward and threw himself upward, using all the power he had learned to summon for the Golmiran death leap. Razor-sharp blades scythed the air inches below his ascending feet, but then he threw his left arm around the upright and was swinging himself up to stand on the horizontal. He looked down at the warriors below him and laughed at their astounded faces. Now they could only come at him on his terms, in ones and twos.

"Once in your new position," he bellowed cheerily, "appraise the situation and wait for the enemy to come to you."

A second spear thudded into the upright beam inches from his head, the wooden shaft juddering. He started to pull the spear out but thought better of it. "Unexpected props may prove useful later," he commented.

He glanced down again and saw that there was a mad scramble as the Brigands ran to left and right and began to clamber up the bales of hay that were piled high on either side of the barn. As Cornelius watched calmly, a man began to edge his way along the length of the horizontal beam; an instant later a second man did likewise from the other direction. They began to converge on Cornelius, their swords held out in front of them. They were big, shambling men, unsure of their balance.

"Once the enemy is in an unfamiliar location, the advantage will be yours," said Cornelius. The first man stepped into sword range and delivered a wild swing at the little warrior's head. Cornelius ducked the blow, aware of the Brigand's huge sword chopping a big wedge out of the upright beam above his head. His own blade whipped across the Brigand's legs and the man lost his balance and fell sideways, to land on the table below with a heavy thud. Now the second man was trying to lean round the upright to take a swing at Cornelius, but the little warrior swung nimbly round from the other direction and ran the point of his sword into the first man's ribs. He too fell, to join his predecessor on the table.

"Never undervalue the element of surprise," said Cornelius.

Now more men were edging out along either end of the horizontal beam, two long rows of them, filing determinedly forward. Cornelius looked left and then right and made his decision.

"Whenever possible, take your enemy in large numbers," he advised.

He reached up his left hand and took a tight hold of the shaft of the spear sticking out of the upright beam. Then he chopped his sword into the horizontal beam by his feet. His first blow cut halfway through it and the Brigands on that side yelled in alarm as they realized what he was doing. Some of them started moving frantically back in the direction they had come from, but Cornelius struck a second time, his blade biting clear through the beam. The end dropped suddenly toward the floor and the five men standing on it came tumbling toward him, flailing their arms in a doomed attempt to maintain their balance. Hanging from the spear, Cornelius lashed at them as they tumbled past him, his blade cutting through chain mail and leather with ease. Five of them crashed down onto the table, dead or wounded, and, unable to support the weight of them, it tipped over, throwing the lot of them onto the floor.

"Remember," said Cornelius, "that your advantage cannot last forever, so make full use of it!"

Now he swung himself round on the spear and his feet connected with the chest of the nearest warrior on the other side of the upright, knocking him backward into the men behind him. He fell and a second man went down; a third was left hanging grimly on when Cornelius's feet thudded down onto his fingers and he let go with a howl of pain. Cornelius was just coming upright into a fighting position when he felt an abrupt impact and the stinging pain of cold metal slicing into his shoulder. He glanced down in dull surprise and saw the handle of a throwing knife jutting out from his chain-mail singlet. He grunted in surprise and irritation and raised his gaze to stare at the man who had thrown it, a tall, lanky fellow who was standing precariously on the beam, looking at his would-be victim with an expression of dread on his grimy face.

"Anger can be useful," growled Cornelius, "but only if it's controlled." He ran along the beam with an ear-splitting bellow, straight at the three men who still stood on it. The knife-thrower panicked and tried to back away, but the other men were still pushing forward and they were in a confused huddle when Cornelius slammed into their legs, scattering them before him. They fell from the beam and added to the large groaning heap of men on the floor.

Cornelius paused for a moment, sheathed his sword and reached up his right hand to pull the throwing knife out of his shoulder, gritting his teeth against the pain of it. Blood spurted down the front of his breastplate. He looked down to the floor and saw that the last few warriors were standing there, staring up at him uncertainly.

"When using a throwing knife," he told them, "remember that it's only effective if it hits the right spot." He raised his arm and brought it down again, sending the knife spinning end over end toward the nearest Brigand. The man saw it coming but was too slow to even try and evade it. The blade thudded into his chest with a loud thunk and he fell backward to the floor, dead. Cornelius smiled down at the three men who were left standing and slid his sword back out of its scabbard.

"Finally," he said, "when confronted with the pathetic remains of a cowardly ambush, be sure and show them no mercy whatsoever."

He made to descend but there was hardly any need. The three remaining Brigands turned and ran out of the barn door. Cornelius could hear their feet pounding across the plain outside. He jumped down, gritting his teeth against the pain in his shoulder as his feet connected with the floor. He glanced at the pile of dead and wounded men and assured himself that nobody there was going to cause him any trouble. He had survived the ambush, but knew that this was not the end of the matter.

King Septimus had sent him out here to his death. Clearly he must have wanted him out of the way for some reason. . . .

"Shadlog's beard!" he growled. "Sebastian!" He did not know what was happening to the boy back at the palace, but whatever it was, he would probably be grateful for some help around now. Cornelius hurried outside, aware that his injured shoulder and the arm beneath it were stiffening up, but there was no time to think of that. He had to get back as quickly as he could and it was a long journey. He found an anxious-looking Phantom still tethered to the bushes and he unhitched her reins and leaped up into the saddle.

"Come on, girl," he whispered into her ear. "Back to the palace as fast as you can. Somebody needs our help."

He drove his heels into her dappled flanks and she sprang into a gallop, going as fast as her little legs would carry her. Cornelius hoped it wasn't already too late.

TWENTY

A FINE MESS

Sebastian looked at the king's purple face and realized that he had said something absolutely unthinkable.

Septimus the Slaphead? Had that really come from him? He had heard *somebody* say it and there didn't seem to be anybody else around who was stupid enough to have uttered the words. It *must* have been him, he decided. But what had got into him? Hadn't Malthus told him that nobody would be reckless enough to say those words in the king's presence?

The king was hunched in his seat, his eyes blazing, his teeth bared in what looked like a ferocious snarl. Beside him, Princess Kerin's face was frozen in an expression of shock, her mouth hanging open. And beside her, Malthus looked like he had just been punched in the stomach, his eyes screwed up, his little mouth puckered into an ooh of disbelief.

And that deep, terrible silence continued.

"S-something I said?" asked Sebastian nervously. He was

aware that his former confidence was melting away like ice beneath the glare of the sun. The drug must be wearing off but it was just a few moments too late to be of any help. "Your Majesty, I . . . I didn't really mean—"

At the back of the room a movement caught his eye and he lifted his gaze. He saw the old crone, Magda, gesturing wildly at him, trying to get his attention. He ignored her, telling himself that she had done enough damage for one evening. In absolute desperation, he decided to try and lighten the king's mood.

"If Your Majesty will permit, I'll try you with a twung-tister . . . er, I mean, a twang-tooster . . . er . . . ting-toaster . . ."

He abandoned his clumsy attempts to explain himself and went into the rhyme itself:

> *"Once upon a barren moor*
> *There dwelt a bear, also a boar.*
> *The bear just could not bear the boar.*
> *The boar he thought the bear a bore.*
> *At last the bear could bear no more*
> *Of that boar that bored him on the moor,*
> *And so one morn he bored the boar—*
> *In turn the boar did gore the bear,*
> *But bear was strong, he tore the boar*
> *And laid him bare and made him soar—*
> *That boar will bore the bear no more!"*

Sebastian smiled and opened his arms in a gesture of finality, hardly believing that he'd got through it without a mistake; but King Septimus showed no sign of even having heard the poem.

His eyes still drilled into Sebastian's with a look of uncompromising hatred. If Sebastian had possessed a spade, he would gladly have dug a hole and climbed into it.

"Oh, come on," he protested. "I'm doing my best here! You could at least give me some encouragement!"

Again he noticed Magda's frantic gestures. He saw now that she was pointing to the disappearing cabinet at the back of the stage, as though she thought this might somehow save the day. Sebastian told himself that he might as well try it. After all, what did he have to lose?

He bowed low. "And now, Your Majesty, I would like to present a very special treat, one that I feel sure you will enjoy."

"You're going to kill yourself?" suggested King Septimus hopefully.

"Er . . . no, my liege. No, I am going to perform for you a miracle of magic! Something you have never seen before. But for this event I will need the help of somebody from the audience!" Sebastian gestured around at the seated courtiers and couldn't help noticing that every single face still held an expression of shock. "It—er . . . it's a wonderful trick," he continued. "One that has mystified the crowned heads of the known world—"

"Get on with it!" snapped King Septimus.

"Umm . . . yes, if I could just have an assistant. I wonder if perhaps the princess would like to . . ."

Princess Kerin started to rise uncertainly from her throne and her uncle gave her an unceremonious shove in the back, propelling her toward the stage and almost knocking her over.

"Ah yes, Princess! Such an honor," mumbled Sebastian. He took her hand and walked her across to the cabinet.

187

"What's the matter with you?" she whispered, her back to the audience. "What made you say that?"

"I don't know," he hissed back. "I think it was something in my wine."

"You're drunk?" she asked him.

"No, not exactly." He turned back to face the audience and bowed again. "Your Majesty, lords and ladies of the court, behold the magic cabinet of Aliminthera!" He reached out and swung the wooden door open. "As you can see, it looks like a perfectly ordinary empty cabinet." He waved his hand around in the interior to prove that it was exactly what it seemed. "Now, if I can ask the princess to step inside." She did as he asked, positioning herself with her back against the wall. Sebastian turned to face her as he pretended to make a last-minute check. "You know what to do?" he whispered.

She nodded, but her face was grim. "I can't help feeling it's you who should be vanishing," she murmured.

There was no answer to that. He swung the door shut, and in the same instant pressed the mechanism at the side of the door that caused the back of the cabinet to silently revolve.

"And now I say the magic words . . ."

"*. . . Alika karamah silika kai!*"

Sebastian's voice came faintly to Princess Kerin through the wood at the back of the cabinet. The mechanism had spun her round on well-oiled wheels and now she simply had to slip through the curtains at the back of the stage and wait there, hidden from the audience, so that Sebastian could spin the entire cabinet round to show the audience that nobody was standing behind it.

After a bit of patter he would return the cabinet to its original position and announce that it was time to bring the princess back again; and that was her cue to return to exactly the right spot, so the mechanism could revolve once more, thus putting her back *inside* the cabinet.

An incredibly simple trick—and obvious really, when you thought about it, but it *did* look amazing; though the mood Uncle Septimus was in, it was unlikely that he would be impressed. It would take all her powers of persuasion to ensure that Sebastian was not punished for this. What could have got into him to make him so reckless?

She slipped through the curtains into the gloom and turned back to peep through a narrow gap just in time to hear the audience gasp in surprise as Sebastian threw open the doors.

"But what's this, Your Majesty?" she heard him say. "It would seem that Princess Kerin has vanished!" A halfhearted ripple of applause greeted the trick, and she was just thinking that maybe everything would be all right when a powerful arm grabbed her around her waist and a huge hand clamped tight over her mouth and nose; a hand that held a cloth—a damp cloth that reeked of some powerful odor. The princess tried to struggle but the hands were too strong and the fumes from the handkerchief seemed to flood her nostrils and expand to fill her whole head. Suddenly all the strength went out of her muscles and she found herself falling into a deep, dark abyss.

As she drifted, she was only vaguely aware of arms picking her up and carrying her away, into the silent shadows at the edge of the stage.

"So, Your Majesty, as you can see, there's nobody behind the cabinet!" announced Sebastian, turning it around fully so the audience could see it from every angle. "Her Royal Highness has been spirited away by the imps of Aliminthera. But fear not, for I can bring her back!"

"Oh goody," said the king dryly.

"All I do is say the magic words"—Sebastian hesitated, wanting to be sure that Princess Kerin had enough time to get herself back in position—"the most sacred and secret words, known only to the high priests of Aliminthera. Words which must, of course, be spoken in the correct sequence . . ." Sebastian pressed the secret button and felt the slight tremble as the mechanism turned. "*Alika karamah silika kai!*" he cried and grasped the handle of the door. "And as you can see, Your Majesty, the princess is"—he flung the door open—"not there," he finished lamely.

There was a murmur of disappointment from the crowd, which Sebastian attempted to defuse with a devil-may-care laugh.

"Ha ha! That was just a test! I . . . I really had you going for a moment, didn't I?" He closed the door again. "Of course, *this* time she will reappear." He waited, longer than he probably needed to. "Yes, I sense that the spirits are releasing her now. They are releasing her and . . . and sending her back . . . back . . . back to the mystical cabinet of Aliminthera. Now, Your Majesty, prepare to be absolutely amazed!"

He flung open the cabinet a second time. To reveal emptiness.

Now there was an audible gasp from the audience and a rising murmur of consternation.

"Where is my niece?" asked King Septimus.

"Oh, relax, sire, she's probably just . . . communing with the spirits." Sebastian closed the door again, then snapped his fingers. "You know, I think it would help if we all called her! Yes, she probably can't hear me behind the curt— I mean, behind the veils of oblivion." He gestured to the crowd to try and get them involved. "Princess Kerin!" he called out. "Princess Kerin? We're ready for you to return to us now. Just . . . get yourself into position and . . . *ta-daa!*" He opened the door a third time. Still horribly empty. Sebastian ducked round the side of the cabinet but there was no sign of her back there.

There was a rising hubbub of concern now and King Septimus had been moved to get up out of his chair.

"Where is Princess Kerin?" he demanded.

Sebastian sighed. There was nothing for it. He would have to own up. "She's behind the curtain," he said. He went over to it and pulled it aside. But the back of the stage was completely deserted. He stood there staring into the gloom in dismay, not wanting to believe that his simple trick could have gone so horribly wrong. *Where could she be?* "She . . . she's supposed to be here waiting," he gasped.

"What are you talking about?" snarled King Septimus. "You said you were sending her to the realms of Aliminthera!"

"Well, yes, I *said* that," admitted Sebastian. "But you don't really think—?"

191

"Witchcraft!" cried somebody in the audience. "He has spirited the princess away!"

"Er . . . no, don't be ridiculous, it's just a trick. I couldn't possibly—"

"Guards!" shouted King Septimus. "Hold him!"

Before Sebastian could make a move, two brawny soldiers had run onto the stage and grabbed his arms. He struggled helplessly in their grasp.

"Your Majesty," he gasped. "I can explain!"

"I don't think there's any need to explain," snarled King Septimus. "You told me, in front of all these witnesses, that you would send the princess away to some magical world and it would seem you have done exactly that. Now I demand that you return her at once."

"I . . . I can't," cried Sebastian. "I don't know where she's gone!"

At this, there was an outcry in the room. Everyone was up out of their seats and shouting at the tops of their voices. Among the cries Sebastian heard several voices yelling for the king to "burn the witch!" He glanced hopefully around the room, thinking that somebody must have realized that Magda was involved; but then he realized that they were actually shouting about him.

"But . . . I'm no witch!" he protested. "This is ridiculous. You've got to let me explain—"

"Take him to the dungeons!" roared King Septimus. "We'll see if the palace torturers can discover the truth."

Sebastian tried to protest but the two brawny soldiers began to drag him away through the crowd. As he was propelled along, people stepped forward to spit at him or launch blows at his helpless figure. He realized with a dull sense of shock that it was all over for him. In the space of a few hours he had gone from hero to zero—and worse still, with Cornelius away on a mission and Max shut up in the royal stables, there was nobody here to help him.

Just before the soldiers dragged him out of the door, he saw Magda standing watching him, a satisfied smile on her ugly face. He opened his mouth to shout at her but a huge fist struck him in the forehead, stunning him, and by the time he had recovered himself, the soldiers were already dragging him down the stairs toward the gloom of the dungeons.

TWENTY-ONE

THE AWFUL TRUTH

Phantom sped along beneath the stars, kicking up a cloud of dust in her wake. Cornelius was hunched forward in his saddle, his teeth gritted against the terrible pain in his shoulder. He still had a good distance to cover and would have given anything to stop and rest for a while.

But he was sure now that something was terribly wrong and was determined not to stop until he was back in Keladon. He slapped the reins against the pony's flanks, willing her on to even greater efforts, as her nimble hooves ate up the distance between her and Sebastian.

Princess Kerin seemed to be rising slowly up from deep below the surface of a pool of warm water. Her head broke the surface and she opened her eyes, but at first everything was a blur. Then her surroundings came sharply into focus and she realized that she was sitting on a chair in a deserted cellar room.

No—not deserted. Somebody was sitting a short distance away from her, a dirty, brutish man with a stubbled chin and a shock of greasy black hair. She recognized him as Golon, the master of the king's dungeons. She tried to get up out of the chair but realized that she was tied into it, and she fell back with a gasp of frustration. She shook her head to try and rid herself of the last threads of sleep and struggled against the rough cords that bound her arms to the chair. Golon noticed her and gave her an oily, gap-toothed grin.

"Calm down, Princess," he told her. "No need to get all excited. You just sit quiet and wait."

"What . . . what's going on?" she asked him. "Why am I tied like this?"

"Just following orders, Your Highness. It's nothing personal."

Now she realized that she was wearing a filthy, ragged dress, the kind of thing that a servant girl might wear.

The full indignity of what had happened hit her like a clenched fist. "How dare you!" she cried. "Release me at once! When my uncle learns of this outrage, he'll—"

"Your Highness, it was your uncle who issued the orders," said Golon bluntly. "He also gave me permission to keep you quiet by any means I choose." He leaned threateningly toward her, his expression grim, his big fists clenched. "So I would shut up if I were you. Unless, of course, you'd prefer to wear a gag."

Princess Kerin opened her mouth to reply, but after a moment's hesitation she closed it again. Her eyes filled with tears of indignation. She could do nothing for the moment but sit there and watch as Golon strutted around the cell, enjoying his power over her. She realized with a dull sense of shock that Sebastian had been right to question her uncle's motives.

After what seemed an age, the door opened and two figures entered the room. Uncle Septimus strode in first, a sardonic smile on his face. Behind him walked a huge, cruel-looking man with a shaven head and a long drooping moustache. He wore the fur robes and animal-hide trousers of a Brigand and he was looking down at Princess Kerin with a malevolent grin on his face.

"Uncle Septimus!" cried the princess, still trying to convince herself that this was some kind of ghastly mistake. "What's going on? Golon says that this has been done on your orders."

"That is correct," said King Septimus coldly.

"But . . . why?"

"Why?" King Septimus threw back his head and gave a mocking laugh. "I should have thought that would be perfectly apparent, even to a dull-witted creature like you. Did you really think that I was going to hand over the keys to the kingdom to a brat such as yourself? That I would happily trade in the power and might of a monarch and go back to being your official wet-nurse?"

"But . . . it was always understood . . . that I would be queen."

"Understood . . . but not accepted. It has always been my destiny to rule Keladon. And I will not allow anything or anyone to stand in my way."

"But . . . I'm your niece! Surely you would not harm a member of your own family?"

King Septimus gave her a silky smile. "Why not? It hasn't stopped me before, has it?"

Princess Kerin's eyes widened in realization. "My parents!" she gasped. "You were behind their deaths!"

King Septimus gave her a mocking bow. "Oh, the croat finally drops!" he said. "You poor little fool. You must have been the only person in the kingdom who didn't suspect me. But yes, I arranged for their . . . removal."

"But why? Your own brother and his wife—"

"Because he was a weakling!" snapped King Septimus. "He was so completely under your mother's influence, he forgot to think and act like a king. He didn't have the first idea what being a monarch was about and he would have steered Keladon into oblivion. Did you know he was thinking of scrapping the system where everybody pays toward the upkeep of the palace? A few years of that and we'd all be living in poverty. So I took steps to remove him; and since your mother would have been quite miserable without him, I made sure that she accompanied him into the next world."

Anger blossomed in Princess Kerin's chest, a great surge of heat that made it hard for her to find the breath to make her reply. "You . . . you plunged our kingdom into a war . . . that lasted for years!" she shrieked. "Thousands of people . . . died because of what you did!"

King Septimus shrugged. "What do I care about *people*?" he snarled. "I became king. Nothing else mattered. And I intend to remain king, whatever the price."

Princess Kerin felt as though she had been wearing a blindfold for years and somebody had just removed it. "Sebastian tried to warn me about you," she said bitterly. "And I dismissed his notions. I couldn't see through your lies, but he could."

"Really? Then isn't it a good job that the elfling will be executed at dawn?"

Princess Kerin shook her head. "No! You mustn't harm him! What has he done to deserve such a fate?"

"What has he done? What has he done?" King Septimus paced around the cell for a moment, as though mulling the question over. "I'll tell you what he's done. He interrupted a carefully laid plan to have you captured by Brigands, that's what. He brought you safely back to the palace when I had fervently hoped to learn of your death!"

Fresh tears trickled down Princess Kerin's face. "You must hate me," she gasped.

"Princess, you have no idea how much," said King Septimus. "All these years of having to pretend to be the loving uncle— always smiling, bestowing gifts, granting favors. When what I really wanted was to throttle the very life out of you."

"But what did I ever do to you?"

The king spread his hands in a gesture of helplessness, as if he'd had no choice in the matter. "You were born," he said. "And that made you one more obstacle in my path to power. But now you are completely at my mercy. That wicked jester has used some kind of dark witchcraft to send you into another realm, a world from which you shall never escape. Nobody will ever see you again, Princess. At least, nobody in Keladon."

"You . . . you are going to kill me?"

The king shook his head. "That would be too easy on you," he said. "A brief moment of pain and then it would all be over. But you see, Princess, such is the enormity of my hatred for you that I want you to suffer. I want you to go on living for years, waking up every morning to the realization of all you have lost. I want you to experience the pain and ignominy of life in the gutter, a world from which your only escape will indeed be death. You will notice that you are dressed for just such an occasion. Allow me to introduce somebody." He gestured to the big shaven-headed man, who stepped forward with an evil grin. "This is Kasim, a trader from the slave markets of Brigandia. He specializes in selling human flesh to the highest bidder. I have paid him in advance and told him that you are to enjoy no special privileges. He will put you on the selling platform as someone of lowly birth, a commoner. This should ensure that whoever purchases you will extract every last bit of work that's in your pampered body. You may last for years like that, washing, cleaning, scrubbing, working your privileged fingers to the bone."

Kasim nodded. "She looks strong enough," he observed. "And she's not bad-looking. I think there will be many who will wish to bid for her."

Princess Kerin shook her head. "I . . . I will tell whoever buys me who I really am!" she protested. "I will offer them a reward if they return me to Keladon."

"Tell them," said the king gleefully. "Offer away! Do you think that anybody in Brigandia will believe you? Particularly when Kasim has warned the buyer that you are a simpleton, given to strange fancies and notions."

"You . . . you evil brute!" shrieked Princess Kerin. "You won't get away with this. The people love me—they won't allow this to happen!"

King Septimus gestured to Golon. "She's beginning to bore me," he said. "Send her back to sleep and prepare her for the journey to Brigandia." He seemed to remember something. "Oh, one last thing." He moved closer to her and gave her a mocking grin. "Happy birthday," he purred. Then he turned away, laughing.

"No, wait . . ." gasped Princess Kerin. "Please, I—"

But then Golon's brawny arms came around her shoulders and one hand was clamping the foul-smelling cloth over her nose and mouth. She held her breath as long as she could, but in the end she had no choice but to breathe in the awful fumes. The strange, shuddering emptiness filled her head and she was sinking into the depths for the second time that night.

Slumped dejectedly on a wooden bench in the deepest, darkest cell in the palace dungeons, Sebastian reflected on his fortunes. It occurred to him that the positive letter he had sent to his mother would not even be a third of the way on its journey yet, and already it was hopelessly incorrect.

His tenancy as resident jester to King Septimus had been woefully short-lived. He hadn't even lasted one full performance, thanks to the wiles of that hideous old crone Magda. If he ever got his hands around her skinny throat, he would ensure that she never tricked another victim as she had tricked him. He thought about how Max had tried to warn him about her and how he had dismissed the buffalope's comments as malicious gossip. But Max had been absolutely right to mistrust her.

And it was blindingly obvious now what King Septimus was up to. As far as the lords and ladies of the court were concerned, he, Sebastian Darke, had used witchcraft to dispose of Princess Kerin. They had seen it happen with their own eyes. It would be useless to protest his innocence and shout that King Septimus had actually kidnapped his own niece. Nobody would believe him for a moment; and it didn't take a genius to work out that he wouldn't be around long enough to do much protesting. The palace executioner was probably already sharpening his axe.

Sebastian swallowed. What was he to do? It was apparent now that Cornelius had been sent away on his "secret mission" simply to ensure that he was out of the way. Who knew what fate might have befallen him? And off in the luxury of the royal stables, Max had no way of knowing what had happened to his master.

There was nothing to do but sit here and await his fate. He felt like crying, and might have done just that if he hadn't been interrupted by the clanging of an iron door somewhere out of sight. He heard the clumping of feet descending the stone steps from the entrance door, and looking up he saw Golon, the big, brutish dungeon master leading the thin figure of Malthus toward him. The two men exchanged words and the dungeon master turned back, while Malthus approached the bars of Sebastian's cell. He stood there, looking in at Sebastian, a glum expression on his face.

"Well," he said at length, "that was quite a debut."

Sebastian spread his arms in a gesture of helplessness. "What can I say?" he said. "If you're going to go out, you may as well do it in a blaze of glory."

"But the things you said! It's as though you had a death wish."

"Yes, well, that was because I drank some wine that Magda gave me. It must have been drugged."

Malthus grimaced. "I wouldn't touch anything that she'd been near," he observed. "She's pure evil, that one."

"A pity you didn't warn me about her earlier."

Malthus moved closer to the bars and lowered his voice. "So . . . what did you do with the princess?" he asked.

"I didn't do anything with her! King Septimus obviously had her kidnapped. He must have had somebody hiding behind the curtain."

Malthus nodded. "Well, I didn't think you'd really made her vanish," he said. "And it isn't exactly a mystery why he'd want her out of the way, is it? Let's face it, when you're the all-powerful ruler of a place like Keladon, you're not going to want to hand it over to a mere girl."

Sebastian stared at him in surprise. "Then you . . . you believe me?" he gasped. "I didn't think you would!"

"Of course I do. I've worked around King Septimus long enough to know that he's an evil and absolutely ruthless man, who'd stop at nothing to get his own way."

"Then . . . you'll help me?" asked Sebastian hopefully.

Malthus gave him a sour look. "Absolutely not. I've no wish to join you tomorrow morning."

"Tomorrow morning?" Sebastian felt his stomach lurch. "Why, what's happening tomorrow morning?"

"You'll be making your final appearance, I'm afraid. A double act with Luther, the Royal Executioner. It's what's known in these parts as a touch of the Percivals."

"I see," said Sebastian mournfully. He swallowed hard. "Oh well, I can't pretend I'm surprised."

"The king is going to have your head displayed at the palace gates as a warning to anyone who dares to oppose him."

"Yes, well, thanks for—"

"I hate it when he does that. The birds come flapping down and peck away at the eyeballs—"

"Yes, yes, that's too much information!" Sebastian gave Malthus a hard look. "I can't believe you're just going to walk away and leave me to my fate. I mean, you know I'm innocent. . . ."

"Yes, and I'm innocent too. It doesn't mean that the king wouldn't have me boiled in oil if I displeased him. You have to understand, Sebastian, I'm a . . . now, what's the word?" He thought for a moment. "Yes, that's it. A coward. And I intend to go on living for a while longer yet."

"You call that living? Serving a master you don't respect? Somebody who you know is evil."

Malthus shrugged. "I admit, it doesn't sound like a dream job," he said. "But it's still an improvement on having my head stuck on a pole. I'm sorry, Mr. Darke, but there it is." He turned to leave.

"Wait!" said Sebastian, getting up from the bench and walking over to the bars. "At least do me one favor. Take a message to my buffalope, Max, in the royal stables. Tell him what's happened to me."

"He'll know soon enough," said Malthus. "The king has organized a free feast for everyone who attends the execution tomorrow. Roast buffalope is always very popular at such events."

Sebastian stared at Malthus. "Oh no!" he said. "Not Max. He's done nothing wrong. Why would anybody hurt a poor dumb animal like him?"

"Not exactly dumb," said Malthus, walking back along the corridor. "He's an animal that can speak and who knows who he might talk to? You honestly think the king is going to risk him blabbing?" He turned back toward the stone steps. "Guard! Let me out, please!"

"Malthus, wait! Come back—please!"

But Malthus climbed the steps up to the heavy wooden door and didn't pause to look back. The door opened and slammed shut behind him. Sebastian returned to his bench and slumped miserably back down on it, his head in his hands. Somehow he felt worse about Max than anything else. He would be terrified when they led him out to be slaughtered. He was a brave and noble companion. All right, so he did tend to complain a lot, but even so. . . .

And then Sebastian thought about his mother and he

205

wondered how long it would take for the news to reach her that her only son was dead. Perhaps she would never learn of his fate, but would wait for his return through all the long, lonely years, until old age carried her away.

It was no use. He couldn't hold back the tears any longer and he was just glad that there was nobody around to see him crying.

TWENTY-TWO

SLENDER HOPE

Once again Princess Kerin seemed to be floating in a deep, warm lagoon, drifting lazily along, propelling herself with the occasional flick of a foot. Above her she could see the rippled surface of the water and knew that if she reached up one hand, she could break through to the air above. But she felt so warm, so sleepy, she had no energy to rise up through the depths.

Then a sound came to her—a voice, oddly familiar, but shattered into a series of incomprehensible noises by the weight of the water in her ears. She made a supreme effort and propelled herself upward. Her head broke the surface and she lay still for a moment, blinking uncertainly around her.

She wasn't anywhere near a lagoon. She appeared to be lying on straw in some kind of wagon, rough wooden walls rising on four sides of her. She tried to sit up, but didn't seem to have any strength in her arms and legs. Instead, she managed to turn her head to one side and felt the gentle touch of air on her cheek. She was inches from a small knothole in the wood and through the hole came that familiar voice, easier to understand now that she had temporarily shrugged off her unconsciousness.

". . . all I'm saying, Osbert, is that it shows you how little he cares about me. I mean to say, he actually threw the thing at me, bounced it right off my head! All right, so it didn't exactly hurt, but it's not nice to be treated like that."

"Max?" Princess Kerin struggled to align one eye with the hole in the wood. In the gloom beyond, she could see a huge horned head, nodding as it continued to speak.

"How would you like it, Osbert, if one of your soldiers marched in here and bashed you on the head with a—?"

"Max!" Princess Kerin managed to find the strength to put some urgency in her voice. She saw the buffalope flinch and turn his head to look toward the wagon.

"Who's there?" he asked.

"It's a ghost!" cried another voice. "Osbert not like ghosts! Osbert leave!" There was the thud of small hooves on the ground outside.

"Osbert!" chided Max. "Don't be silly, it's just—" He broke off, puzzled, and moved closer to the wagon. A moment later his warm wet nose was snuffling at the knothole. "Who *is* that?" he asked suspiciously.

"It . . . is I . . . Princess Kerin. . . ."

"Princess? What on earth are you doing in a—?"

"No time!" gasped Princess Kerin. "Can't stay . . . awake . . . drugged."

"Drugged? This is an outrage! Who would do a thing like—?"

"Max! Please listen! They have kidnapped me. They are taking me to . . . to Brigandia. They are going to sell me as . . . a slave." Princess Kerin could feel a fresh wave of unconsciousness sweeping toward her like a wave, threatening to swamp her once again. "You must tell . . . Sebastian," she whispered. "And Corn . . . Corn . . . eli—"

And then the warm wave crashed down over her and she sank once again, deep beneath the surface of the lagoon, into a sleep from which she could not escape.

"Princess? Princess, speak to me! Who has kidnapped you?"

Max stood there looking at the cattle wagon in agitation, wondering if he had the strength to smash through the wooden walls. But what would be the point if the princess was drugged? She wouldn't be able to help herself. No, he needed to find Sebastian, but even that was no easy task. For a start, somebody had closed the stable gates for the night; and even if he could get out of here, a buffalope could hardly go wandering through the palace looking for his master.

He was just pondering the dilemma when the main gates at the top of the stables creaked open. Two men entered and came walking up the central aisle toward the wagon. One was short and hunched, with dirty hair and a scruffy beard. The second was a huge, cruel-looking man with a shaved head and a long drooping mustache. He pointed into one of the stalls.

"Hitch up those equines," he said, "and be quick about it. I want to be on our way as soon as possible." He noticed Max standing by the wagon and gave him a suspicious look. "What's that ugly brute doing there?"

Max opened his mouth to say, "Look who's talking!" But something prompted him to keep quiet. The man looked hard, dangerous, capable of anything. So Max just stood where he was, gazing back at him. The man's companion emerged from the stall, leading two heavy equines by their halters.

"Oh, it's just an old buffalope, Master Kasim. I wouldn't worry about him."

But Kasim wasn't so easily persuaded. "I'm not so sure. Some of them can talk, you know."

The little man laughed dismissively. "I've encountered a few who've managed to pick up the odd word, but nothing you'd write home about."

Kasim shook his head. He reached for the curved scabbard at his side and slid out his sword with a bright hiss of steel. "Better not take the risk," he said. "It won't take a moment to make sure he never speaks again."

Max swallowed hard but tried to keep his expression blank. If this man suspected for a moment that he could understand every word, he was finished.

"I don't know if we *should* kill him," argued the little man. "This is the royal stables. He might be a favorite of the king."

"What, a stinking old creature like that?" Kasim was studying Max's expression, as though searching for any sign of recognition. "What would the king want with a buffalope?"

The little man shrugged. "He's *in* here, isn't he? There must be a reason. Most of the common livestock are kept out in the stockades."

"Hmm." Kasim held out his sword until the point was inches from Max's throat. "Well," he murmured in a soft, silky tone, "what do you say, Mr. Buffalope? Can you talk?"

There was a long silence while Max steeled himself for what he knew he had to do. It was almost more than he could bear, but it was a necessary deception if he was to live long enough to help the princess. He opened his mouth and let out a long, stupid sound.

"Mooooooooo!" he said.

The two men stared at him for a few moments; and then they both burst out laughing.

"Oh yes, a real intellectual," chuckled Kasim. "I don't think we need to worry about him." He slapped Max across the rump with the flat of his sword and Max put his head down and trotted away toward the end of the stables, where he noticed that the men had left the door open. He glanced back and saw that they were busy hitching the equines up to the wagon. He edged forward and peered out of the open doors, across the stretches of carefully tended lawns at the back of the palace. This was his opportunity, he decided.

And he stepped out into the night.

As Cornelius approached the mighty wooden gates of the city, the voice of a lookout on the walls above called down to him.

"Who goes there, friend or foe?"

"Friend!" shouted Cornelius, reining in Phantom and gazing

211

up to the parapets. "Captain Cornelius Drummel of the Crimson Cloak."

There was a long silence and Cornelius wondered at the wisdom of riding straight up to the gates like this. Supposing the king had issued orders to have him killed on sight. But no, he reasoned, most likely the ambush had been arranged in secret. King Septimus would not want many people to know that he had betrayed his newest recruit.

After a few moments the voice shouted back, "Enter, friend," and the doors creaked slowly open. Cornelius gave Phantom's flanks a light squeeze and the pony took him on inside.

A big ruddy-faced officer stood at the gates, smiling at him. "You're out late," he observed. "Everything all right?"

Cornelius nodded and indicated his bloody shoulder. "Had a bit of a dustup with some Brigands," he said. "One of them sliced my shoulder. I had to treat them very severely."

The officer grinned. "Made short work of them, did you?" He chuckled, then looked dismayed. "Oh, look, sorry, I didn't mean . . ."

"That's all right," said Cornelius. He was about to say something else but was interrupted by the sound of a creaking cattle wagon approaching out of the darkness, pulled by two powerful equines. A couple of villainous-looking men were sitting in the driving seat, and as the wagon approached, one of the men, a bald-headed ruffian with a drooping mustache, waved a piece of paper stamped with the king's royal seal. The officer nodded and waved the wagon through, but stared after it with a look of distaste.

"It seems they'll let anyone into Keladon these days," he muttered. "Those two are Brigands, if I'm not mistaken." He waved to the men who tended the buffalopes harnessed to the machinery that operated the gates. The men turned the beasts round and set them walking in the other direction, causing the gates to swing shut again. Cornelius caught a last glimpse of the cattle wagon bumping speedily away into the night.

"Where are they off to at this time of night?" he muttered.

"Who knows?" said the officer. "But we'll all sleep better in our beds for their absence." He nodded at Cornelius's bloody shoulder. "You'd better get over to the surgeon's tent—get a dressing on that shoulder. Looks nasty."

"Later," said Cornelius. "First I need to speak to my friend Sebastian Darke."

"The jester?" The officer grimaced. "You a friend of his? I wouldn't mention that to anyone if I were you."

"Whyever not?"

"Well, you've been away, so you won't know." The officer moved closer and lowered his voice as if to impart a secret. "He spirited Princess Kerin away, didn't he? Made her vanish into thin air, just like that! Nobody knows what's become of her."

Cornelius glared at the man. "What are you babbling about?" he snapped.

"The jester. He's some kind of dark magician. The king's had him thrown into the dungeons. He's to be executed tomorrow morning."

"By Shadlog's beard! I hope you jest with me!"

"No, I wouldn't joke about things like that. I'm trying to change my shift. Haven't seen a good execution in ages."

"Where *are* the dungeons?" demanded Cornelius.

"I'll take you to them," said a voice in the shadows to his left; and the officer snapped suddenly to attention and saluted. Cornelius turned his head to see Captain Tench riding toward him, his face expressionless. "I appreciate that the jester is a friend of yours and you'll doubtless want to speak to him before he is . . . dealt with."

Cornelius studied the man's gaunt face for a moment and didn't trust what he saw there for an instant. But he decided to play along. "That's very kind of you, Captain," he said.

"Not at all. I was going that way." He started off along the avenue and Cornelius nudged Phantom forward to catch up with him. The two men rode together in silence for a while.

"Looks like you've been in the wars," said Captain Tench at last, looking down from his saddle.

"Nothing I couldn't handle," replied Cornelius calmly. "Bunch of skulking cowards, lurking in ambush. It seems somebody wanted me out of the way."

"Really?" Tench raised his eyebrows. "I can't imagine why."

"Perhaps some kind of treachery is afoot," suggested Cornelius.

"Treachery?" murmured Tench, as though unfamiliar with the word. "How do you mean?"

"I mean, perhaps some sneaking rat wanted to do something underhand. Without my interference."

Tench made no reply and they rode on in silence until they

reached the palace courtyard. Tench dismounted and hitched his equine to a rail. Cornelius did likewise and turned to stroke Phantom's muzzle.

"I'll be back soon," he whispered. Then he turned to Captain Tench, who led him across the stone flags to the main doors of the palace. A couple of armed guards saluted Tench and swung back the doors. Cornelius and Tench stepped through and their boots clumped on the smooth white marble floors.

"I'd say you're overestimating your worth," said Tench at last. "What could you possibly interfere with—a little fellow like you?" He led the way through an arched opening and down a long flight of steps.

Cornelius let the remark pass. "Perhaps somebody thought I might try to help Sebastian," he suggested.

"Help him? What, to make the princess disappear, you mean?"

Cornelius chuckled and shook his head. "Let me tell you something," he said. "I know Sebastian pretty well. He wouldn't have the first idea how to make a person vanish. At least, not by magic or witchcraft."

"But everybody saw it happen!" protested Tench. "The whole court was there. He put her into a magic cabinet and she vanished into thin air. Then he was unable to bring her back again."

"If that is what truly happened, then somebody else must have been involved," said Cornelius. "Sebastian adores the princess; he'd never allow any mishap to befall her."

They had come to a long low-ceilinged corridor. Tench

215

allowed Cornelius to go ahead of him and pointed to a solid wooden door at the far end of it.

"There's the entrance to the dungeons," he said. "Golon!" he yelled. "Open the door. The jester has a visitor."

There was a sound of footsteps scuffing up another flight of stone steps on the far side of the door. Then a huge bolt was drawn back and the door creaked slowly open. An ugly unshaven face peered out at Cornelius.

"Isn't it a bit late for visitors?" growled Golon irritably. It was evident from his bleary eyes that he had just been woken from sleep. Cornelius noted a sour smell of wine on his breath.

"Not at all," said Captain Tench, who was still standing behind Cornelius. "It's never too late for new customers." There was the sudden rasp of steel as Tench's sword was unsheathed. Cornelius turned round calmly. He was not at all surprised by the turn of events. Indeed, he had been expecting something like this. "The little man will not be visiting the jester but sharing his cell," said Tench. "And tomorrow we'll have a double execution." He appraised Cornelius for a moment. "We might need to tell them to get a smaller axe."

Cornelius gazed up at Tench in disgust. "It's as I thought," he said. "You knew about the ambush. You probably organized it."

Tench shrugged. "I did as my sovereign commanded," he said. "Now, are you going to go down those stairs quietly, or would you prefer to go down them with a sword in your ribs?"

Cornelius looked thoughtful. "Well, let me see now. What would be preferable?" He deliberated for a moment, then allowed his eyes to widen as though a thought had just occurred to him. "Wait," he said. "I've got a better idea." He pointed at Golon and then at Tench. "What about if we all go down the stairs together? The three of us."

"Together?" growled Tench. "How do you propose we do that?"

"Like this," said Cornelius. And made his move.

TWENTY-THREE

BREAKING OUT

Sebastian had been on the edge of dozing off when he was suddenly shaken fully awake by a fearsome crash, mingled with yells of surprise. He jumped up off the wooden bench and ran forward to peer through the bars of his cell. The crash was followed by a series of thumps, grunts and bellows, as three men came tumbling down the flight of stone stairs into the cellar. Sebastian recognized Golon and two uniformed soldiers, one of whom was very small.

"Cornelius!" he yelled.

But the manling was in no position to answer right now. He was clinging onto the right wrist of the other soldier, trying to hold back the sword that was clutched in the man's huge fist, as the three figures rolled over and over in an ungainly tangle of limbs. Finally they thudded down onto the hard floor of the dungeon. Golon landed first, facedown, and gave a final grunt of pain as the larger of the two soldiers came down on top of him, with Cornelius crouched on his chest. Now Sebastian could see that the other soldier was Captain Tench and that he was trying his very best to kill Cornelius.

But the struggle didn't continue for long. Cornelius pulled back one fist and struck Captain Tench hard across the chin. The man's body went limp and he collapsed back onto the unconscious figure of Golon. Cornelius stooped down and snatched up the keys from the jailer's belt. Then he hurried across to Sebastian's cell.

"I don't know," he said. "I leave you alone for one night and look what happens."

"The princess," began Sebastian. "She was helping me with a disappearing trick and—"

"I know all about it," Cornelius interrupted him. "I heard it from one of the men on the gate." He began to sort through the keys on the bunch, trying them one by one in the lock on the cell door. He had to stand on tiptoe to do it. "Looks like we were right to have misgivings about King Septimus," he said.

"You're injured," observed Sebastian, looking at the crust of dried blood on the little warrior's shoulder.

Cornelius nodded. "The king organized a small ambush for me," he said. "Twenty Brigands against one Golmiran."

Sebastian smiled. "Pretty much equal odds then," he said.

Cornelius gave a nod of satisfaction. He tried another key and this one slotted into the lock with a satisfying click. He turned the key and the well-oiled door swung silently open. "Come on," he said. "We need to get out before somebody notices what's happening down here."

"What about Max? They're planning to have him roasted to-morrow."

"Really?" For a moment Cornelius looked quite pleased by the idea. Then he shook himself. "We'd better collect him, I suppose. We'll go by the royal stables on our way out and see if there's any sign of him." They started toward the stairs. Cornelius stooped, picked up Captain Tench's sword and handed it to Sebastian.

"What about the princess?" asked Sebastian grimly.

"What about her?" Cornelius looked up at him, his face expressionless.

"Well, she's been kidnapped, hasn't she? We have to help her."

Cornelius shook his head. "Right now I'd say our priority is saving our own skins. She could be anywhere." He fixed Sebastian with a hard look. "She could be dead."

Sebastian stared down at him in shock. The thought hadn't even occurred to him. He was going to say something else, but Cornelius had started up the stairs and there was no real option but to follow him. As they ran toward the open doorway at the top, a soldier appeared carrying a tray of food. He was probably bringing Golon his supper. He saw the two men approaching and stood there staring at them, unsure what to do. But Cornelius didn't hesitate. He ran forward and slammed into the man's legs, tipping him off balance. Sebastian, following on Cornelius's heels, grabbed the man by his shoulders and pulled hard, ducking under him as he fell. The man, still holding the tray of food, tumbled over Sebastian's back and went

somersaulting down the steps to join the two unconscious men below. He struck the ground in a scatter of broken crockery and didn't move.

Cornelius led the way out of the dungeons and along the corridor beyond, his sword held ready to meet anybody who opposed them. But it was late and there didn't seem to be anybody about. They made it out to the main hall of the palace itself, and it was then that Cornelius remembered the heavily armed guards who were standing on the other side of the main door.

"There's two soldiers out there," he warned Sebastian. "You take the man on the left, I'll take the one on the right."

They approached the door. Sebastian took the handle in one hand and prepared himself to fling it open; but then he paused at the sound of a familiar voice. He glanced at Cornelius in surprise.

"That sounds like Max," he whispered.

They listened intently and could just make out the words through the thick slab of wood.

". . . and I tell you, you must let me enter. This is a matter of the utmost importance."

"Allow a buffalope into the palace?" cried one of the guards. "The king would have our guts for garters."

"Not when he hears what I have to tell him. It's about the princess."

"Go on, clear off, before I put a spear in you!" growled the second guard. "We're not going to take orders from a filthy beast of burden."

"I don't much care for your tone!"

Sebastian and Cornelius looked at each other. Cornelius nodded and began to count.

"One . . . two . . . *three!*"

Sebastian wrenched the door open and they both jumped out, taking the guards by surprise and punching them to the ground before they even had a chance to react. Max stood there in openmouthed surprise, looking down at the two unconscious men.

"Well!" he complained. "They *were* being rather rude, but I can't help feeling you overreacted."

"Never mind about that," said Cornelius. "Here, Sebastian, grab their weapons. We may have need of more than one sword apiece."

Sebastian crouched down and helped himself to the nearest guard's sword and scabbard. "What was this news that was so important?" he asked Max as he buckled on the belt.

"Princess Kerin," said Max. "She's been kidnapped."

"I could have told you that," said Sebastian.

"Yes, but I spoke to her just a little while ago."

"What?" Sebastian looked at Max incredulously.

"It's true, I swear! I talked to her. She was in the back of a cattle wagon."

"Max, are you sure?"

"Of course I'm sure. She's been taken to Brigandia to be sold as a slave."

Cornelius remembered something. "Shadlog's teeth!" he said. "I passed such a wagon as I came in! The two men driving it looked like Brigands—the officer on duty remarked upon it. But they were carrying a pass marked with the king's seal."

"What more proof of treachery do we need?" cried Sebastian. "Cornelius, we have to go after her."

Cornelius gazed up at Sebastian thoughtfully, as though considering the request. Then he shrugged. "I suppose you're right," he admitted. "Though it seems to me we'd do far better simply to get as far away from here as possible." He sighed. "They have a bit of a start on us, but it shouldn't be too hard to overtake them on the plain and deal with them." He thought for a moment, then seemed to come to a decision. "Well, come on, we'd best get moving." He ran toward the hitching post at the edge of the courtyard where Phantom still waited and swung himself up into the saddle. He indicated Captain Tench's equine.

"I trust you can ride?" he asked Sebastian.

"No problem." Sebastian moved to the captain's mount. He hadn't ridden in ages, but he figured he'd be all right. He pulled his lanky frame up into the saddle and patted the equine's neck. "We should still stop by the stables. We'll need to grab some water—and there's a couple of other things I need to get from my caravan."

"Well, we'd best be quick," Cornelius warned him. "It won't be long before somebody raises the alarm."

"How will we get past the guards at the gate?" asked Sebastian.

"A good question. I haven't quite figured that out yet. It was an easy enough matter to get in, but once they see you, we'll most probably have to fight our way out."

Max shook his head. "There's too many guards," he said. "They'd drag you down by sheer force of numbers. No, you get off to the stables and grab the provisions. Leave the gate to me. Just let me have a few moments alone with those buffalopes who operate the machinery. And when you come, come quickly."

Sebastian and Cornelius looked at each other doubtfully but Max was already trotting away along the approach to the palace.

"What do you suppose you're going to do?" hissed Sebastian; but Max didn't hesitate and within a few moments he was out of earshot.

"What do you think?" asked Sebastian.

"I don't know," admitted Cornelius. He hefted a sword and swung it around his head a couple of times, the razor-sharp blade hissing on the air. "Whatever happens, we'd best go prepared for the worst," he said. "Come on!"

And the two men galloped off in the direction of the royal stables.

Max turned the bend at the end of the avenue and saw the massive wooden gates up ahead of him. Guards were ranged in their posts along the length of it, but he was glad to see that they all seemed to be sleeping.

He saw the two huge buffalopes standing in position, harnessed to the machinery that operated the gates, and he felt a wave of pity for them. They had probably lived most of their lives chained here. When he had first arrived at Keladon, he'd spoken to them in the human tongue and they had ignored him completely. It was only afterward that it had occurred to him that they'd probably have reacted if he'd spoken in buffalope. After all, these were manual laborers; they probably weren't the brightest sparks in the campfire. It was years since Max had said anything in his native tongue, but he thought that he could probably manage to make himself understood. He hoped so, anyway. Because he had a plan. . . .

He slowed to a walk and sidled carefully up to the buffalopes, noting as he did so that their keeper was asleep on a blanket only a few steps away. The buffalopes were dozing on their feet, but they both opened their eyes as Max approached them.

Max opened the conversation with a snuffling grunt, which in buffalope meant *Greetings, brothers*.

"Hello," said the first one grudgingly; his companion just grunted.

"I bring you glad tidings," said Max.

"Oh yes," said the first buffalope. "Don't tell me, we're going to get a day off from operating these flipping gates."

"Er . . . no, it's not that. I bring you the word of the great god Colin."

Their eyes lit up. Now he had their undivided attention. He had counted on them being devotees of the buffalope god, and it had paid off.

"What does Colin say?" asked the second buffalope eagerly.

"He wants all his followers to rebel against humankind," said Max.

"What?" The first buffalope looked puzzled. "And how exactly are we supposed to do that?"

"By doing the exact opposite of what they tell you," said Max. The two buffalopes exchanged puzzled looks.

"Why does he want us to do that?" asked the first buffalope.

"It's a test of your resolve. He says that only buffalopes who obey him to the letter will be allowed to join him in Buffalope Paradise—the Great Wallow in the Sky."

"You're sure this is the word of Colin?"

"Oh, absolutely. He came to me in a vision and he said, 'Max, your job will be to spread the word.' So here I am."

"What did he look like?" asked the second buffalope.

"Oh, quite regal really. Big curling horns. Very nice features. You could see he comes from an impeccable background." Max glanced nervously over his shoulder but there was no sign of his friends yet. "And he was shimmering with this strange light all around him. And through his nose—"

"The world, hung from a silver ring." The first buffalope sighed. "Blimey, I wish I'd seen him."

"Oh, you will! Once humankind is overthrown he's planning to reveal himself to us all."

"Really?" The second buffalope looked eager. "I can hardly wait."

"Yes, well, how about a little practice?" suggested Max.

"Umm . . . OK," said the second buffalope.

"Right, pretend I'm your master. I'll give you an order and—"

"We do the exact opposite," said the second buffalope. "Yes, I think we can handle that."

Max glanced over his shoulder and saw to his alarm that two riders had just appeared at the end of the avenue.

"Right, first of all make sure those gates are properly closed!" he said.

"Which means—" said the first buffalope.

"—that they should be open!" concluded his companion.

Dutifully the two buffalopes began to walk to their left, causing the huge wooden cogs to start turning. The gates slowly began to creak open.

The sound served to rouse the beast-master from his sleep. He stared at the two buffalopes for a moment, then glanced suspiciously at Max. He lifted his head, looked toward the gates and then came fully awake.

"Stop that!" he shouted at the buffalopes. They glanced at each other but continued with what they were doing. The gates continued to swing open.

"You stupid brutes," growled the beast-master. He got to his feet, grabbed a leather riding crop that hung from his belt and started to beat the buffalopes across the back with it. They winced but kept on opening the gates. "Stop it!" roared the beast-master. "Shut those gates!"

Max frowned. He felt terribly guilty for causing the buffalopes such discomfort but these were desperate times. He lowered his head and pawed the ground. The beast-master stopped what he was doing and looked at Max warily.

"What do you think you're doing?" he snarled.

"Getting ready to knock a big stupid bully off his feet," said Max in the human tongue; and he charged, lowering one horn to get it under the man's legs. He flipped his head upward and the beast-master was thrown through the air with a bellow of fear. He came down heavily onto a stack of barrels, causing one of them to split open. He slumped unconscious amongst the wreckage. The noise of the collision had woken some of the other guards. They were getting to their feet and looking in dull surprise at the ever-widening gates of the city.

"What the—? Shut those gates!" roared the ruddy-faced officer, the man who had admitted Cornelius a little while earlier. But the buffalopes redoubled their efforts and the gates swung even wider. The officer was going to shout something else, but he suddenly became aware of the thudding of hooves behind him and turned just in time to see two equines bearing down on him, one tall and majestic, the other tiny but galloping for all it was worth. The officer fumbled for his sword, but then they were past him and racing out into the night.

"Guards!" he yelled. "Fetch equines! We need to go after those men."

"Colin wants you to *close* the gates now," Max told the buffalopes; and he galloped after his friends.

The two buffalopes stopped obediently in their tracks, twisted round in their traces and started walking in the other direction. The gates began to swing shut again. Max managed to get through the narrowing gap just in time.

"No!" roared the officer. "*Open* the gates! We need to get after them! Open the bloody gates!"

The buffalopes simply stepped up their pace. The officer ran to the gates and tried desperately to hold them back, but to no avail. "Help me!" he roared. Other soldiers ran to assist him, but they could not compete with the strength of two fully grown buffalopes and the doors slammed shut with a mighty thud, trapping everyone inside.

Sebastian, Cornelius and Max galloped across the plains, following the wheel ruts in the general direction of Brigandia. Cornelius turned in his saddle and stared back toward the palace.

"Nobody seems to be following us!" he shouted. "In fact it looks like they've closed the gates."

Sebastian looked at Max, who was racing along with a self-satisfied smile on his face. "How did you manage that?" he asked incredulously.

Max glanced up at him. "Never underestimate the power of religion," he said mysteriously. And that was all he had to say on the matter.

PART THREE

TWENTY-FOUR

IN CAPTIVITY

The three friends stood on the ridge in the gathering morning sunlight and gazed despondently down into the valley below them. They saw the sprawling city of Brigandia, dwarfed by distance and laid out like an intricate model on the dusty plain. There were no walls around this lawless place because only the brave and the foolhardy would dare to venture into that maze of narrow streets. Even as they stood there looking down, a tiny cattle wagon was kicking up a trail of dust as it raced under the huge stone arch that marked the main entrance.

"I can't believe it," said Cornelius angrily. "They only had a little start on us. By rights, we should have caught up with them before daybreak."

"It's my fault," said Max woefully. "I'm not as young as I used to be. I couldn't keep up that kind of pace all night. I told you to go on without me!"

"It's as much our fault," said Sebastian. "What a pity we don't have a map of this area."

"Who needs a map?" growled Cornelius. "I've never had any use for such a thing, I just follow my instincts."

"Well, all right, but you have to admit that we lost our way for quite a while back there. I still say we should have taken the left-hand fork when we came to that dead tree. But you were convinced it was the one on the right. . . ."

Cornelius sighed and shook his head. "Well, whatever the reasons, the whole rescue has just become much more difficult," he said. "It's one thing to fight a couple of Brigands in the middle of nowhere. It's quite another to wander into their stronghold and take on the entire population."

"We're not giving up on Princess Kerin," Sebastian warned him.

"I didn't say we were! But it's going to require some planning, that much is obvious." Cornelius turned away and went to sit on a nearby rock. "I don't suppose you thought to grab any food before we left the royal stables?" he said. "I'm absolutely starving!"

Sebastian walked over to Captain Tench's equine and unslung a large waterskin from the saddle. "Only water," he said. "Sorry." He carried it over to Cornelius and handed it to him.

"So what else have you got in there?" demanded Cornelius, indicating a set of bulging saddlebags. "You certainly spent enough time rooting around in your caravan before we left. I assumed you were getting provisions."

"I picked up a few things I thought might prove useful," said Sebastian mysteriously. "Things that belonged to my father."

"What things?" asked Max suspiciously.

"Thunder-sticks."

Max looked suddenly very wary. "Oh no, not the thunder-sticks," he said. "I didn't even want you to bring them in the caravan, let alone in your saddlebags."

"What in the name of Shadlog are thunder-sticks?" demanded Cornelius.

"They're these things my father brought back from his visit to the mountains of Kanderban," explained Sebastian. "You light the end of them with a tinderbox, and after a few moments they go off with a bang! The Kanderban tribesmen use them in their festivals. My father planned to incorporate them into his act but when he tested one, the explosion was far too powerful—"

"Blew a great big crater in the middle of the field," said Max. "I advised the young master to get rid of them before there was some terrible accident. But of course nobody ever listens to me."

Cornelius frowned. "I dare say they might come in useful," he admitted. "We could use them to create some kind of diversion perhaps. But listen, it might not come to that. As I see it, there's nothing to stop us from riding straight in there. And there's no reason why we can't bid for the princess in the auction—it will probably be open to the public."

"So," murmured Sebastian, "you're saying we can just buy her back?"

"Well, we can *bid*. I don't know about you, but I've only got a few croats to my name." He shook his head ruefully. "It's maddening! There was a whole stack of gold coins back at that ambush. If I'd only thought to grab them after the fight, we'd probably have enough money to purchase her."

"Well, I've nothing either," said Sebastian. "It's a pity King Septimus didn't give me some of my wages in advance."

They both looked at Max.

"Obviously I haven't got any!" he told them. "I'm a buffalope."

"So we'll have to find another way," said Cornelius. "Grabbing the princess should be easy enough; getting out of there in one piece—that's a different matter. Chances are every Brigand in the city will be on our heels." He actually seemed to brighten at this prospect. He lifted the waterskin to his lips, took a swig, then handed it to Sebastian. "I suggest we just make our way down there and do a bit of sniffing around," he said. "Try and get the lie of the land. I don't suppose they hold the slave auctions every day: we need to find out where and when they are."

Sebastian nodded. He took a swig of water himself. "I hope she's all right," he said.

"Oh, I've seen that one fighting lupers," Cornelius reminded him. "I reckon she'll manage until we get there. Come on, let's make tracks."

They returned to their mounts and climbed up into the saddles. They started back along the trail that led to Brigandia. Max remained on the ridge for a few moments, staring mournfully down at the city, only too aware of its terrible reputation.

"Brigandia," he muttered, "City of Thieves." He sighed. "And it all seemed to be going so *well*!"

He shrugged his massive shoulders, turned away and followed the two equines down the hillside.

*   *   *

Peering through the knothole, Princess Kerin saw a swift succession of images flashing by as the wagon clattered along the narrow streets. She saw groups of ragged, tattered people staring suspiciously at the wagon as they loitered around roadside stalls selling food and homemade wine; she saw tall white-painted buildings with rugs and tapestries hanging from the windows, and strange humpbacked, long-necked animals carrying sacks of grain.

Here sat a street conjurer sending a small child up a rope, which seemed to rear up into thin air; and over there were beggars, squatting in doorways, holding out their hands for coins. There were armed groups of warriors swaggering drunkenly around the streets and large gangs of children yelling and shouting as they chased a ball. She saw servants carrying an ornate velvet chair on which a rich merchant and his wife were sprawled, and a huge gray animal with big flapping ears and a strangely elongated snout. Finally she noticed a sign, crudely painted on a slab of wood, which said: TO THE AUCTIONS.

She pulled her face away from the knothole and realized that the wagon was slowing down. As it came to a halt, she heard the jeering voices of men outside the wagon. Then there was the clank of a chain being untied and the doors of the wagon burst open, allowing sunlight to glare into the interior. The one called Kasim stood there, grinning in at her. Behind him was a small wiry man with a scruffy beard.

"We have arrived at our destination, Your Highness," said Kasim, giving her a mocking bow. "Now shift your royal backside and get out here."

"I will not," Princess Kerin told him.

"Then allow me to help you," said Kasim. He lunged forward, grabbed a handful of her hair, and as she screamed and struggled, he dragged her out into the open and dumped her in the dust. She sat there staring up at him in astonishment, totally lost for words.

"Forget your life of privilege," he told her. "It counts for nothing here. You either do as you're told or you'll feel the toe of my boot in your arse." He looked at the wiry man. "Take her to the holding pen," he said. "And try not to damage her too much. I don't want her covered in bruises for the auction tomorrow."

"Yes, Master Kasim." The little man grabbed her by the arm and yanked her to her feet. Kasim moved away, shouting orders to other men.

Princess Kerin looked around quickly. They were in a wide, open marketplace, one side of which was dominated by a high wooden platform, with steps leading up to it. Ahead of them stood a low stone building with a metal door set into it. As they approached, the wiry man shouted, and the door was unbolted from within. A brutish-looking guard in a chain-mail jerkin stood back to allow them to descend a steep flight of steps, then slammed and bolted the heavy door behind them.

Princess Kerin was ushered into a dank, airless underground room, lit only by a couple of oil lamps. In the dim light she could see two huge metal cages, in which groups of people had been placed. One cage held men, the other women, but all the captives looked dejected and ragged and scared.

The guard walked over to the women's cage, produced a

bunch of keys and unlocked the door. In his free hand he held a heavy cudgel, ready to swipe at anyone who tried to make a dash for freedom, but nobody did. Instead, they shrank back, looking as though they were well used to being hit.

"I've got a new cell-mate for you," announced the wiry man. "She's friendly enough, but she's completely mad."

"Ignore him!" cried Princess Kerin. "I am Princess Kerin of Keladon, the niece of King Septimus. I have been kidnapped against my will. I command you all to rise up and help me."

"See what I mean?" said the wiry man. "Loopy." He gave the princess an unceremonious push in the back and launched her into the cell with such force that she tripped and fell flat on her face. There was some laughter from the other prisoners. "Have a nice evening, *Your Majesty*," said the wiry man, bending his skinny body in a mocking bow. "I trust the accommodation meets with your approval!"

"How dare you!" screamed the princess, getting back to her feet and throwing herself against the bars. "You'll pay for this, you wretch! Nobody lays hands on me and gets away with it!" But the guard was already letting the man out of the door and locking it behind him. "Come back!" she screamed. "You can't leave me in here!" She turned back to look at the other women, who were keeping as much distance between themselves and her as the small cage would allow. "I . . . I realize it sounds like I'm crazy," she told them, "but I'm telling the truth. I really am a princess!"

"Yes, dear," said a middle-aged woman with lank gray hair. "And I really am an actress—I'm just between performances!"

This elicited some laughter among the other prisoners.

"You must believe me," pleaded Princess Kerin. "Surely one of you has been to Keladon. You might have seen me at the royal palace!"

"I've been to Keladon," said one ratty-looking little woman, "and I've seen the princess many times."

"Yes? And . . . ?"

"She didn't look anything like you. She was a handsome girl in a red velvet dress, wearing beautiful jewels."

"But that's . . . You have to imagine me in those clothes and then—" The princess broke off. They were all looking at her, and the only expression she saw in their eyes was one of pity— not pity because she was a princess robbed of her birthright; but because she was clearly quite mad and there was no help for her. She turned away, went over to a corner of the cage and slumped down on her haunches. Covering her face with her hands, she began to cry.

TWENTY-FIVE

IN BRIGANDIA

As Sebastian, Cornelius and Max moved slowly through the narrow streets of Brigandia, they were aware of eyes staring at them from every window and every doorway.

It was a deeply unsettling feeling, because none of the people watching them had anything like a friendly demeanor. The Brigands looked at the visitors with open suspicion because they were strangers, and in this city your face needed to be known, otherwise you were considered a potential enemy. And it wasn't just a few people. Everyone stared, from the groups of ragged barbarians striding by, to the women washing clothing in the communal water trough, to the bands of ragged children playing wild games of tag up and down the street.

Sebastian had never felt so vulnerable in his life. He glanced down at Cornelius, who was trotting along beside him on Phantom. "This really isn't my idea of fun," he said through gritted teeth.

"Ignore them," advised Cornelius. "Just keep your gaze fixed straight ahead. Never look around or they'll think you're afraid of them."

"We *are* afraid of them," said Max. "Some of them look like they'd chop you up and roast you over a fire just for the fun of it."

Cornelius gave a dismissive snort. "Remember, they're just Brigands and we are gentlemen. They could never hope to be in our position."

"I'll try to remember that when they're attempting to stick a sword into me," said Sebastian glumly. But, he reminded himself, he was hardly in a position to complain. After all, he was the one who had insisted on mounting this rescue mission in the first place. He just hoped that it wasn't already too late. If the slave auctions had taken place that morning, Princess Kerin might already be on her way to a place of employment and there would be little hope of ever finding her.

The three friends turned a corner in the main street and found themselves entering a large open square. At the top end of it there was a raised wooden platform with steps leading up to it.

"This must be the slave market," said Cornelius. "But clearly nothing's going on at the moment." He guided Phantom across the square to a hitching rail and climbed out of the saddle. Sebastian followed suit and Max stood there sniffing the air uncertainly.

"I don't like this place," he muttered. "It smells of despair."

Cornelius gazed around thoughtfully. "Whatever it smells of, this is where they'll be bringing the princess to auction. And

242

this is where we'll have to make our move." He pointed to a ramshackle building across the way from them. Smoke and noise issued through the open doorway, and above the door there was a painted sign depicting a heavily armed warrior in full battle cry and the words THE BRIGAND'S ARMS. "We'll go into that tavern and ask a few questions," he said.

As if in warning, there was a sudden crash and a man came hurtling headlong through the window. He hit the dirt road with a loud thud, rolled over a few times and came to rest on his back. He made a halfhearted attempt to sit up but groaned drunkenly, and slumped back unconscious.

"Clearly a charming establishment," observed Max. "You're not seriously thinking of going in there, are you?"

"A tavern is the best place to get information," Cornelius told him. "Everyone knows that. Come on, Sebastian, show them a brave face."

The two men started toward the doorway but stopped when they realized that Max was following them.

"Where do you think you're going?" Sebastian asked him.

"Into the tavern, of course."

"You can't go in there!" protested Cornelius. "People are staring at us already. What do you think they'd be like if we took you with us?"

"Well, I don't fancy staying here by myself," whined Max. "It's not safe."

"You'll be all right," Cornelius assured him. "Besides, we need you to keep an eye on our equines. Don't let anybody get near them."

"Oh, and how am I supposed to stop them?" asked Max. "Say, 'Excuse me, Mr. Brigand, would you mind awfully leaving those equines alone?' Fat lot of use that would be!"

"You'll think of something," Sebastian assured him. He reached out and patted Max's head. "If in doubt, put your head down and charge. It works for most eventualities. And don't worry, we'll be back in a few moments."

As he said this, a man came flying out of the doorway, to crash face down in the dirt. Gales of raucous laughter spilled out of the tavern. Sebastian swallowed hard and glanced at Cornelius.

"Perhaps we *should* take Max in with us," he said.

"Don't be ridiculous! Come on."

Cornelius marched on and Sebastian reluctantly followed him. They stepped through the open doorway into a fog of pipe smoke and alcohol fumes and stood for a moment looking around. The interior of the tavern was packed with dirty, ragged men, all in various stages of inebriation, all talking and laughing and joking at the tops of their voices. But at the entry of the two strangers, it fell suddenly, shockingly silent; and every pair of eyes in the room turned to look at the newcomers.

It was a bad moment. Sebastian wanted to turn and run but he knew he couldn't do that. Cornelius stood looking coolly around the room, returning the stare of everyone in turn and showing them that he was not intimidated. Then he jerked his head at Sebastian and started toward the bar. In the silence, their footsteps sounded unnaturally loud on the bare wooden floor and it seemed to take them an age to cross the intervening space. But then they were at the counter, which was presided over by a fat, red-faced landlord in a leather jerkin. He was polishing a tankard with a cloth that looked like it had previously been used to mop out a cesspit. He glared at Sebastian.

"You're a brave lad coming in here by yourself," he observed.

Sebastian was puzzled for a moment but then realized that the man couldn't actually *see* Cornelius, who was hidden behind the counter.

"He's not by himself," said Cornelius. He pulled over a vacant chair and clambered up onto it, so that his head and shoulders poked above the countertop.

The landlord nodded. "A midgeling, eh? Haven't seen one of your kind in here for a long time. The last one we had complained about the quality of the drink."

Sebastian steeled himself for trouble but Cornelius just smiled.

"Midgelings can be fussy creatures," he admitted.

"Yes, well, we Brigands don't like being criticized. That's why we drop-kicked him out of the window. Managed to get him clear across the street and into the cattle trough opposite."

Cornelius allowed himself a wry smile. "Luckily I'm not a midgeling, but a Golmiran," he said. "However, Golmirans can be pretty fussy too, so I had best mind my manners." He glanced around the room again and the other drinkers averted their eyes and returned to their conversations. The hubbub of voices began to rise back to its former level. "I am Cornelius Drummel, formerly of the Golmiran army," he told the landlord. "This is my good friend Sebastian Darke, jester and adventurer."

245

Sebastian glanced at Cornelius in surprise, wondering at what point he had been promoted to the rank of "adventurer."

The landlord nodded. "And I'm Garth Bracegirdle, landlord of the Brigand's Arms. Now, what can I get for you fine gentlemen?"

"We're looking for information," said Cornelius.

Bracegirdle shook his head. "In case you hadn't noticed," he said, "this is a drinking establishment. I don't give out information to anyone who isn't drinking."

Cornelius and Sebastian exchanged glances.

"In that case," said Cornelius, reaching into his pocket and slapping a couple of croats on the counter, "we'll have two tankards of your finest ale."

Bracegirdle grinned, revealing a lot of gaps in his teeth. "That's the spirit," he said. "Have, er . . . have either of you tried Brigandian ale before?"

The two shook their heads.

Bracegirdle busied himself filling two tankards, ladling in a murky brew from a huge open barrel that stood on the ground beside him.

"I only ask because it's something of an acquired taste," he said. "The locals have a name for it. They call it Swamp Fever. It's brewed to an ancient recipe handed down from father to son for generations. It has a little more 'kick' than most ales."

He set down the tankards on the countertop and Sebastian looked doubtfully at the scummy gray foam that was spilling over the brim. As he watched, something bobbed to the surface—something round and glistening. It was the eyeball of an animal. At least, he hoped it was an animal. Sebastian felt his stomach lurch.

"Hey, lucky you!" said Bracegirdle, slapping him on the shoulder. "You don't get many of those in a barrel!" He leaned in close. "Don't tell the others," he whispered. "They'll all want one."

"Now, about that information . . . ," said Cornelius.

"No, no, lads, first you must drink! Here's to your health." Bracegirdle filled a third tankard from the same barrel and, lifting it to his mouth, he indicated that the two strangers should do likewise.

Feeling distinctly nauseous, Sebastian lifted his own tankard, reached into it and picked out the eyeball. He set it down on the countertop. "I think I'll save that for later," he said weakly.

"Aye, that's the ticket!" bellowed Bracegirdle. "Drink up now!"

Sebastian raised the tankard to his lips, took a deep breath and gulped down a mouthful of the brew. At first he was pleasantly surprised by the taste, which wasn't that bad—sweet and strangely satisfying—but then he felt a jolt in his stomach, like he'd just been kicked by a buffalope, and his legs almost went out from under him. He grunted in surprise and had to put his free hand on the bar to steady himself. Glancing at Cornelius, he saw that his friend had almost fallen off his chair.

"Delicious, eh, lads?" grinned Bracegirdle, licking a crescent of foam from his lips. "And good for the health. I drink ten of these a day!"

"Ten?" echoed Cornelius incredulously. And then added in a deeper voice, "Yes, that, er . . . seems about right." He set down his tankard carefully, as though afraid he might drop it. "Now, about the slave auctions . . ."

"Oh, so you're here for the auctions, eh? Well, you've come to the right place! There's not a more convenient spot in Brigandia. They start first thing tomorrow morning. Have you gentlemen got any lodgings for the night?"

"Er . . . no," said Sebastian. "Why, can you recowhere some mend?" He shook his head, marveling that after just one mouthful of ale he was already feeling drunk. "I mean, can you recommend somewhere?"

"Well, normally I'd say right here in the Brigand's Arms, but I just rented out my last room to that gentleman over there." He pointed to a table across the packed bar, where a huge, heavily muscled man was arm wrestling with a shabby-looking Brigand, the two of them grunting and straining as they tried to force each other's hands down to the table. Eventually the big man prevailed and gave out a bellow of triumph as he did so. "Lovely room it is too," continued Bracegirdle. "Looks right down onto the auction platform. You could have made your bids straight out of the window."

"Is that a fact?" Cornelius looked thoughtful for a moment. Then he started to climb down from his chair.

"Where are you going?" Sebastian asked him.

"Thought I might try my hand at a bit of arm wrestling," said Cornelius with a wink. "You stay here and enjoy your drink."

"Umm . . . right." Sebastian picked up his tankard and raised it cautiously to his lips again, but this time he kept his free hand braced on the countertop. When the shock hit him, it was no less savage, but this time he was ready for it.

"He's not serious, is he?" asked Bracegirdle. "Little fellow like that. That big brute will murder him."

"Oh, you don't know Corneliush . . . Corneliosh . . . you don't know him," finished Sebastian lamely. He glanced over at the table and saw that the manling had climbed up onto the bench opposite the big man. He was offering up his arm, resting his elbow on an upturned tankard in order to make it the same length as that of his opponent. "You just watch this," said Sebastian. "This will amaze you."

But it was Sebastian who was amazed, because Cornelius only put up a token show of resistance before the big man pushed the back of his tiny hand down to a horizontal position. Sebastian frowned and Bracegirdle laughed.

"Well, that's exactly how I expected it to turn out," he said. "Not much of a surprise at all."

Sebastian opened his mouth to make an excuse but then he heard Cornelius speaking to the big man.

"Well, look," he said, "why don't we make it the best of three? And let's make the stakes a little more interesting. You see, my friend and I have nowhere to sleep tonight. . . ."

Sebastian smiled. He saw what the little man was up to now. The oldest trick in the book. Make your opponent think you had no chance and they'd agree to bet just about anything.

"Now," continued Cornelius, "I understand you have a room right here in this tavern. Why don't you bet that?"

"What?" jeered the big man. "Against a couple of lousy croats? I don't think so."

"Well, now, I tell you what. Outside the tavern I've got two fine equines complete with saddles, bridles and loads of supplies;

plus a good strong buffalope. Supposing I wagered all those against your room?"

The big man looked around as though he couldn't believe his luck. "Seriously?" He laughed. "You've got yourself a deal, shorty!"

Sebastian winced. It probably hadn't been a good idea to call Cornelius that. As he watched, the manling was rolling up one sleeve and looking at the big man with a confident smile.

Sebastian leaned forward over the counter, raised his tankard and winked at Bracegirdle. "Cheers," he said. "Good health! And, er . . . one more thing. What time do you serve breakfast around here?"

TWENTY-SIX

AN ALLY

One moment the princess was crying her eyes out. The next, she stopped in surprise as a hand stroked her hair.

"There, there, m'dear, don't take on so. You'll be all right."

Princess Kerin dashed the tears from her eyes and looked up, cheered by the first kind words she had heard in ages. She found herself looking at a plump, freckle-faced young woman, with ginger hair tied in two bunches and kind, blue eyes. She was dressed in a shapeless sack dress and she was kneeling beside the princess, smiling at her reassuringly. She smelled pretty bad, as did everybody else in the cage. Princess Kerin regarded her warily.

"What do you want?" she asked suspiciously.

"I don't want nothing," said the woman. "Just to talk, that's all."

"If you've come to make fun of me—"

"No, I wouldn't do that, miss. Ain't much here to laugh about, not for any of us, I reckon."

Princess Kerin softened a little. "I realize you probably think I'm mad," she said.

"I don't think you're mad," replied the woman. "Leastways, no worse than any of the rest of us. If you tell me you're a princess, who am I to say different? I've lived long enough to know that in this world just about anything's possible. Why, my old father, he had this pig back on the farm when I was little and he taught it to sing. I swear he did!"

Princess Kerin felt as though a weight had been lifted from her back. She smiled back at the woman and blinked away the last of her tears. "What's your name?" she asked.

"I'm Peg," said the girl. "Peg o' the Hills, they call me. I'm a shepherdess from the hills of Torin. Or at least I was afore Kasim and his slave-drivers passed through our village." She sighed. "I got a family back there, I have. A fine strong man and two lovely children. They was away visiting his ma in the next village when the slavers came—and thank goodness, otherwise most like he'd be dead and my children would be on sale tomorrow alongside me."

Princess Kerin swallowed nervously. "We're being sold tomorrow?"

"Oh, aye, miss. It's a big day, there's people comin' from all over the country for the sale. Least you won't have too long to wait. I've been stuck in this stink hole for days."

"It's disgusting!" said Princess Kerin. "How can people sell other people as though they were cattle?"

Peg looked at her thoughtfully. "Don't they have slaves in Keladon, miss? That is where you said you came from, ain't it?"

Princess Kerin felt awful. Yes, of course there were slaves in her city, thousands of them: the grand palace had been built through the sweat and tears of such people, but somehow she'd never given the matter any thought before.

"Well, I'll tell you something, Peg. If I ever get back there and take my rightful place on the throne, I'll make sure that slavery is abolished. The rich merchants can start paying people to work for them. Nobody has the right to own another person."

"Well said, miss. But it ain't gonna help us much." Peg turned aside and sat down beside the princess on the straw-covered floor. "You got a husband, have you?" she asked.

"No. Though I'm supposed to be marrying soon. Prince Rolf of Bodengen. Have you heard of him?"

Peg giggled. "I should say I have! He's supposed to be very good-looking, ain't he?"

"Hmm. Well, not as good-looking as his paintings make him out to be. To be honest, he doesn't exactly set my heart aflutter. . . ."

Peg gave her a sly look. "Ah, but there's somebody who does, though, ain't there, miss? I can tell by that sparkly look in your eye."

"Hmm. Yes, there *was* somebody. To tell you the truth, I'd only known him for a few days and yet there was something about him. Something . . . special."

"You talk about him as though he's not around anymore."

Princess Kerin nodded, trying to keep her emotions under control. "I believe he's dead, Peg. Killed by an executioner's axe. And . . . it's all my fault." She felt herself on the verge of tears again but Peg took her hand and gave it a squeeze.

"Tell me about him," she said.

"He . . . he was an elfling . . . from the town of Jerabim."

"Ah, yes, they do say as how the elflings have special powers that mortal men do not. A kind of sixth sense, it is. They're supposed to be able to look at a person and straightaway know their true nature."

"Really?" Princess Kerin felt a terrible twinge of guilt at these words. "So it's no wonder he saw right through my uncle and his lying words."

"Your uncle? That would be . . . ?"

"King Septimus of Keladon," said Princess Kerin bitterly. "The uncle I trusted for years. The man who arranged to have me taken into slavery so that he could remain upon my throne."

"Oh, miss, that's terrible!"

The princess gazed at Peg through a misty veil of tears. "Then you . . . you really do believe me?"

"Yes, I do. I know a mad person when I meet one—and believe me, I've met a good few of them in me time. But you're not one of them—I'd be willing to bet on it. Thing is, how does it help you that one such as I believes?" She gestured at the gloomy crowd of prisoners slumped around the cage. "We'll never convince this lot; and I don't think none of the guards will listen to your story neither."

"Then I can only hope," said Princess Kerin softly.

"Hope, miss?"

"That somebody knows where I am."

Max had been waiting outside the tavern for what seemed like ages. He'd had some pretty tense moments when gangs of ruffians had come past and showed more than a casual interest in the contents of Sebastian's saddlebags. He'd been obliged to speak to the people concerned, and in each case they'd been so startled, they'd chosen to move on without too much trouble; but he was starting to wonder whether he wouldn't be better advised to wander into the tavern and look for his master.

And then, right on cue, Sebastian and Cornelius came out, looking very red-faced and breathing noxious fumes in his general direction.

"You've been drinking!" observed Max, horrified.

"Yesh," agreed Sebastian, looking quite pleased with himself. "But it couldn't be helped."

"Well, that's marvelous, isn't it? Poor Princess Kerin is held captive somewhere in this city and you two are in the local tavern getting pie-eyed. A fine rescue party indeed!"

"It's not like that," Cornelius told him. "Besides, it's only Sebastian who's drunk. I only *pretended* to drink the ale."

Sebastian looked at him in dull surprise. "You . . . pretended?

"Of course. You don't think I'd be so stupid as to drink that filth, do you?"

Sebastian frowned. "Er . . . well, anyway, it's all right because Corneliush did a bit of arm wrestling and he won. Wish means we don't have to give you and the equines to somebody elsh."

"What are you blathering about?" asked Max. "What about the princess?"

"We have to make our plan of action," said Sebastian. He had managed to totter over to his mount and, with some difficulty, was unstrapping the saddlebags. "We're going to go up to our room and deshide what to do."

"Your room?" Now Max really was indignant. "You're not leaving me here again, are you?"

"Shush," said Cornelius, holding a finger to his lips. "We have to. We can hardly bring a buffalope into a tavern bedroom, can we?"

"Oh, wonderful. So I get to stand around here all night while you two sleep in a luxurious bed."

"We won't be sleeping," Cornelius assured him as he unhitched his own saddlebags from Phantom. "We'll be drawing up our plans. And, Max, you will have a very important role to play. We'll need you to stay alert because the auction starts first thing tomorrow morning."

"And we need you to guard the equinsh," Sebastian reminded Max, "becaush we can't make our eshcape without them." He slung the saddlebags over his shoulder and weaved his way unsteadily back toward the door. "Good night, old friend," he shouted back over his shoulder.

"Yes," said Cornelius, starting to follow. But then he paused and turned back to look at Max. "You know," he said, "I put you up as part of a bet in an arm-wrestling contest. And just for a minute there . . . just for a minute . . . I seriously thought about losing." He smiled, shook his head. "But good sense prevailed. Good night, Max!" And he went after Sebastian.

Max stood and watched them go in mild disbelief. The door slammed behind them. He looked at Phantom and shook his head.

"That's typical, isn't it?" he complained. "Off they go into the nice warm tavern. They'll probably have a slap-up evening

257

meal and a nice goblet of wine. Meanwhile, we haven't had a thing to eat all day, not even a handful of mulch. It's at times like this that you realize where you figure in the grand scheme of things. If you've got two legs, you're laughing. If you've got four, you barely register a giggle. It's enough to make you really depressed."

He looked at Phantom, who just snorted and stamped one foot.

Max sighed. "Sometimes being an educated animal is a mixed blessing," he said. "It really is."

In the safety of their room, Cornelius opened the window, and he and Sebastian looked out onto the deserted, moonlit square. Sure enough, there was Max and the two equines, hitched to a rail away to their right, and directly beneath the window was the broad sweep of the wooden auction platform.

"That must be where the prisoners will be led out tomorrow," observed Cornelius thoughtfully.

"So where are they now?" asked Sebastian.

"My guess would be that they're down there." Cornelius moved his index finger to his left, pointing out the rear of the stage and a barred metal door, which appeared to lead into an underground chamber. "That will be the holding cell. You notice there are no windows of any kind."

"Maybe we should jusht launch an attack on that?" reasoned Sebastian. "Why wait till all thosh crowds are around tomorrow?"

Cornelius shook his head. "There's only one way in," he observed. "And nobody would open the door for somebody they didn't know. Besides, you're not in the best condition to do any-

258

thing right now." He frowned. "So it will have to be tomorrow, I'm afraid. As you said, there will be a lot of people around, so we're going to have to depend on the element of surprise."

He began to pull the various pieces of his miniature crossbow from the compartments in his belt and quickly slotted them together. He took out a short wooden bolt with a heavy three-pronged metal head. And finally, from his saddlebag, he drew a long coil of fine silken thread. He fastened the end of the latter to the crossbow bolt and slotted it into the bow. Then he walked to the window and peered thoughtfully across the square.

"What are you doing?" Sebastian asked him.

"Shush! You'll spoil my aim. Here, grab hold of this." Cornelius handed the free end of the thread to Sebastian. He glanced quickly around to ensure that the square was still deserted, then lifted the crossbow to his eye line and took long and careful aim. Peering over the little man's shoulder, Sebastian saw that he was aiming for a slightly lower building on the far side of the square, which had what looked like battlements adorning its roof. Finally, Cornelius squeezed the trigger. The bolt shot out of the window, taking the length of thread with it. It flew in a tight graceful arc and landed right between a couple of the notches. "Perfect," said Cornelius. "Now, pull back on the thread . . . gently."

Sebastian did as he was told, and after a few moments the hooked head of the bolt snagged itself on the stonework at the edge of the roof. Cornelius came over and pulled harder, checking that the bolt was now stuck fast. He pulled the thread tight and directed Sebastian to climb up on a chair and fasten it securely to one of the wooden beams that traversed the low roof.

"There!" he said at last, twanging the thread like the string of a finely tuned instrument. "Done!" He led Sebastian back to the window and showed him how they now had a secure line running in a gentle downward slope some ten feet above the centre of the stage.

"What's it for?" asked Sebastian, mystified.

"What's it for? Why, it's the quickest route possible down to that stage! When the time comes, you just loop a short length of rope over it, jump from the window and go shooting across the square. When you get to the middle, you let go and you drop right onto the center of the stage!"

Sebastian looked at Cornelius warily. "I can't help noticing that you're shaying 'you.' I hope you're not exshpecting me to go down that thing."

"Why not? You'll be fine."

"Cornelius, I don't have your exshperience of soldiering."

"Oh, you don't do so badly. Besides, it *has* to be you. I'll be too busy causing the diversion." He pointed to some small openings under the wooden stage. "I'm the only one small enough to get under there," he said.

"Yesh, but this thread doeshn't look strong enough to take my weight!"

"Nonsense. It's made from the web of a Golmiran tunnel spider. It's one of the strongest substances known to man. And don't worry, you'll only be on it for a few moments. Now, show me how these thunder-sticks work. . . ."

A moment later Cornelius had the powerful firework devices out on the bed and was fashioning shorter fuses for them, trying to estimate how long it would take him to light them and get out from under the stage before they went off. And as he worked, Sebastian noted, there was a look of glee on his face; like a little boy anticipating a favorite game. It never seemed to occur to him that he could be hurt, even killed.

Sebastian sighed and turned to look down once again at the empty square, concentrating on the small rectangle of light issuing from the barred doorway of Princess Kerin's prison. He wished he could warn her about tomorrow. She must be entirely without hope now, he decided. How he wished he could talk to her, stroke her soft shining hair. . . .

A sudden sense of panic came over him as he realized for the first time the full depth of his feelings for her. It was madness, he told himself. He was a commoner and she was destined to be queen. What was more, she had already told him that her duty lay in marriage to Prince Rolf of Bodengen. Yet for all that, it was for her that he had made the journey into this most dangerous of cities; and it was for her that he would be risking his life the following morning.

But now there was nothing to do but sit and watch Cornelius making his preparations for what promised to be quite a party. . . .

TWENTY-SEVEN

THE BIG AUCTION

Princess Kerin woke to the touch of a hand on her shoulder, shaking her gently and intruding into the dream she had been having.

"Sebastian," she whispered. "Not yet. A few more minutes . . ."

And then she was quite suddenly awake, and she realized she was cold and muddy and lying on a scattering of straw. She looked up and saw that the face smiling down at her was not Sebastian, but Peg.

"So that's his name, is it?" she said good-naturedly. "Sebastian."

"I was dreaming," said Princess Kerin. She sat up and glanced around the interior of the cage, where everybody seemed to be in a state of some agitation. "What's going on?" she asked.

"It's morning. They'll be coming round with the food in a bit."

"Food." Princess Kerin remembered that she hadn't eaten anything since leaving Keladon. "Thank goodness," she said. "I'm starving! What do they serve? I wouldn't mind some eggs—"

"I wouldn't get your hopes up, miss," Peg warned her. "It's only a few old scraps of bread."

"Oh." She tried not to let her disappointment show. "Well, I . . . I quite like bread."

"You only get some if you fight for it," Peg warned her.

"Fight for it?" The princess was horrified. "I'm not fighting for food. I can't think of anything more humiliating."

"Well, miss, that's how it works here. They throw in the scraps and everybody scrambles for a bit. Remember, this is the last we'll get till we're sold and taken off by our new masters."

Princess Kerin nodded numbly. She felt that she had woken from a dream to find herself in a nightmare. Somehow, sleep had made her forget about what was going to happen to her.

The metal gate creaked open and brilliant sunlight spilled momentarily into the gloom. A big, brutish soldier came in carrying two metal buckets. "Mornin', little piggies!" he jeered. "Time for your din-dins."

He approached the men's cage first and, lifting one of the buckets, he threw the scraps of food in through the bars. Immediately there was a commotion within as everybody, young and old, flung themselves down onto the straw to try and claw up a taste of the food. Blows were exchanged and some of the older men were shamelessly pushed aside as their younger, stronger cell-mates grabbed the lion's share of the pitiful amount that was on offer. As the men grabbed something, they moved off to

263

different parts of the cage to crouch down, cramming the bread into their mouths like animals.

Now the grinning soldier picked up the other bucket and approached the women's cage. "Hello, ladies!" he giggled. "Missed me, 'ave yer?"

"Get ready," Peg urged Princess Kerin.

The soldier stood there for quite a while, the bucket raised, knowing full well how tantalizing it was to the hungry women in the cage. Then at last he flung the scraps in through the bars and watched with a satisfied smile on his face. Princess Kerin started forward but was immediately knocked aside in the rush of prisoners moving in from behind her. The mound of scraps was immediately surrounded by a scrum of women, pushing and shoving each other in their haste to claim a little sustenance. They pulled at hair, clawed at faces, lashed out in anger. The princess thought of the sumptuous banquets she had attended in Keladon, the plates piled high with rich food that she'd pushed aside, barely touched, and her eyes filled with tears of shame. She turned away in disgust and went back to slump down in the corner.

But a moment later Peg returned, clutching two crusts of bread. She squatted down beside the princess and handed one of them to her.

"No." Princess Kerin shook her head. "You have them, Peg. I don't deserve any."

"Course you do." Peg pressed the hunk of bread into her hands. "You got to eat, miss, keep your strength up. You never know when you'll get the chance again. Go on." She kept insisting until finally Princess Kerin gave in. She lifted the bread to her mouth and took a bite. It was old and stale but it was the only food that had passed her lips in ages and she ate hungrily, devouring every last little bit of it, savoring the taste on her tongue. And as she ate, she swore to herself that she would not turn her back on poverty ever again, as long as she lived.

She was just finishing up the last mouthful of bread when the outside door swung open again and a familiar figure stepped arrogantly into the room, his heavy boots stirring up swirls of dust that seemed to dance in the rays of sunlight. It was Kasim, grinning an oily grin and looking very pleased with himself. He strode into the center of the room and stood there, one hand on his hip, the other holding a plaited leather whip. He gazed around at the occupants of the cages.

"Slaves," he said, "the moment you have been waiting for is at hand. It is time to find out what your miserable lives are worth." He focused his attention on Princess Kerin and his eyes seemed to glitter with a cold, mocking light. "Some of you will fetch a good price," he said. "Others will be worth nothing but a few paltry coins. But it's all good profit for me." He sneered. "Bring them," he said and, turning on his heel, he strode back toward the open door.

Princess Kerin looked at Peg and the woman smiled reassuringly.

"Come on, miss," she said, taking the princess's hand. "Wherever we end up, it's got to be better than this filthy hole."

Princess Kerin nodded. She was grateful that she had an ally, even if it was only for a short while. She and Peg followed the other prisoners out of the cage toward the exit.

* * *

The blaring of trumpets alerted Sebastian to the fact that some-thing important was happening. He stared down from the open window of his room at the vast crowds of people gathered around the stage. Cornelius was down there somewhere, he knew, but he had lost sight of him ages ago and had no idea what had happened to him. He could see Max and the two equines, standing in the midst of the crowd, a short distance from the foot of the stage, and supposed that Cornelius could not be far away from them. Hopefully he would be under there now, planting his explosive charges. Sebastian hoped the little man had made the fuses long enough, otherwise they were li-able to go up while he was still beside them and even Cornelius would have trouble surviving that. . . .

Now Sebastian could see a big bald-headed man climbing the steps at the back of the stage. He stepped out onto the wooden platform, waving a hand to people in the crowd whom he rec-ognized. Behind him trailed a long line of ragged women, who were being herded by a few uniformed soldiers armed with spears. Sebastian looked desperately for Princess Kerin but for an uncomfortably long time he didn't see her. He was coming to the conclusion that she wasn't in the group, when suddenly he *did* spot her, looking frail and scared, holding hands with an-other woman who appeared to be speaking to her.

Sebastian picked up the short length of rope from the bed—his means of getting down to the stage. He looped it around the long stretch of thread leading out from the window, but for the moment he did nothing. Cornelius had told him to wait until Princess Kerin stepped up onto the selling block, a small rostrum that stood a few inches higher than the main platform. The crowd became rowdy as the various bidders discussed the merits of the women on sale, and eventually Kasim had to hold up his arms for some silence.

"Greetings, people of Brigandia," he roared. "Welcome to our monthly slave-mart!" The crowd shouted back its approval, and Kasim turned to look at the straggle of women who were now ranged behind him. He turned back to the crowd and raised his arms for silence again. "You know me," he shouted. "Honest Kasim. My slaves are gathered from around the known world and every one of them comes complete with my personal guarantee of satisfaction. If any slave purchased fails to give a minimum of one year's service, I will replace it free of charge with a similar model!" A roar of approval greeted this offer. "If any slave fails to give adequate service, I will call round personally to administer a little on-site maintenance!" He cracked his whip in front of him, winked at the crowd and was rewarded with gales of laughter. "I have slaves of all kinds," he promised them. "Big, small, short, tall, fat, thin, young, old—whatever you're looking for, you're sure to find it here! Plus, don't miss this week's special. Buy two slaves and get a third half price!" More yells of approval. It was clear that Kasim was a popular man here in Brigandia.

Sebastian looked at Princess Kerin standing helplessly on the stage and felt like going down and showing Kasim that not everybody liked what he did, but he knew he had to wait for the appropriate moment, otherwise they'd never stand a chance of getting out of here alive. He wondered how Cornelius was doing under the stage. . . .

*   *   *

Deep in the crisscrossed timbers beneath the platform, Cornelius was at work, tying his last pack of thunder-sticks to one of the main supports. He had linked all the short fuses together so they could be lit simultaneously, and he figured that once ignited, he had perhaps to the count of ten to get out of there and shield himself from the blast. He glanced upward at a small gap in the boards, through which he could catch occasional glimpses of what was happening onstage.

It would be impossible to see the exact moment when Princess Kerin stepped up onto the rostrum, but he had told Max to issue a loud moo at the appropriate time and that would be the signal to light the fuses. Once the explosives went up, it would be anybody's guess what happened next, and Cornelius had to admit that he didn't really have a clear idea of where it went from there. With any luck the explosion would stun people long enough to allow them to escape from the crowd—but Cornelius had had no idea it would be as big and jam-packed as it was.

He finished tying the last fuse and reached into his pocket for his tinderbox and a small candle he had borrowed from his room at the inn. Crouching down, he gathered a little straw together and struck the flint against the box, scraping repeatedly until he produced a big enough spark to get the kindling smoldering. By carefully blowing on the kindling, he eventually managed to produce a tiny flame, and from this he set the wick of the candle alight. He crouched there, ready to ignite the fuses the moment he heard Max's alarm. From above him he heard the deep voice of Kasim, calling out to his public. . . .

*   *   *

From where he stood near the front of the stage Max had a perfect view of the proceedings. Kasim spread his hands in a dramatic gesture.

"So, my friends," he roared. "We're all set. Let the auction begin. Bring me the first one!"

A soldier moved into the line of captives and emerged holding a skinny, tangle-haired woman by the arm. He pushed her toward Kasim, who gestured with his whip, indicating that she should stand up on the raised wooden plinth in front of her so the crowd could get a better view. Clearly terrified, the woman did as she was told. She stood there, looking anxiously around.

"Now, here's a real *beauty*," roared Kasim sarcastically, and the crowd laughed. "All right, there's not much meat on her bones, but I dare say she can work hard enough. She'd be good for scrubbing floors and cleaning out latrines and I've no doubt she can cook and sew. Who'll start me off at one croat?"

Somewhere in the crowd a hand went up, and the auction was under way.

Max could see the tears of humiliation in the woman's eyes. It must be a terrible thing, he decided, to be treated like this. Not that his kind weren't used to such things. Most buffalopes got sold at some point in their lives and it was always humans that did the bidding. But to bid for their own kind like this! How degrading. No buffalope would ever sink so low.

"I wish that big hairy brute would move," said a voice immediately to his right, and Max turned his head in surprise. A short distance away, four slaves were struggling to hold up an opulent sedan chair so the occupants could have a clear view of the auction platform. On the chair, reclining on rich velvet and brocade cushions, lounged a fat merchant and his equally fat wife. They were looking toward the stage with interest, but the woman was holding a silk handkerchief over her nose, as though a smell was bothering her. She pointed a stubby, jewel-encrusted finger at Max. "Can't you get him to clear off, Archibald?" she asked her husband. "You know how sensitive my nose is."

"I don't see how he *can* move," replied the merchant. "We're all hemmed in here. Mind you, I don't know who'd be stupid enough to leave such a creature there in the first place." He lifted a hand to make a bid. "Three croats!" he roared.

"You're not bidding for that sour-faced old baggage, are you?" protested the woman. "What would you want her for?"

"The woman who tends the cesspits is getting too old for the work," said Archibald. "She can barely stand. I don't mind paying a few croats for somebody with a bit more energy."

From the stage, Kasim surveyed the crowd. "Three croats, I'm bid. Do I hear four?" He gazed around, looking for a sign among the crowd. "Anybody? At three croats, then . . . going . . . going—"

"Four croats," said Max, in as loud a voice as possible, while keeping his head well down.

"Four croats, I'm bid!" Kasim waved a hand in Max's general direction. "Will anybody make it five?"

There was a long pause before Archibald said, "Five croats."

His wife gave him a disapproving look over the top of her silk handkerchief. "Don't bid any higher," she advised him. "She wouldn't be worth it."

Archibald smiled. "Don't worry, nobody's going to pay more than—"

"Six croats!" said Max.

"Six croats, I'm bid," said Kasim. "Do I hear seven?"

The fat merchant was staring around the crowd, trying in vain to spot whoever it was that was bidding against him. "Who was it?" he asked his wife. "Somebody very cultured, by the sound of it. I bet it was that jumped-up little oil seller, Antonius. He's always trying to go one better than me."

"Forget it," she advised him. "It's no great loss. You can bid for another one. Somebody younger, stronger . . ."

But the merchant ignored his wife's advice. "Seven croats!" he roared defiantly. Clearly this was a man who was used to getting his own way. "Let's see Antonius beat that," he said to his wife with a smug smile.

"Twenty croats!" said Max. There was uproar in the crowd. Kasim couldn't believe his good fortune.

"Did I hear twenty croats?" he cried. "That's fantastic." He was scanning the crowd now, trying to see who the bidder might have been. "Only the first sale of the day and people are already digging deep in their purses. Now then, is there any advance on twenty?"

The merchant was looking around in openmouthed awe. His wife, meanwhile, was pointing at Max. "It was that animal!" she cried. "I saw its mouth move!"

"What?" Her husband stared at her in astonishment. "Don't

271

be ridiculous, dear. It was Antonius. I know that slimy voice when I hear it. Well, he's not getting the better of me!"

The merchant was clearly going to bid again, but his wife grabbed his arms and held on tight until Kasim had dismissed the bidding.

"Going . . . going . . . gone for twenty croats!" Kasim pulled the woman down off the rostrum and pushed her unceremoniously toward the stockade where the winning bidders could collect their slaves. Then he gestured to his soldiers to pick out another one.

Max was giving a satisfied sidelong glance at the sedan chair, where the red-faced merchant and his wife were having a very loud argument.

"I'm telling you it was the buffalope! I saw its mouth move."

"D'you think I'm stupid, woman? Antonius has had it in for me ever since we put that shop next to his."

"It wasn't Antonius! Don't you know those animals can be trained to speak?"

"Oh, really—as if a great shaggy brute like that would have the intelligence to bid at a slave auction! Now, shut up, this one looks very interesting."

"I'm not sure I approve. She's too pretty for my liking."

Max turned his head back toward the stage and his eyes widened in surprise. He had expected to have to wait ages before they got to the princess, but no, here she was being prodded along at the point of a spear, while a second soldier restrained the plump woman she'd been standing with. Now she was climbing reluctantly up onto the rostrum. Max glanced up toward the window and saw Sebastian crouched in position, all ready to go. But first he had to give the signal. For a terrible moment he couldn't remember what it was. He started to panic, but then remembered: it wasn't a word or anything complicated. It was that degrading sound again. Still, he thought, at least this time it was for a good cause.

He lifted his head, gathered all the power in his lungs and let out a great bellowing "*Mooooooooooooooooooooo!*"

TWENTY-EIGHT

TO THE RESCUE

Under the wooden platform the noise was so sudden and so loud that Cornelius jolted as though from a dream. He reached out a hand to grab the candle, but caught it awkwardly with the tip of a finger, knocking it over. It immediately went out.

"No!" he gasped. He fumbled in his pockets for his tinderbox, knowing that he would have to go through the whole process of lighting the candle again—and that Sebastian would have already launched himself at the sound of Max's call. He got the tinderbox in his hand, detached the flint and started frantically striking sparks. . . .

Sebastian took a firm grip on each end of the short length of rope, snatched in a deep breath and jumped out of the window.

At first he just dropped, and he had the horrible sensation that he was going to keep dropping until he hit the cobbled street below; but then he reached the point where the support thread snapped him back up again and he began to move toward the stage, slowly at first but with increasing momentum. Below him he saw the wide stretch of the wooden platform and Princess Kerin, gazing anxiously out at the massed crowd; and as he looked down at her, he was aware that his pace was quickening dramatically, the short rope sliding easily over the long stretch of silken thread. He snapped his gaze up to the end of it and it was then that he saw the grappling arrow pull a big chunk of masonry out of the roof opposite.

The rope ahead of him went suddenly, horribly slack and he was left flying through the air, forward and downward, carried by his own momentum. He opened his mouth to yell something, but then the crowded stage was whizzing up to meet him, so he forgot about yelling and concentrated instead on trying to land in one piece.

Cornelius struck and struck again, and the big sparks fell onto the mound of straw, fizzled and went out. He kept on striking repeatedly with the flint, his hands slippery with sweat and then, just when he thought it was no use trying any more, a spark caught, glowed red and burst into a tiny orange flame. He snatched up the candle, held the wick ever so carefully to the flame and finally managed to get a light.

"Yes!" he hissed; and almost blew the candle out again.

He put the flat of his hand around the flame, sheltering it from any other breath that might emerge from his mouth. Now he transferred the candle to the jumble of intersecting fuses gathered in the middle of the main beam, and immediately a bright hissing flame flared in his face. He crouched there for a moment, gazing at the rapidly shortening fuse; then remembered that he didn't have much time, so he turned round and started crawling frantically on his hands and knees, back to the opening at the front of the stage. And that was when his chain-mail jerkin snagged on a nail, leaving him stuck as the fuses burned rapidly closer to their explosive charges. . . .

Max stared up in horror as Sebastian's gangly body fell through the air. He was pretty sure that this last development wasn't intentional, and looking at the way Sebastian was flailing downward, it was hard to know which particular bit of the stage he would land on and whether he would arrive feet- or headfirst. But there was no time to dwell on it: Max had to get on with his part of the plan. He nodded at the two equines, who were standing just ahead of him, closer to the stage.

"All right," he said. "On my command. One . . . two . . . *three!*"

And he and the equines turned quickly round so they were facing away from the stage. Max's main role, once Sebastian, Cornelius and the princess were mounted, was to clear a path for the escape. He noted, with more than a hint of satisfaction, that the fat merchant and his wife were right there in front of him. He saw the startled expressions on their faces and just couldn't resist speaking to them.

"Lovely day for an auction, isn't it?" he said brightly.

Sebastian steeled himself for the impact of the wooden stage against his skinny body, but at the last possible moment something softer intervened: Kasim. Sebastian had a brief impression

276

of the slave-master's startled face an instant before he slammed into him. He felt the man grunt in surprise as all the air was knocked out of his body. Then the two of them fell, and Kasim's shoulders hit the wooden stage scant seconds before Sebastian came crashing down on top of him. Kasim's eyes bulged in pain and he opened his mouth to yell, but he couldn't get any breath. Sebastian rolled over onto his back and found himself looking up at an astonished Princess Kerin.

"You!" she gasped. "Where did you come from?"

Sebastian gestured vaguely toward the upstairs window of the tavern opposite, but he too was unable to catch enough breath to make a reply.

He got back to his feet, drawing his sword as he did so, aware that the soldiers were all staring at him in astonishment, too surprised as yet to make a move. He also knew that this situation wouldn't last long. He stepped up to Princess Kerin, threw an arm around her waist and began to pull her toward the edge of the platform, wondering what had happened to the explosion. What if the fireworks had failed to ignite? He heard a groan from beside him, and glancing down, he saw that Kasim was struggling upright, an angry expression on his face. He was still holding his whip in one massive hand.

"What happens now?" asked Princess Kerin.

It was a very good question.

Cornelius struggled to free his chain-mail singlet from the nail, but a link of metal had caught in the head and it was refusing to budge. He glanced desperately toward the thunder-sticks and saw that the fuses were burning down at terrifying speed, only a fingernail's length away from the explosives.

"Shadlog's beard!" he growled. He summoned all his strength and pulled hard. He was rewarded with a ripping sound and then, quite suddenly, he was free and scrambling frantically toward the opening at the edge of the stage. . . .

"I don't know how you got here, Elf-man," snarled Kasim, advancing toward Sebastian, his whip raised. "But when I'm finished with you, you'll wish you'd stayed in Keladon to face the executioner's axe."

Behind him, the other soldiers were advancing too, their swords and spears raised. Sebastian pushed Princess Kerin behind him and lifted his own sword in defiance as Kasim closed on him. He remembered something he had heard Cornelius say and tried to follow his example.

"Step right up here if you think you're hard enough," he said, as calmly as he could manage. "And I'll take that great ugly head off your shoulders."

Kasim grinned unpleasantly, showing several gold teeth dotted in among his natural ones. "Brave," he observed. "But so stupid." He flicked his wrist almost casually, and something hissed through the air, wrapped itself around Sebastian's sword and pulled it clean out of his hand. It went clattering away across the wooden platform. Sebastian stared after it in dismay. "Still feeling confident?" asked Kasim. He flicked his wrist again and this time the whip lashed Sebastian across the cheek, a stinging blow that almost knocked him off his feet. "Now," purred Kasim, "are you going to come quietly or am I going to—?"

The remainder of his sentence was lost in a great roar of smoke and flame that came belching up through the middle of the platform, flinging splintered wood in all directions. A couple of soldiers who were close to the blast were thrown headlong through the air, their arms and legs waving like frantic puppets. One of them collided with Kasim and sent him sprawling for a second time, but by then Sebastian had already grabbed Princess Kerin and jumped off the edge of the platform, into the chaos of panicking people all around it. As his feet thudded onto the earth, he saw a tiny figure crouched at the foot of the stage, beckoning to him. Cornelius indicated the two equines waiting patiently for their riders, just a few steps away. His face was black with soot and he was grinning like a maniac.

"What a blast!" he roared. "Did you see it? Fantastic!"

A great wave of smoke washed over them as Sebastian moved over to his equine and clambered up into the saddle. He reached down and pulled Princess Kerin up behind him. Even in the heat and excitement of the moment, he registered how good it felt to have her arms clasped around his waist. He glanced down at Cornelius and saw that he had just vaulted onto Phantom's saddle. But ahead of them now lay a seemingly impenetrable press of yelling, shoving people. How were they ever going to get out of here?

"Max!" yelled Cornelius. "It all depends on you now."

Max lowered his head and pawed the ground a couple of times while he gathered every last bit of strength into his massive shoulders. He looked up briefly and saw the fat merchant and

279

his wife sitting in their sedan chair, staring at him white-faced and terrified.

"So," said Max quietly, "I smell, do I?"

And he put his head down again and charged. He felt the impact of the wooden chair against his horns, and then he tossed his head to the side and the thing went tumbling away, flinging the two screaming merchants onto the heads of the crowd. Max didn't hesitate. He continued on his way, driving everyone and everything before him, a chaos of running, shouting people, braying animals and clattering vehicles—it was all the same to him. As he moved on, he closed his eyes, concentrating on utilizing every ounce of power at his disposal, and he was aware only of a series of impacts against his head, things that broke or moved aside or went flying over his mighty shoulders, and he told himself he was not going to stop now, not for anything. . . .

Princess Kerin hugged herself tight against Sebastian, hardly believing that he was still alive, that he had come all this way and risked so much to help her. She looked across and saw Cornelius, crouched low in the saddle of a tiny equine, racing along beside her. Just behind him, she was astonished to see another familiar figure on an equine. It was Peg, and she was urging her mount along like there was no tomorrow, and a sense of joy sprang up in Princess Kerin's heart to think that her new friend would escape and make her way back to her husband and children. Their eyes met and Peg shouted something, but the princess could not hear her words over the tumult of yelling people.

She opened her mouth to shout something back, but the

words died as the head of another equine moved into her line of vision and she saw that the rider was Kasim. He was hunched down in the saddle and he was urging his mount to go faster as he closed on the princess, one huge tattooed arm outstretched to make a grab at her. He wasn't finished yet and he was clearly intent on preventing her escape.

"Sebastian!" she yelled; but if he heard her, he was too focused on the way ahead to take any notice, and now she was aware that the slave-master's fingers were brushing against her arm, looking for a hold, seeking to pull her back out of the saddle. His mouth curved into a grin of satisfaction as he sensed victory. . . .

Princess Kerin turned back to try one last shout into Sebastian's ear—

And then a huge wooden fruit barrow came flying through the air, thrown up by Max's horns and flung recklessly backward. Sebastian saw it and ducked, pressing the princess down with one arm as he did so. Peg saw it and ducked; and Cornelius was so near the ground already that he had no need to duck; but Kasim didn't see it at all—not until it crashed full into him and sent him tumbling backward off his mount with a scream of mingled pain and terror. Then he was gone, lost in the rapidly thinning crowd as Max powered his way to the very edges of it.

And quite suddenly they were free, moving out from the crowds of people and racing along the main street that led to the entrance arch and out onto the plains beyond.

TWENTY-NINE

SEIZE THE DAY

Around midday they came to a shallow valley with a small stream meandering through it and they finally dared to stop for a while. Cornelius spent some time up on the ridge scanning the plains behind him with his telescope, just to assure himself that nobody was following; and it was only then that he allowed everyone to descend into the valley.

"At last!" groaned Max. "I couldn't have gone on another step without a drink." He waded straight into the shallow water and began slaking his thirst in a series of noisy gulps. Sebastian could see that his mighty horns were dented and splintered from the ferocious battering they had encountered back in Brigandia. He helped Princess Kerin climb down from his mount and she immediately hurried across to Peg. The two women met midstream and hugged each other delightedly.

"Peg, I'm so glad you escaped," said the princess. "It all happened so suddenly back there, I had no time to even look for you."

Peg smiled. "When you went off the edge o' that platform, I followed three steps behind. There was this nobleman sitting on an equine just a little way off. I persuaded him to part company with it." Peg looked down ruefully at her knuckles, which were badly grazed. "He took some convincing," she added.

Princess Kerin laughed delightedly. "What will you do now?" she asked.

"Me? Oh, I shall make my way back to the hills of Torin. I reckon a couple of days' hard riding should get me back to my family. I'll just have to hope that they're safe and well . . . and that they haven't forgotten me in the weeks I've been away."

"I doubt they will have done that," the princess assured her.

"But more important, what will *you* do now, miss?"

"Yes," said Cornelius, who had just walked up to the water's edge with Sebastian. "A very good question. What will you do, Your Highness?"

Princess Kerin frowned and looked down at the clear water swirling around her feet, as though seeking an answer in those glittering shallows. "I really don't know," she admitted. "I do not think that I can ever go back to Keladon."

"Why not?" demanded Sebastian. "It's rightfully yours."

She laughed at that. "Oh yes! And do you think my dear uncle Septimus will ever allow me to set foot inside the palace again? He would have me executed in an instant." She shrugged her shoulders. "But then, where else am I to go? It's been my home since I was born. I don't know anywhere else."

Cornelius took off his helmet and sat down in the sand at the edge of the stream. For a few moments he trailed one tiny hand in the water, as though deep in thought. Then he scooped up a handful and splashed it over the still raw wound in his shoulder. He gritted his teeth against the pain, then shook his head.

"I know what *I* would do," he said at last.

Princess Kerin looked down at him. "Tell me," she said.

"I would go back and claim what is mine."

"That's easy to say," she told him. "But not so easy to do. Uncle Septimus has a mighty army at his disposal. He would crush any resistance we could organize without a moment's thought."

"He won't be expecting any resistance. As far as he knows, you've been sold as a slave in Brigandia."

"But it won't take more than a day for news to reach him of our escape," said Sebastian. "He'll know by . . . tomorrow afternoon at the latest."

"Which is exactly why we must make our move before then. First thing tomorrow morning our army must be ready to make its attack."

"Army?" Princess Kerin stared at him. "What army? I *have* no army!"

"Princess, you have the hearts and minds of every man, woman and child in Keladon," said Cornelius. "I have seen the way you are adored by them. If they were to learn of your uncle's treachery, I don't doubt that every one of them would be willing to fight to put you back where you belong."

"It's true enough," agreed Sebastian. "They all know that you're the rightful queen. And no matter how powerful an army he has, it cannot stand against everybody in the city. And I believe that many of those troops would switch their allegiance in a moment if they knew what had happened. Remember, as far as they're aware, I've used witchcraft to make you vanish. You'd only have to walk back through those city gates and tell them what really happened to you."

Princess Kerin was still doubtful. "I don't know," she said. "Supposing we try and fail?"

"Better that than to skulk in the shadows while a liar and a coward lords it over your kingdom," said Cornelius. "But, Princess, I'm only airing an opinion. It's entirely up to you to do what you think is right and just."

There was a long silence, during which the trickling of the stream seemed to rise to a roar. Then Peg spoke.

"Your Highness, if it be your wish, I'll come with you and fight at your side."

Princess Kerin smiled at her friend and shook her head. "No, Peg. I thank you from my heart, but your rightful place is with your husband and children."

"And yours is with your people. Listen to what your friends are telling you, I believe they too speak from the heart."

"I do not doubt it. Now, Peg, please be on your way and may good fortune guide you safely home to the arms of your loved ones."

The two women embraced again and then Peg stepped away, grabbed the bridle of her equine and swung herself nimbly up into the saddle. But she hesitated a moment and leaned down until she was close to the princess.

"I'm off then; but if you ever want the help of Peg o' the Hills, you just come looking for me. Whatever happens back in

Keladon, there'll always be a hot meal and a roof over your head, should you have need of it." She glanced quickly across at Sebastian, then smiled slyly. "You was right," she whispered. "He is a good-looking lad!"

The two women clasped hands for a moment; then Peg kicked the flanks of her equine and it moved off across the stream and up the gentle slope of a hillside. When she crested the rise, she reined in her mount for a moment and waved. Then she was gone, racing down into the valley beyond.

Princess Kerin stood gazing after her for a while. Several moments passed and then she realized that three pairs of eyes were watching her. Max too, having slaked his thirst, had stopped drinking and had ambled back downstream a little to see what would happen next.

She walked over to him and stroked his battered horns with her hand. "I haven't thanked you, Max," she whispered. "You were absolutely magnificent back there."

Max considered this for a moment. "I was pretty incredible, wasn't I?" he said.

"Your poor horns, they're absolutely ruined. I wish I could do something to make them better."

"Hmm . . . you haven't got any fresh pommers on you, by any chance?"

"Max!" said Sebastian.

"Oh, all right, it was worth a try!"

Princess Kerin turned away. "I . . . I need some time alone. To think," she told them; and she moved to the edge of the stream and away along the riverbank.

"Don't take too long, Your Highness," Cornelius called after her. "Don't forget, somebody may have followed us from Brigandia."

But she didn't reply. Sebastian sighed and slumped down beside his friend at the water's edge. He felt tired and travel sore, but he knew that there was still more to do. He wrenched off his boots and cooled his feet in the river, letting out a great sigh as he did so.

"Oh yes," he said. "That's good." He glanced at Cornelius and the thick crust of dried blood that had seeped through the chain mail at his shoulder. "You should let me clean that wound," he said. "It could become infected."

Cornelius made a dismissive gesture. "I'll clean the wound when all this is over," he said. He stared along the bank to the solitary pacing figure of Princess Kerin. "I don't envy her the decision," he said. "It'll take guts to go back in there after what's happened."

"But what else can she do?" asked Max. "That's the trouble with being a member of royalty. You're not equipped to do anything else with your life." He gave Sebastian a sly look. "Perhaps she could try being a jester. She couldn't be any worse than some people I've heard."

"You watch it," Sebastian told him, but there was no real venom in his voice. The truth was that he thought Max had been positively heroic back in Brigandia. Without him, they'd never have got out of there. He was about to say something to that effect but Cornelius punched him on the arm.

"Hey up!" he said.

Sebastian turned his head to see that Princess Kerin was striding back toward them with what looked like new determination.

"You're right," she told them as she drew near. "Why should
I take this lying down? It's him that's in the wrong, not me."

"To Keladon?" asked Cornelius.

"To Keladon," she said. "To take back the city . . . or die
trying!"

They camped that night within sight of the walls of Keladon, a
short distance from the main road that led to the city gates, so
that they'd be able to see if anyone approached from the direction of Brigandia. Nobody did.

"Probably too busy licking their wounds," Sebastian told
Princess Kerin. "Let's face it, Kasim won't be in too much of a
hurry to tell Septimus that he's let you escape."

He and the princess sat with their backs against a mighty tree,
watching the road for signs of life.

"Where has Cornelius got to?" she wondered. "He's been
gone ages."

The little warrior had headed off toward the main gates some
hours back and appeared to have had no trouble getting in.

"He said there were a few things we needed," said Sebastian.
"I hope one of them is food, because I'm absolutely starving."

Princess Kerin shook her head. "I don't see why we didn't all
just go in there. I feel like we're wasting time, sitting here."

"We need to wait for the right moment," Sebastian told her.
"Tomorrow morning, when the market is at its peak. Half the

population will be out on the streets and the rest of them within earshot." He smiled at her. "And don't worry, they'll listen to what you have to say."

She studied him for a moment. "You know, I haven't even thanked you, have I?"

"Thanked me? For what?"

"For coming after me. For risking your life for me back in Brigandia."

Max, browsing on the grass a short distance away, gave a meaningful cough.

"Yes, you too, Max. All of you. I will be forever in your debt."

"Oh, don't be silly," protested Sebastian. "I just . . . we just . . ."

"I know it would have been easy for you to slip away and leave me to my fate. But you didn't. Why?"

"Because . . . well, because I . . ." Sebastian sat there looking at his feet, unable to say the words that were in his heart. "What I'm trying to say, Princess, is that I . . . I really—"

"He loves you," interrupted Max. "Quite obviously."

Sebastian shot a withering look at the buffalope. "If you don't mind, I'll speak for myself!"

"Well, I'd get on with it if I were you. She's liable to be an old lady by the time you get around to it!"

"Is that true, Sebastian?" asked the princess.

"What, that you'll be an old lady?"

"No, you idiot! What Max just said."

He turned back to look at her. Her lovely face was inches from his own and his heart was pounding in his chest. "Oh, well, I . . . I suppose it is. . . ."

Her eyes were burning into his. He had the impression that every muscle in his body had turned to jelly. He just sat there, staring back at her.

"I think she would like to be kissed now," said Max quietly.

"Will you please attend to your own business!"

"I'm only saying—"

"Shush!"

He took the princess in his arms and pulled her closer to him. The world seemed to stop turning. For a long, impossibly beautiful moment, there was nothing but the two of them, clinging warm to each other under the glittering canopy of stars. Then he leaned forward to kiss her—

"Ahem!"

"Not now, Max!"

"*Ahem!*"

It wasn't Max. It was Cornelius, who was standing a short distance away, a couple of parcels tucked under his arms. Sebastian and the princess broke apart quickly and sat there looking distinctly sheepish.

"I hope I'm not interrupting anything," said Cornelius.

"Nothing too spectacular," said Max.

"Good." Cornelius moved closer. He sat cross-legged beside them, set one of the paper parcels aside and began to unwrap the other. "I managed to scrape together a few croats for food," he said. "It's not much. Some bread and cheese, a gourd of local wine . . ." He opened out the sheet of paper and set the food down in front of them.

"Cornelius, you're a marvel!" said Sebastian. He tore off a

hunk of bread and a slice of cheese and handed them to Princess Kerin. As she took them, her hand touched his and they exchanged smiles. They all ate for a while in silence. There were no goblets, so Cornelius passed around the gourd and they each took a swig. The brew was rough but warming.

"What's it like in the city?" asked the princess as she handed the gourd back to Cornelius.

"Ripe for revolution," he told her. "Everywhere you go, people are talking about you, wondering if they'll ever see you again. Some of them have bought the idea that you've been spirited away by an evil magician. . . ." He nodded at Sebastian. "Many others are not convinced by the story at all. I heard quite a few voicing their suspicions about King Septimus. Believe me, it won't take much to tip those people over the edge, and if they go, the others will follow."

"I wish I had your confidence."

"You'll be fine." Cornelius set aside his food and reached for the other parcel. He handed it across to her. "This is for you," he said. "I think it will help tomorrow. I didn't have the money to pay for it, so I had to find a merchant who was willing to accept my personal promise of payment. Luckily, as a member of the Crimson Cloak, my credit is quite good."

Princess Kerin hesitated for a moment, then tore open the paper to reveal a beautiful dress in a vivid shade of red. "Cornelius," she said. "It's beautiful!"

He shrugged. "Tomorrow, when we ride through those gates, you must look every inch a princess," he told her. "We'll only get one chance at this. Let's give it our very best shot."

She leaned forward and kissed him on the cheek. "You've both been so wonderful—"

"Ahem!"

"Sorry, Max. You've *all* been so wonderful. I won't forget it. When all this is over—if it goes the right way for us—I will reward you both."

"Let's not worry about that now," said Sebastian. "Let's just get through tonight. We should try to get some rest."

It was easy to say but much harder to do. The three of them sat beneath the stars, talking and making their plans, until the first light of dawn colored the eastern sky.

THIRTY

POWER TO THE PEOPLE

They waited until the sun was well up and they knew that
the marketplace would be at its busiest. Then Cornelius announced that it was time to make their preparations.

The princess stole away behind some bushes and put on her
new dress. She found a little pool of water and used a strip torn
from her old dress to scrub the dirt and smoke from her face. As
she did so, she thought about how much she had changed in just
a few days. The spoiled child she used to be would never have
tolerated such a lowly act as this. When she emerged, she looked
more like her old self. She walked slowly back to the others and
they both instinctively went down on one knee before her.

"There's no need for that," she told them.

"Princess, there's every need," Sebastian told her. "You are the
rightful queen of Keladon. Of course we bow to you." He got
back to his feet and stepped closer to her. "About last night . . ."
he said.

"Let's not talk about it now," she urged him. "This could well be our last day together. . . ."

They stood looking at each other for a moment, and once again Sebastian wondered if she was waiting for him to kiss her. But instead he took her hands in his and squeezed them gently. There was a long silence.

"Well, we've a lovely day for it," observed Max, a little too loudly.

Sebastian and the princess stepped back from each other.

"It's time," said Cornelius.

They mounted up, then took a few moments to arrange Princess Kerin's dress around her to achieve the look they wanted. Cornelius insisted it was an important detail. Then they set off at a brisk canter to cover the short distance to the city gates. As they drew near, a voice from the ramparts shouted down the standard inquiry.

"Who goes there? Friend or foe?"

There was a brief silence.

Then Princess Kerin spoke in a clear, confident voice. "Soldiers of Keladon, it is I, Princess Kerin!"

There was another silence. A few men appeared on the ramparts, gazing down in astonishment. Then, from within, they heard the sound of the beast-master shouting an order. "Close the gates!" he roared. There was a long moment while the three of them sat there in total bemusement. Then the gates began to creak slowly open. Sebastian glanced inquiringly at his companions.

"I'll explain later," said Max.

They rode through into the courtyard beyond. A cluster of

astonished soldiers were gathered around the entrance. Cornelius recognized the red-faced officer he had spoken to a couple of nights before. The man stared at Princess Kerin for a moment and then went down on one knee.

"Your Highness," he said. "I . . . I am delighted to see you. I was told you were gone, sent to some terrible place by . . . by . . ." He recognized Sebastian and pointed an accusing finger. "By him!" he snarled. "Guards, take that man and clap him in irons!"

"*No!*" Princess Kerin's voice stopped them in their tracks. "Hear me now, all of you. This man, Sebastian Darke . . . and this man, Captain Cornelius Drummel, are my good and trusted friends—"

"Ahem!"

"*And* this loyal animal here—he too is my friend. If any one of you harms them in any way, you will answer to me. Do I make myself clear?"

The red-faced officer bowed his head. "As you command, Your Highness. Now, please, allow me to send a man to the palace to tell your uncle of your safe return."

Princess Kerin shook her head. "Send no one," she told him. "I would rather . . . surprise him." She looked around at the uniformed men kneeling in front of her. "I want you to get your men onto their equines. Leave just a couple to guard the gate. You will escort me to the marketplace, where I will address the people of Keladon. If you have a trumpeter, make sure he comes with us."

The red-faced officer looked doubtful. "Your Highness, I'm not sure that—"

"Do you disobey my command?" snapped Princess Kerin.

The officer bowed obediently and shouted an order to his men. "Saddle up! We go with the princess."

Cornelius pointed to a big wooden hay wagon standing alongside the gatehouse. "Harness our buffalope to that wagon, will you?" he suggested. "The princess can address the people from the back of that."

"A hay wagon?" The officer looked horrified, but the princess gestured to him to do as he was told and he ran to obey.

"What's your thinking about the wagon?" muttered Sebastian.

"It'll be a suitable chariot for a warrior queen," replied Cornelius. "And with Max to pull it, there won't be much that will stand in its way."

Max groaned. "Oh no, not again," he protested. "You're always using me as some kind of battering ram."

"My dear fellow," said Cornelius. "Revolution never happens without a cost. We must all be willing to pay the price."

"Yes, yes," said Max dolefully. "It's just that sometimes I feel people are taking advantage of me!"

Within a few moments everything was done. The three friends dismounted, Cornelius got up behind the reins of the wagon and Sebastian and the princess climbed in the back. The troop of mounted cavalry formed a protective guard on either side of them. Cornelius clicked the reins and Max started forward along the main street. They traveled the short distance to the main square, the hub of the marketplace. As they had hoped, it was packed with people. And as soon as they caught sight of the princess in her brilliant red dress, they abandoned whatever they were doing and clustered delightedly around the wagon, their heads bowed in reverence.

"Trumpeter, sound a fanfare," said Princess Kerin. "I want to be sure to speak to everyone."

The trumpeter lifted his bronzed instrument to his mouth and blew a loud blast. Sebastian looked nervously down the road, but told himself that they were still too far from the palace for it to be heard there. At the sound of the trumpet, more people appeared, spilling out of shops, cafés and houses, moving as close as they could to the wagon, until it was encircled by a press of excited humanity.

Princess Kerin got slowly to her feet. "Well, here goes!" she whispered under her breath. She walked to the very center of the wagon and raised her head, her hands on her hips. She took a long slow look around her, gazing openly at the mass of puzzled faces, waiting a moment to allow anticipation to build. She drew in a deep breath and tried to fight the nervousness that was knotting itself in her stomach. Then she began to speak, as loudly and clearly as she could.

"People of Keladon. Your princess has returned to you!"

At this there was a great roar of approval and she had to hold up her hands to ease them back into silence.

"Many of you have been told that this man, the jester Sebastian Darke, was responsible for my disappearance. I tell you now that this is not the case! It is only with the help of Mr. Darke and his friend, Captain Drummel—and even the mighty buffalope that pulls this wagon—that I am free to stand before you now." She paused for a moment and gazed sternly at the sea of bemused faces that surrounded her. "I was not transported to a mystical world by supernatural powers. That was a lie, perpetrated by the people who had me kidnapped."

At this, there were gasps of dismay from every direction. The princess waited to ensure that everybody had heard her correctly.

"Yes, kidnapped—not by witchcraft or sorcery, but by very real people who still reside in the palace along the road. What's more"—she paused for effect—"kidnapped on my birthday!"

More gasps—and a gradually rising note of discontent.

"These people plotted my downfall. Like the skulking cowards they are, they arranged to have me sold into slavery in the markets of Brigandia!"

Now another roar came from the crowd. The City of Thieves was hated by them all, and the thought of their princess even going near the place was abhorrent to them.

"Yes, it's true!" she assured them. "I stood upon the auction platform before the lowest scum of Brigandia, like some piece of livestock; and it was only the daring of these two men—and their buffalope—that saved me from being sold to the highest bidder."

Now the sounds that came from the crowd were ones of anger and outrage. Fists were being shaken in the general direction of the palace, even though it was not visible from this point.

"And now, good people of Keladon, I come to the worst part of my story. Prepare yourselves for the awful truth of this sorry tale. The person who betrayed me—the person who cast me into so miserable a fate—was my own uncle, King Septimus!"

For a moment there was complete and utter silence. The feelings of shock were apparent. But then another roar came from the crowd, one so loud that Sebastian was obliged to put his hands over his ears. The princess waited for it to die down a little before she continued.

"Yes, your king—your *temporary* king—decided he did not

want to hand over the kingdom to me. He decided that he would do anything, no matter how despicable, to keep his position secure. And to explain what had happened, he constructed a cold and callous lie to ensure that nobody would ever know what he had done. But I have escaped to expose him for what he is. A liar, a thief and, most terrible of all . . . a murderer!"

At this there were cries of disbelief.

"Yes, I swear it on my own life!" cried the princess. "I have learned a terrible truth about my uncle Septimus, a man I trusted above all others. It was he who arranged the death of my parents—your former king and queen. He . . . he and his wicked consort, Magda, arranged to have them poisoned!"

Now the tumult that spilled from the crowd was overpowering—and after a few moments Sebastian could detect the sound of a chant building from somewhere in the very heart of it. It was just a few people at first, but it grew steadily louder and louder and began to spread as more and more voices took up the cry.

"Down with the king, down with the king, *down with the king!*"

"So now, people of Keladon, I ask you to come to my aid," yelled Princess Kerin, struggling to make herself heard over the noise. "I ask you to take up whatever arms you can lay hold of and come with me to the palace, where I intend to take back the throne which is mine by right!"

Cheers followed this announcement. Then there was a scuffle on the edges of the crowd as several mounted soldiers approached from the direction of the palace. Sebastian saw that the squad was led by Captain Tench. He was staring around, steely-eyed, at the huge gathering.

"What's going on here?" he demanded. "Who gave permission for this? Return to your homes immediately!" He caught sight of the princess standing up on the wagon and his jaw dropped open. He sat there in complete astonishment for a few moments, unable to find his voice. Then he noticed the mounted soldiers who were guarding her. "What . . . what are you men doing?" he cried. He pointed at Cornelius and Sebastian. "Arrest them, bring them to the palace!" But the soldiers just sat there looking at him in silent accusation and Tench began to realize that his position of power had suddenly evaporated. Terror overcame him. He tried to turn his equine round in a clumsy attempt to flee the scene.

"Stop them!" cried Princess Kerin. "Do not let them escape!"

Instantly a sea of hands reached up to grab at the mounted soldiers.

"Get your hands off me!" bellowed Captain Tench. "How dare you? How—?"

But he was pulled headfirst from the saddle and dragged, kicking and struggling, into the crowd of people. Fists rained down upon him as he fell into their midst and he did not get up again.

"Take their weapons!" yelled Cornelius. "Take their equines. Find what other weapons you can. People of Keladon, you have been lied to, you have been bled dry by a man who does not deserve to lick the boots of the rightful ruler. But the hour of vengeance is at hand. We go to the palace!"

He flicked the reins and Max started forward slowly, moving with difficulty through the masses of people. They moved aside to let him through, and after a few moments the wagon emerged at the very edge of the crowd. The mounted soldiers lined up on either side of it and behind them pressed their army. Looking around, Sebastian saw that the market stallholders were passing out anything that resembled a weapon, and others were running in and out of their homes, bringing anything they thought would be of use. He saw pitchforks, crossbows, ancient rusting swords and spears that probably hadn't seen service for years.

"It's a pretty motley crew we've gathered," he observed quietly.

"We've got truth and justice on our side," said Cornelius. "Plus, of course, my old favorite. The element of surprise."

"Think that'll be enough?"

Cornelius grinned. "Ask me again in a little while," he said.

Somebody leaned over and handed Sebastian a couple of swords. He passed one of them to Princess Kerin, and as she took it, their eyes met.

"How did I do?" she asked him.

"You were every bit the queen of this land," he told her. "These people will follow you anywhere."

"I just hope I'm not leading them to their doom," she said. Then she moved to the front of the wagon and steadied herself by clutching the wooden seat in front of her. She held her sword aloft so that everyone could see it.

"People of Keladon!" she cried. "Forward to victory!"

Cornelius snapped the reins and Max took off at speed. The soldiers urged on their equines and the angry rabble followed, waving their weapons or their fists as they raced along the wide uphill road that led to the palace.

THIRTY-ONE

DOWN WITH THE KING

King Septimus was feeling rather pleased with himself.

He had risen early, despite a night of drunkenness and gluttony, had eaten a hearty breakfast comprising all his favorite delicacies, had soaked himself in a hot bath steeped in oils and perfumes and, with the help of Malthus, had just finished dressing himself in his finest robes. It certainly felt gratifying to know that he was now the undisputed king of Keladon and that there was nobody around who might challenge him for the throne. He wondered where Princess Kerin was now and amused himself by imagining her dressed in rags, down on her hands and knees, scrubbing the floor of a latrine.

He lounged on a silken sofa in the royal chamber, wondering exactly what he would do with the rest of his day.

"I may pay a visit to the royal treasury later on," he told Malthus. "It's quite a while since I went through my coffers and counted up what I own."

"Four days, sire," said Malthus, without a trace of irony.

"Hmm. That long? Well—"

"While you are there, sire, you might be kind enough to consider the little matter of my salary."

"What about it?" growled King Septimus.

"Well, sire, the last time we spoke on the matter, you told me that you might consider actually letting me *have* one."

Septimus pulled a sour face. "You mean to tell me, Malthus, that as well as having the illustrious honor of waiting on me, you also expect to be *paid* for it?"

"Yes, sire! Er . . . I mean, no, sire, of course not. I just—"

"Empty out my chamber pot. And before you do so, open the shutters and allow in a little air."

"Yes, sire." The manservant hurried across to do his master's bidding. He unlatched the shutters and pulled them back to reveal a beautiful summer morning. There was a clear view of the main road leading downhill to the marketplace, and as Malthus looked out, he saw something unexpected. A crowd of people was coming round the bend in the road. A sizeable crowd. He kept expecting it to fizzle out, but it didn't. There seemed to be rather a lot of people. Thousands of them, in fact, and judging by the way they were waving their fists—and what looked like a fearsome collection of weapons—they evidently weren't here to do some sightseeing.

Malthus opened his mouth to say something, but thought better of it. It had occurred to him that it would be in his best interests to get out of here as quickly as possible and he didn't want a command from the king to keep him in place. So he turned quickly away from the window, grabbed the king's chamber pot and started toward the exit, moving so fast that the contents of the pot began to slop over its sides.

"Malthus, you imbecile, be careful!"

"Sorry, sire." Malthus didn't slow his pace. He kept right on going.

"What's your hurry, man?"

"A . . . pressing engagement, sire!" And Malthus was out of the door and heading for the stairs. Septimus heard a sudden crash as the chamber pot was discarded in the rush.

"What the . . . ? Malthus? Malthus!"

No reply. The king got to his feet and paced around the room for a moment, sensing that something wasn't quite right. Then a distant sound of shouting voices brought him to the open window. He stared out in complete and utter horror at the great mob of people who were racing toward the palace. Even at this distance he recognized the figure in the bright red dress, standing in the wagon that led the crowd. He opened his mouth in sheer disbelief, not wanting to believe this was happening. Then he snapped back to reality and, turning, he ran out of the room.

The two guards who stood at his doorway jumped smartly to attention.

"Sound the alarm," cried King Septimus. "An armed mob approaches the palace. Send the Crimson Cloak up here to defend me—the rest of you, get out there and deal with it. Barricade the doors. They are to be defended with your miserable lives!"

"Yes, sire." The two men turned and hurried away down the staircase, shouting an alarm.

King Septimus was about to retreat to his quarters but he noticed a frail figure emerging from one of the corridors to his left. It was Magda and she was carrying a large bag over her shoulder, while supporting herself with a stout walking stick.

"Magda," he said. "Going somewhere, are we?"

She was evidently not pleased to see him. "Your Majesty!" she cried. "What a pleasant surprise. I was just . . . er . . . planning to pay a little visit . . . to my . . . mother."

"Your mother?" King Septimus smiled sweetly. "I had no idea your mother was still alive. Why, she must be . . . what? A hundred and twenty, a hundred and thirty?"

Magda smiled, showing brown stumps of teeth. "She *is* a goodly age, sire, and in poor health. She needs my herbs and potions to make her strong. I'll be back in a day or so."

"Hmm. It wouldn't be the case, would it, that you have gained knowledge of the angry mob that is approaching the palace? The mob led by Princess Kerin. It couldn't be, could it, that you are attempting to run out on me?"

Magda feigned a look of sheer amazement. "A mob, Your Majesty? I had no idea!"

"Oh, well then. Fair enough. You didn't know about it. I suppose you'd best get along to your mother, hadn't you?"

"Thank you, sire." Magda started hobbling toward the staircase as fast as her ancient legs would carry her.

"How are you proposing to get there?" asked King Septimus, drawing closer to her and placing one hand on her shoulder.

She swallowed nervously. "I, umm . . . thought I'd take a carriage," she said quietly.

"Oh, surely not. A woman of your magical talents? I think

you'd get there much faster if you employed a more . . . super-natural form of travel."

"What do you mean, sire?" she asked him.

"I mean you should bloody well *fly!*" he roared; and with that, he grabbed the back of her dress with both hands and threw her down the staircase. He watched with interest as her frail body went tumbling and crashing down the marble steps, and noted with a hint of satisfaction that she managed to hit every single one of them on the way.

Her lifeless body came to rest at the feet of a group of armed men wearing deep red cloaks. The king's bodyguard. They looked down in shock at the old woman's sprawled figure.

"Don't just stand there gawking like idiots!" snarled the king. "Get your idle carcasses up here and form a protective line at the top of these stairs. If anyone tries to get up here, hack them to pieces."

The men hurried up the stairs to do as they were told. After all, they had sworn to protect the king with their lives, even if he *was* in the habit of throwing little old ladies to their deaths. They turned at the top landing and drew their swords.

"I might as well tell you," said the king, "that this rebellion is being led by Princess Kerin. It could be she who leads the attack against you. Put aside any notions of her royal connections. You will treat her as you would treat any other person who threatens the sovereignty of your king. I command it. Now, get to it, you scum. I'll be in my chambers."

He went back inside and hurried across to the window. The mob was close now—uncomfortably close. He could see the occupants of the wagon: Princess Kerin, holding a sword aloft and shouting like a madwoman; the little Golmiran, gripping the reins and urging that fleabag of a buffalope to go faster; and, crouched at Princess Kerin's side, that meddling breed of a jester.

King Septimus said something very uncouth beneath his breath. Let them try to take him, he thought. He would not go down without a fight.

Down on the bucking, shuddering wagon Sebastian could see the palace doors fast approaching; and as they drew nearer, the doors swung open and ranks of uniformed soldiers came spilling out of it, holding shields and brandishing swords and spears. There seemed to be a lot of them and they were lining up in protective rows right across the courtyard, their shields held out and linked to form what looked like an impenetrable wall of bronze.

The last man out of the doorway had to stoop to avoid bashing his head. It was Klart, the king's champion, clad in heavy body armor and clutching a cudgel the size of a small tree. As he stepped out and took his position, the doors slammed shut behind him, and Sebastian knew that whoever was left inside would be barricading it against the attack.

Now the wagon was approaching the short flight of steps up to the palace courtyard. Sebastian had assumed that they'd have to stop here and climb down from the wagon. But Cornelius had other ideas. He slapped the reins against Max's haunches and urged him to go faster still. He glanced back over his shoulder.

"Hold on tight," he bellowed; and Sebastian and the princess both grabbed hold of the sides of the wagon.

Max went up the steps at speed. There was a terrible impact as the wagon's heavy wheels connected with solid marble, and for a moment Sebastian thought the ancient vehicle would smash itself to pieces. But then the wheels gripped, and the wagon crashed upward, shuddering and shaking like a thing possessed.

In an instant they were back on level ground and crossing the broad expanse of courtyard to where the soldiers waited for them. Looking back, Sebastian saw the angry crowd swarming up the steps behind them. He turned just as Max slammed headlong into the wall of shields, scattering soldiers before him like ninepins. And then the world turned into a mad mêlée of shouting, yelling people. Soldiers were clambering up on the wagon and Sebastian was flailing at them with his sword, knocking them down again, but no sooner was one man down than another replaced him. They seemed to come from every side and he had to fight for his very life.

For a while he caught only glimpses of the action around him. He saw Princess Kerin, laying about her like a professional sword fighter and yelling aloud for her followers to keep going. He saw Cornelius, standing on the wooden seat of the wagon, grinning like a madman and scything down soldiers as a farmer cuts down wheat. Then Sebastian saw Klart, raining down blows with his mighty cudgel, but failing to hold back the unstoppable horde of people swarming over him like ants. They pinioned his arms and legs, tripped him and then descended on him, hitting and stabbing with whatever they had to hand. In a moment he disappeared from view under mounds of struggling people.

And, quite suddenly, the soldiers stopped coming at the wagon. Looking around, Sebastian saw that the force around the doors had been vanquished. Not one of them was left standing. Cornelius jumped down from his seat and began to unhitch Max. As soon as he was free, the buffalope moved away, looking for new targets to attack, but for the moment at least they were in short supply. Cornelius clambered back up onto the wagon and shouted a command to the people around him.

"The wagon!" he roared. "We'll use it as a battering ram!"

"Makes a change from using me," muttered Max.

The crowd ran to obey him. People pressed in around it and eager hands seized its heavy wooden frame.

"Now, all together!" shouted Cornelius. "One, two, three . . . go!"

And the wagon was propelled headlong across the courtyard toward the palace doors, people scattering out of the way to allow it passage. The front of the wagon slammed against wood and the doors bucked inward, but they sprang back again. The impact knocked Sebastian and Princess Kerin off their feet and they lay for a moment, looking at each other.

"Maybe we should get down off this thing," said Sebastian.

She shook her head. "The people need to see me," she told him.

"Again!" yelled Cornelius. The wagon was pushed backward, right to the very edge of the courtyard. "One, two, three . . . go!"

This time the impact was heavier and the door buckled in on itself with a loud splintering sound.

"Again! We're nearly through!" roared Cornelius. The wagon rumbled backward.

Sebastian reached out and squeezed Princess Kerin's hand. "This time," he assured her.

There was a long, deep silence as they waited.

"One, two, three . . . *go!*"

All those pushing put every ounce of strength they possessed behind the wagon and it seemed to fly forward as though shoved by the hand of an invisible giant. The impact when it slammed against wood jarred every tooth in Sebastian's head, but whatever was holding the doors in place snapped like a twig beneath the onslaught. The doors crashed open and the wagon thundered through into the foyer of the palace, slamming into the ranks of soldiers that had remained inside.

Princess Kerin jumped back to her feet and waved her sword. "Onward!" she screamed. "Victory is at hand!" A great yelling tide of people spilled through the shattered doorway and swept the remaining soldiers before them, pushing them back into the depths of the palace. The princess leaped down and went with them, completely lost in the moment. Sebastian clambered down too, intending to follow her, but he felt a sharp tug against the hem of his jerkin and, looking down, he saw Cornelius. He was pointing toward the big staircase, at the foot of which lay the dead body of the witch, Magda.

"Up here," said Cornelius. "The king's chambers. That's where he'll be hiding."

Sebastian flung a last anxious glance after the princess, then nodded. He followed Cornelius up the stairs, realizing as he did so that the main force was still below, chasing the last soldiers through the labyrinthine corridors of the ground floor. The two men hurried up the giant staircase and then hesitated as they got to the top.

Ranged across the landing in front of them was a row of men in distinctive uniforms. The king's bodyguard, the Crimson Cloak.

THIRTY-TWO

THE FINAL CONFLICT

Cornelius halted a short distance from the line of bodyguards. He scanned each of their faces before he spoke.

"Men of the Crimson Cloak," he said, "I do not wish to fight you. I have only been a member of your organization for a few days, but I think of you as brothers-in-arms."

A tall bearded man who seemed to be the natural leader of the group replied. "And as a member, Captain Drummel, you, like us, are sworn to protect the life of the king. Why are you attacking his palace?"

Cornelius frowned. "For the best of reasons. When I swore that oath, I thought I was vowing to defend an honest man—not a tyrant who would send his own niece into slavery in order to prevent her from being queen."

Sebastian had expected some gasps of astonishment from the men but there was no reaction at all. He began to experience a sinking sensation.

"Who tells you this?" sneered the bearded man.

"Nobody told me. I saw it for myself. My friend Sebastian and I rescued the princess from the slave markets of Brigandia only yesterday. And that is not the end of this so-called king's treachery. He arranged the murder of the former king and queen. He even laid a trap for me on my first mission, sending twenty Brigands to try and silence me. Let me assure you, the man skulking in those chambers is not worth defending."

The bearded man smiled sarcastically. "And supposing I were to tell you, Captain Drummel, that we knew all about the ambush—and about the king's plans for the princess. Supposing I told you that each of us was paid handsomely to pretend we saw nothing? What would you say then?"

Cornelius's eyes widened in realization. An expression of disgust came to his face. "I would say that the Crimson Cloak is a mockery," he snarled. "And that I no longer have any wish to be a member."

"What if we offered you the same arrangement?" said a second man. "You would be rich beyond your wildest dreams."

"But I would have no honor," Cornelius told him. "And my life would be as worthless as yours."

The bearded man laughed. "Oh, come now, Captain Drummel, you cannot hope to make a stand against us. We are the finest warriors in the land. We will cut you down like chaff."

Cornelius bowed from the waist. "Gentlemen, you are most welcome to try," he said.

Sebastian started forward to stand beside Cornelius, but the little warrior motioned him back.

313

"This is serious stuff, young friend," he said. "No offense, but I don't want you to get in my way."

"Cornelius—"

"No. I tell you, stand back!"

Sebastian shrugged and reluctantly retreated a few steps. There was a long silence while the men appraised each other. Then the bearded man stepped forward, his sword raised. Cornelius waited, his expression calm. The man launched an attack, and once again Cornelius performed that lazy, almost imperceptible flick of the wrist. His opponent took a couple more steps forward, his eyes staring straight ahead, a bright pool of blood blossoming on his chest. Then he missed his step and went tumbling down the staircase.

The other members of the bodyguard exchanged looks of disbelief. Then, as one, they charged toward Cornelius. For an instant he was lost to sight, buried amidst a scrum of struggling bodies; but then he broke free and somersaulted upward, away from the mêlée, to land gracefully on the stone balustrade alongside his opponents. His sword performed a couple of deadly thrusts and two more men fell dead on the stairs.

"And now, gentlemen," he said, "I think it's time you were introduced to the Golmiran death roll."

He threw back his head and bellowed at the top of his lungs. Then he launched himself upward, spinning around until his body was a blur, somersaulting across the staircase to the far balustrade, and as he passed overhead, his sword zipped around in a deadly arc, cleaving the helmets of three more opponents and dropping them in their tracks. Sebastian had to press back to one side as the bodies went tobogganing past him down the steep slope to join their comrades.

Cornelius came out of the spin and landed on the far balustrade, laughing like a maniac.

The remaining five bodyguards were beginning to get the message. They faltered, backed away and ran past him down the stairs, abandoning their weapons as they did so. As Sebastian watched, they clambered over the bodies of their fallen comrades and went out through the gap in the smashed doorway. He heard their feet racing away across the courtyard. He turned back to his friend.

"Cornelius, you were—"

He broke off in horror as he saw the little warrior crumple and fall from the balustrade onto the staircase. Sebastian hurried to him and kneeled beside his sprawled body, turning him onto his back. He saw the bright splash of fresh blood oozing through the torn chain mail at his stomach.

"Someone . . . must have . . . caught me a lucky blow," observed Cornelius through gritted teeth. "Shadlog's breath!" He tried to struggle up but sank back with a groan. The death leap had completely exhausted him.

"I'll go for help," Sebastian told him.

"No . . ." Cornelius gestured toward the door of the king's chambers. "Don't waste time. Get . . . Septimus. It's . . . up to you now." He gave a little shudder and his body went limp.

"Cornelius!" Sebastian put an ear against the little warrior's mouth and heard breathing, but it was slow and shallow. He didn't dare hesitate any longer. He got to his feet, his sword

315

held ready, and strode across the landing to the door of the king's chamber. He paused for a moment, gathering his courage. Then he lifted a foot, kicked the door open and ran inside. At first glance the room looked empty. Then he heard a thud behind him and turned to see that King Septimus had been waiting behind the door. He had just slid a huge metal bolt into position, locking it. In his other hand he held a fearsome-looking curved sword.

"So," he said. "Alone at last. The jolly jester and I." He raised his sword and slashed it around in the air, making a series of imaginary feints and jabs. "Got any good jokes for me, have you?"

Sebastian shook his head. "Not really the time or place," he said.

"And how are you with that sword? Any good?"

Sebastian shrugged. "I'm not so bad," he said.

"Glad to hear it," said King Septimus mockingly. "I, on the other hand, am a champion. Three times winner of the Keladonian fencing tournament. I don't wish to blow my own trumpet, but I am considered unbeatable. And it's going to give me such joy to end your interfering little life." He stepped forward, sword raised. "Sometimes, it's the simple things that give the most pleasure, don't you think?"

Sebastian didn't have time to reply. The king came at him with brutal force, swinging the heavy blade straight at his head. He only just got his own sword up in time, and the impact of metal against metal struck sparks and sent shock waves along the length of his arm. King Septimus grunted, pulled the blade away and swung low at Sebastian's legs. He jumped, the razor-sharp blade cleaving the air inches below his feet; and in the same instant he threw out his left fist and punched the king full in the face.

King Septimus reeled back with an oath and lifted a hand to wipe at a smudge of blood on his lips. "You cheated!" he said. "You'll pay for that."

"You were right," Sebastian told him. "It *is* the little things that give pleasure."

King Septimus sneered but his face was dark with fury. "Funny man," he said. "We'll see if you're still laughing in a few moments."

He came at Sebastian again, driving the blade with such force that when Sebastian parried the blow, he stumbled backward, tripped and went sprawling over a low wooden table. He hit the floor on the far side of it, aware that the king was still coming at him, lashing out with the sword. Desperately Sebastian grabbed a leg of the table and pulled it toward him, trying to use it as a shield. The king's blade hacked a chunk out of it inches from his head. Sebastian got his feet in behind the table and kicked hard, launching it off the ground toward his opponent.

Septimus stepped nimbly aside but it gave Sebastian time to get back to his feet. Now the two men circled each other, looking for an opening.

"You've been lucky so far," observed Septimus calmly. "But you can't evade me forever. After all, I'm a king and you are nothing but a breed."

317

"I know what I'd rather be," Sebastian assured him. "And by the way, you're no longer a king. Your reign ended the minute the people of Keladon turned against you. Whether you kill me or not, you'll still be finished here."

"It will be a hollow victory for you," King Septimus assured him. "Trying to perform your pathetic act with no head."

He had artfully backed Sebastian into a corner against a stout wooden door. Sebastian was about to edge away from it when Septimus leaped at him with a vicious flurry of blows, each more powerful than the last. Sebastian just managed to block them; but the final one knocked him backward again and the door behind him opened unexpectedly. He found himself in a narrow corridor with a spiral of stone steps leading upward behind him. He just had time to register that this must be the famous tower of King Septimus; and then his adversary was upon him once again and he was forced to retreat, stumbling backward up the staircase, blocking the endless succession of blows that were thrown at him.

In the subdued light, Septimus's eyes seemed to glow with some deranged fire. He was laughing as he attacked, driving Sebastian upward, higher and higher. Sebastian's arms ached and the sweat flowed from every pore of his body, but he could find nowhere on the smooth stone steps to make a stand; and then, a particularly vicious blow smashed the sword clean out of his hand. It went skittering away out of reach.

Septimus grinned, his eyes malevolent. "Oh dear," he said. "Not looking too good, is it? Better start begging for mercy,

Elf-man!" He came forward and Sebastian did the only thing he could do: he ran.

"Yes, run!" gloated Septimus, climbing the steps at his leisure. "But there's nowhere to hide, Jester. Nowhere at all."

A few turns round the spiral and Sebastian came to a painted wooden shield hanging on the wall. He reached up and tried to pull it down but it was securely mounted and he was horribly aware of Septimus getting closer. He made an almost super-human effort and the shield came down, pulling chunks of stone with it. He slid the shield onto his left arm and crouched low, pressing himself against the inside wall. As Septimus came round the spiral to face him, he leaped up and smashed Septimus in the chest with the shield, knocking him back several steps, but he didn't fall. He gathered himself and came right back at Sebastian, swinging the sword so hard that it hacked shards of wood from the shield. Sebastian reeled under the impact and once again began to reverse up the staircase. Passing by an arrow slit, he saw that the ground was already a long distance below them.

"Come on, Jester, this is making me weary," complained Septimus. "Give me a clear shot at that head of yours and we can end all this."

"How about . . . you give me . . . the first shot?" gasped Sebastian. He was almost at the point of exhaustion now, the sweat raining from his face, and he didn't think he could go on much longer.

"No," snarled Septimus. "I asked *first*!"

He lifted his arm and struck downward with such force that

the shield split in two and Sebastian felt the razor-sharp blade slice deep into his shoulder. Galvanized by pain, he lashed a fist at his opponent's face, but Septimus ducked under it and retaliated with a punch of his own, which hit Sebastian full on the nose. He fell backward and his shoulders crashed against wood. Something gave way behind him and he fell through another door and emerged into a sudden blaze of sunlight. A flight of birds, disturbed by his arrival, flapped noisily upward into the clear blue sky. He lay there for a moment, staring up at them as they wheeled away, his head spinning. He realized that he had reached the very top of the tower. Septimus had been right. There was nowhere to hide.

With a supreme effort, Sebastian got back to his feet and stumbled the short distance to the parapet. He gazed over and saw a great crowd of people swarming far below. From this vantage point they looked like an army of insects. A great roar came drifting up as they caught sight of him, and he saw a tiny figure in a red dress come running out of the palace doors, her face turned upward to look at him. He was going to shout out her name but a hand grabbed his injured shoulder, spinning him round and making him cry out with the pain of it.

Septimus punched him hard in the face. He almost went over the parapet, but the king grabbed him by the hair, twisted him back round and held the blade of the sword to his throat. He could feel the razor edge grazing flesh.

"Not so fast, Elf-man!" growled Septimus into his ear. "Look down there. There she is, your beloved princess. I want her to see what happens to you. I want her to be the last thing you see as you die. Now . . . any final words?"

Sebastian's mind was reeling; but through the red mist that gathered at the edges of his consciousness, one last desperate idea came to him and he knew he had to try it.

"Just one thing . . . ," he croaked. "Something I've always wanted to know. . . ."

"Yes?" whispered Septimus.

"Is it . . . is it a wig?"

Septimus jerked back as though somebody had stabbed him. "What are you talking about?" he hissed.

"Your hair . . . it looks too perfect to be real."

"Of course it's real!" bellowed Septimus. "Everyone knows it's real!"

"All right . . . if you say so." And with that, Sebastian flung up a hand, grabbed a handful of hair and pulled hard. There was a terrible moment when the hair held fast, as though stuck securely in place—but then there was a ripping noise and it came off in one piece, revealing a king who was as bald as a boiled egg. From down below, sounds of laughter drifted up.

"Give that back!" roared Septimus, throwing his sword arm over his head and reaching for the wig with his free hand. "Give it back, I say!"

Sebastian retreated along the parapet, holding the wig out like a lure. "You want this?" he asked. "You want it?" He leaned dangerously out over the parapet, holding it at arm's length. "We'll send it down to the people, shall we?" he said. "Then they'll all see!"

"No! No, give it to me!" Septimus was leaning over too, trying to reach for the wig, his fingers inches away from it. Then . . .

"Oops!" said Sebastian; and he let it fall.

"*Nooooo!*" Septimus made a last desperate grab for it, and in that same instant Sebastian ducked down, grabbed the king's legs and heaved him up and over the edge. Septimus teetered for a moment on the parapet, his arms flailing wildly as he tried to find a hold.

He gave one dismal squeal of terror. Then he slid forward and fell into empty air.

Sebastian watched as the king went twisting and turning downward, his legs pumping madly as though he were trying to run. Below him the crowds of people scattered in all directions, not wanting to be flattened.

The wig, caught by the wind, didn't fall as quickly as the former king. He seemed to catch up with it moments before he hit the ground.

Sebastian snapped his gaze away at the last moment; and when he could bring himself to look again, the crowd had swarmed around the smashed body and it was lost from sight.

Wearily Sebastian staggered back through the open doorway and started down the staircase, slipping and sliding on the smooth steps, having to hold himself up with his uninjured arm. It seemed to take an age to get down to the king's chambers. He could hear the sound of fists pounding on the door, but weak as he was from loss of blood, he had to struggle with the heavy bolt before he could get it open.

The door swung back, revealing a crowd of shouting people on the landing. He had a glimpse of a beautiful face in among the others and he said her name and reached for her, but that was when unconsciousness claimed him. He fell forward into her arms and didn't even feel the many hands that lifted him gently and carried him back down the stairs to safety.

THIRTY-THREE

TO BE A QUEEN

Sebastian waited impatiently outside the door of the queen's chambers. Three moons had passed since the final battle for Keladon and the palace was beginning to return to some semblance of normality. The shattered front doors had been repaired and Sebastian's arm had nearly finished healing. Cornelius too was well on his way to a full recovery. Sebastian had visited him in the hospital only that morning, and the little warrior had been full of energy and raring to get back into action. He had also mentioned that he had something to tell Sebastian; something that would have to wait until they could speak in private.

Over the past weeks, Sebastian had barely had a chance to speak to Queen Kerin. To begin with he had been in the hospital, unconscious and feverish. He had missed her triumphant coronation. True, she had visited him a couple of times later on and had thanked him profusely for his help. But the two of them were aware that their conversation could be overheard by patients in the surrounding beds, and there had been no opportunity to speak of what was in their hearts.

Now at last she had summoned him for a private audience. He felt nervous and slightly sick, which he knew was an indication that he was in love. But he did not really know what he was going to say to her. It had been difficult enough when she was a mere princess. But a queen? What did you say to a queen?

The door of the chambers opened and Malthus came out, looking well pleased with himself. Sebastian had not entirely approved when he heard that the skinny manservant had been appointed to the queen's staff. He remembered how Malthus had refused to help him when he was locked in the cells and knew that he wouldn't have lifted a finger to fight for the princess's right to the throne. But he was a survivor, the kind of man who would switch his allegiance at a moment's notice. The rumor was that things were really looking up for him. He was actually receiving a wage these days.

He smiled at Sebastian. "Ah, Mr. Darke. I trust you are well."

"Well enough," said Sebastian. "No thanks to you."

"Oh, come along, you don't harbor a grudge, do you? I was only looking after my interests."

"As you still are."

Malthus smiled thinly and gave a polite bow. "Her Majesty will see you now," he said, and ushered Sebastian inside, closing the door behind him.

She was standing in front of the marble fireplace, dressed in one of the beautiful brocaded gowns she had recently taken to wearing. Her face was dusted with white powder, her long hair tied up in an intricate bun, and he thought that she seemed so much older than when he had last seen her. She smiled at him, but it was a polite, reserved smile.

"Sebastian," she said. "You are quite healed, then."

He went down on one knee and bowed before her. "I am the better for seeing you," he said.

"Ah, ever the charmer. And how is Cornelius?"

"Nearly mended. He'll be out any time now."

"I'm pleased to hear it." She gestured to him to sit in a nearby chair. She chose another a short distance away. They sat looking at each other in silence for a moment. It felt decidedly awkward, as though they were meeting for the first time. Finally the queen spoke.

"Sebastian, the kingdom of Keladon wishes to express its gratitude to you for the services you have rendered to us. It is my intention to give both yourself and Captain Drummel the freedom of the city and the annual sum of three hundred gold crowns to be spent on whatever is your wish."

He stared at her. She sounded so cold and aloof, as though she were speaking to a stranger.

"The money is to be paid on—"

"Why are you talking to me like this?" he interrupted her. "We're friends, aren't we? After everything we've been through together, I would have thought that we could at least talk to each other like normal people."

"I think I *am* speaking normally. Now, the money is to be—"

"Forget the money! I'm not interested in money! I came here because I wanted to tell you what was in my heart."

She shook her head. "Sebastian," she said quietly, "I know that you once had feelings for me—"

"What do you mean, 'once'? Nothing's changed . . . has it?"

She studied her feet for a moment. "Alas, everything has changed. I'm Queen of Keladon now and must behave like one. I can no longer act on whims and fancies." She lifted her gaze to look at him. "Sebastian, the adventure we had will always be with me. But now my duty is to my people. I told you, what seems like an age ago, that my first real act as monarch would be to marry Prince Rolf of Bodengen."

"Yes, but that was before . . . before we . . ." Sebastian got impulsively up from his chair and moved toward her. He kneeled before her and took her hands in his. "You don't love him," he said. "I *know* you don't. You're doing this because of a royal duty. But I believe that you care for *me*."

"No." She shook her head. "I don't. You are mistaken." But tears glittered in her eyes as she said it. "You must understand, my life is no longer my own. It belongs to the people of Keladon, the people who fought—and in some cases gave their lives—so that I could sit upon the throne. By making this alliance with Bodengen, I will be ending centuries of bloodshed between our two kingdoms."

"But what about *you*? What about your happiness? And mine? Don't we deserve any?"

She was trying hard to maintain her dignity. "Sebastian, ask whatever you wish and if it is in my power, I shall grant it. But not that. I cannot give you that. I'm sorry."

He let go of her hands and got back to his feet. He felt crushed, desolate. He walked across the room and stood looking moodily into the empty hearth. "Then do not ask me to stay here and watch you throw your life away," he said. "I will leave. . . ."

"No, Sebastian, stay here. You can make a good life for yourself. You'll meet a nice girl who you'll fall in love with—"

"I thought I already had." He glared at her. "But somehow it got complicated."

"Well then." She thought for a moment. "The offer of money still stands. I wish to reward you for what you have done. Won't you at least allow me to do that?"

He shook his head. "Please arrange to have the money sent to my mother in Jerabim. I have no need of it." He bowed politely and then turned toward the door.

"Sebastian!" For a moment her regal poise slipped and she sounded like the girl he remembered. "Please, tell me that you don't hate me."

He looked at her long and hard, and for a moment he forgot who she was. "Oh, Princess," he said, "I could never do that." He felt his own eyes filling with tears and hurried to the door. He glanced back once and saw that she was sitting in her chair, her head bowed, her shoulders moving gently up and down. Tears were making lines in the white powder on her face.

He wanted so much to go back to her but knew in that moment that he could not. She had shut herself off from him and would never allow him to get close again. He closed the door and walked quickly away.

He went to the royal stables, looking for Max; and was surprised to find that Cornelius had discharged himself from the hospital and was sitting on a hay bale, chatting to the buffalope. Sebastian paused for a moment outside the stall, listening to their conversation.

"Did you see those soldiers go flying when I slammed into their shields?" asked Max. "It was incredible. They should call me Max the Mighty."

"Well, you should have seen my Golmiran death roll on the staircase. I don't like to boast, but it was a personal best. I still haven't worked out how one of them managed to wound me."

"Maybe you're a bit out of condition."

"Nonsense! Why, I'm in my prime. Once this wound finishes healing up, I'll be ready for just about anything."

"What about more adventures?" asked Sebastian, stepping into the stall.

Cornelius grinned. "Why not?" he said. "It's getting a bit too quiet here for my liking."

"Oh, I don't know," said Max. "Let's not be hasty. The food here is excellent—they really know how to look after you." He gave Sebastian an inquiring look. "How did it go with the queen?"

Sebastian sat down on a bale and tried not to let his disappointment show. "Not great," he admitted. "She's going to marry Rolf of Bodengen."

"I see," said Max. "Well, no, not exactly a result." He thought for a moment. "Maybe she'll keep you on as her 'bit on the side.'"

Sebastian glared at him. "I hardly think either of us would be happy with that arrangement." He looked at Cornelius. "You knew this would happen, didn't you?"

The little warrior shrugged. "I . . . suspected as much. Sebastian, you have to understand, she's the queen now. There are all kinds of things she'll have to do. I'm sure she cares for you but, let's face it, you're just—"

"A jester. And once again, it would seem, an unemployed one."

"I'm sorry, my friend, but I'm afraid only fairy stories have happy endings."

"Hmm. Well, it's not all bad news. She's giving you a gift of three hundred gold crowns a year."

Cornelius stared at him. "You are joking," he said.

"No, I'm deadly serious. We both get the same. Except I don't want mine. I've arranged to have it sent home to my mother."

"A wonderful gesture." Cornelius thought for a moment. "My parents are already disgustingly rich, so there's not much point in me making a similar arrangement."

"Did she mention giving *me* anything?" asked Max hopefully, but the two men ignored him.

"So," said Sebastian, "there's not much point in hanging around here. I have no wish to see her marry that slope-headed oaf."

"Absolutely not," said Cornelius. "Which brings me to some rather interesting news." He paused for a moment and looked around, as though nervous of being overheard. "You left the hospital well before me, but you remember the old fellow in the bed next to me?"

"Vaguely. He was in a bad way, wasn't he?"

"Yes, he'd been wounded in the final battle at the palace. Nathaniel, his name was. I could see that he wasn't going to last very long, so I spent quite a bit of time talking to him. He'd been an adventurer when he was a young man; spent most of his life in the port of Ramalat on the east coast. He'd been planning to head back that way for one last adventure, but realized now that he would never see it again."

"How very sad," said Max. "I wonder if they'll be bringing round some dinner soon—"

"Shush!" said Sebastian. "Go on, Cornelius."

"Well, in his final hours, when he knew it was all over for him, he gave me something." Cornelius glanced round again, then reached into his tunic and pulled out a folded piece of yellow parchment. He opened it and passed it across to Sebastian. It was clearly ancient, mottled by the passing of time. It appeared to be some kind of a map.

"What is it exactly?" asked Sebastian, turning it this way and that to try and catch the light. "This brown ink is so faded, I can barely read it."

"It's not ink," said Cornelius. "It's written in blood. And it's a treasure map. It shows the location of the lost treasure of Captain Callinestra."

"Captain who?" asked Max.

"Callinestra!" said Sebastian. "Surely you've heard of him? Father used to tell me stories about him when I was little. He was this legendary pirate king who was said to have amassed an incredible treasure and hidden it in a secret location. But . . . I always assumed it was just a story."

"Not according to Nathaniel. He told me that when he was a youngster, he was cabin boy on the captain's ship, the *Ocean Star*. It seems that he was entrusted with the map when the ship was finally overrun by a band of rival pirates. Nathaniel escaped, but the captain and all his crew perished."

Max sniffed suspiciously. "If he had the map all that time, how come he didn't go back for the treasure himself?"

"He did. He tried three times over his lifetime, and each expedition was hounded by ill-fortune. On his third attempt he barely escaped with his life. He was planning to have one last try when he was injured in the battle for the palace. He knew his time had come and he must have decided that somebody else should have a chance at it."

"Huh." Max tossed his head contemptuously. "He was probably stark staring bonkers. Most likely drew the map himself. I wouldn't have any faith in an old scrap of paper like that."

Sebastian looked at Cornelius. "But *you* believed his story?" he asked.

The little man nodded. "Every word," he said.

"Well, that's good enough for me," said Sebastian. "We'll leave just as soon as you're completely healed."

"Just a minute!" said Max. "I don't understand. You've just turned down the offer of gold crowns, so clearly *money* doesn't have that much interest for you. So why go chasing after treasure?"

"For the adventure," said Cornelius. "The thrill of finding something that nobody else has ever found."

"Yes, but let's not be too rash about this. I mean, we're onto a good thing here, we don't want to just throw it away . . . do we?"

Sebastian smiled. "Don't worry, old friend. If you'd rather stay here, I'll understand."

Max looked at him for a moment and then shook his head. "You know I can't do that. I promised your mother I'd look after you."

"She'd never know," Sebastian told him. "You could just settle down here, eat everything in sight and get nice and fat."

Max sighed. "It's an inviting prospect, sure enough," he said. "But, no, I suppose I'd better come with you. It's going to involve traveling on water, isn't it? Buffalopes don't like water."

"Buffalopes don't like a lot of things," murmured Cornelius.

Sebastian handed the map back to him. "Here, keep this safe until we're ready to leave," he said. "Judging by the look of you, I'd say a few more days should put you right." He glanced at Max. "As for you, I'd advise you to eat every last scrap they give you. Once we're on our way, the food isn't going to be quite so plentiful."

"It's marvelous, isn't it?" said Max disgustedly. "No sooner do you get comfortable in one place than the young master has a desire to move on again. Honestly, sometimes I could just spit, I really could!"

At that moment the gates at the top of the stables opened and the ostler came in carrying buckets of food.

"Oh goody," said Max, cheering up considerably. "Din-dins!"

EPILOGUE

It was time to go. Max had just eaten his final leisurely meal at the royal stables and now he was being harnessed once again to Sebastian's caravan. Cornelius had saddled up Phantom and filled the saddlebags with provisions for the long journey.

There was to be no ceremonial send-off, no bands playing, no trumpet fanfares, all of which suited Sebastian fine. He was glad to be getting away because later today, he had been told, Prince Rolf of Bodengen was due to come visiting; and Sebastian knew that he could not bear to stick around and watch that.

He was just about to climb up into the seat of the caravan when Cornelius gave a polite cough. Sebastian turned to see somebody approaching: the cloaked and hooded figure of a woman.

She removed the hood from her face and Sebastian and Cornelius went down on their knees.

"Would you leave without saying goodbye?" she asked reproachfully.

Sebastian frowned. "I thought we had already done that," he said. "And you shouldn't be out by yourself. It's dangerous to go without an escort."

"I thought this occasion was worth the risk," she told him. "You know that you are all very special to me."

"Clearly not special enough," muttered Sebastian.

"Don't be bitter," she told him. "It doesn't suit you." She indicated that he should stand and she came closer until she was facing him. "I have made arrangements for your mother to receive the yearly payment of gold crowns. A trusted messenger has already left with it. Now you need have no worries on her behalf. She will have enough to live out her life in luxury." She reached under her cloak and handed a heavy cloth bag to Cornelius. "And here is a full year's payment, Captain Drummel. For services rendered."

"Thank you, Your Majesty," said Cornelius, bowing low. "I am grateful for your kindness."

She looked at Sebastian. "And since you would take no reward for yourself, I have something else for you." From around her neck she produced a pendant hung on a leather thong. It was beautifully worked in gold and precious jewels and was fashioned in the shape of an eye, with a glittering blue pupil. She reached out and hung it around his neck.

"This amulet," she said, "is supposed to keep the wearer safe from harm. It has been in my family for generations. It is really only supposed to be given to members of the royal family, but I think in this case we can make an exception."

Sebastian lifted the amulet in his fingers and examined it. "You are kind," he said.

"I don't suppose it's worth asking where you are bound?"

Max opened his mouth to reply but snapped it shut again as Cornelius elbowed him in the ribs.

"We're not sure ourselves," Sebastian told her. "We're simply going wherever the wind takes us."

"Well then, I pray that one day it will blow you back in this direction. Then perhaps you will stay awhile and tell us of your latest adventures." She thought for a moment and smiled. "Remember how we met?" she asked. "How I nearly brained you with that chamber pot?"

Despite himself, Sebastian smiled too. "And I called you a stupid girl," he said. "I couldn't get away with that now." He paused. "It's strange, but it seems like so very long ago. And only a few moons have come and gone since then."

There was a silence while they stood looking at each other.

"I will always remember our time together," she assured him. "When I am old and gray, I will tell my children of my adventures with Sebastian, Cornelius and a buffalope called Max." She looked across at his companions. "Look after him for me. Don't let any harm come to him."

"We won't, Your Majesty," said Cornelius. "You can count on us."

She nodded, and Sebastian saw that once again there were tears in her eyes. She reached forward and kissed him softly on the cheek.

"May good fortune go with you," she said. And she turned and walked quickly out of the stables, pulling up her hood as she did so. Sebastian stared after her, the fingers of his right hand playing with the amulet. There was a long, long silence.

"Well!" said Cornelius, rather more loudly than was necessary. "The time's passing. We've got quite a distance to travel before nightfall."

"My feet are aching at the mere thought of it," muttered Max. "You don't think we should put it off for a few more days, do you?"

"No," said Sebastian, turning back to the caravan. "We've put if off for long enough. Come on, let's go."

Cornelius vaulted into Phantom's saddle; Sebastian climbed up into his seat and slapped the reins against Max's flanks.

"Here, go easy!" complained the buffalope. "We're not even out of the blooming stable yet, and already you're being heavy-handed. My hide is still surprisingly tender, you know!" But he started obediently forward and they moved away from the stables, round the side of the palace and out onto the road beyond.

"We've a fine day for it," observed Cornelius, gazing up at the wide blue stretch of sky.

"Yes," agreed Sebastian. "It couldn't be better. Here's to adventure and the open road." He glanced back toward the palace and thought he caught a glimpse of a white-powdered face gazing down at him from an upstairs window; but when he looked again, there was nobody there. So he turned to face the way ahead and he didn't look back again.

Follow the adventures of
Sebastian, Cornelius, and Max
in Book Two

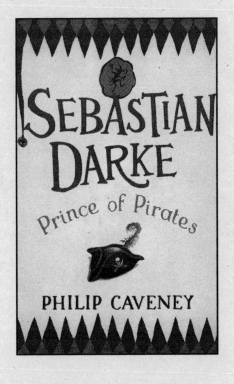

SEBASTIAN DARKE

Prince of Pirates

PHILIP CAVENEY

Excerpt copyright © 2009 by Philip Caveney
Published by Delacorte Press
an imprint of Random House Children's Books
a division of Random House, Inc., New York

CHAPTER 1

THE FOREST OF GELTANE

The ancient wooden caravan had been crossing the wide stretch of plain for several days. Pulled y a single buffalope, it was making decidedly slow rogress. Now the caravan creaked to a halt a short istance from the edge of a mighty forest.

The owner of the caravan sat perched on the wooden seat, clutching the reins and staring houghtfully into the trees. He was what many lainspoken people referred to as a "breed"—the ffspring of a human father and an elvish mother. Ie was not yet out of his teens and his tall lanky rame was loosely draped in the colorful uniform of jester, one that had clearly been designed to fit a nuch bigger man. A garish three-pronged hat was erched on his head.

On the sides of his caravan were painted the

words SEBASTIAN DARKE, PRINCE OF FOOLS. The word "Sebastian" looked somehow different to the rest. It had been added in a wobbly, amateurish hand clearly overpainting another name that had been there before.

Alexander, his father, had been a very successful jester. After his untimely death Sebastian had tried to take up where his father left off, but his recent visit to the city of Keladon had taught him one valuable lesson: that whatever skills he possessed, he was not cut out to be a jester. His future lay in a different direction, and this journey, more than anything else, was his attempt to discover what that future might hold for him.

"This looks depressingly familiar," said the buffalope in a slow, gloomy voice. He too was gazing straight ahead into the thick green ranks of the forest, his apprehension fueled by a journey through those self-same woods in the not-too-distant past. "I can't believe we're going through there again."

"What's the problem?" asked a voice to their left and they both turned to look as a little warrior on a tiny pony came riding abreast of them. Though his voice was deep and sonorous, the face that stared out from under his bronze helmet was smooth and baby-like, completely devoid of hair. His large blue eyes showed not a trace of concern. "Surely, Max, it

you've passed through the forest of Geltane once before—"

"It was no picnic," interrupted the buffalope. "There are *things* in there. . . ."

"Things?" The little warrior shrugged. His name was Cornelius; he was a Golmiran and, like most of his proud northern race, he didn't know the meaning of fear. He looked up at Sebastian. "What's he talking about?" he muttered. "What *things*?"

The elfling considered for a moment. "Things that slither," he said at length. "You couldn't see them and yet you knew they were there. You could hear them moving in the trees high above you." He frowned, remembering. "And then there were the lupers, of course. We never encountered any in the woods, but we heard them howling every night."

"We've seen off lupers before now," said Cornelius dismissively. He reached down to rest his hand on the intricately crafted handle of his sword. "Like all creatures, they have a healthy respect for a length of sharpened steel. And they're not so fearsome. Why, even Max managed to fight off two of them."

Max fixed Cornelius with an indignant stare. "What do you mean, *even* Max? I'll have you know, among my own kind I'm considered quite a warrior."

"Quite a worrier, you mean! You haven't stopped

complaining. It's one thing after another. Your hooves ache, your shoulders hurt, your snout itches—"

"It's all right for you—you don't have the task of pulling this blooming caravan. I said before we ever left the city that the two of you had packed more equipment than we needed. I understand that we have to bring provisions, but you brought enough to supply an army!"

Sebastian sighed. Cornelius and Max had been bickering like this all the way from the city. It was unbearable, particularly when he was in such low spirits. In leaving Keladon, he had also left Queen Kerin, the woman he loved with all his heart. But she had told him that they simply could not be together. She had said it with tears in her eyes, but she had meant it just the same. And any day now she would be marrying some slope-headed dummy of a prince from the neighboring kingdom, even though she had freely admitted that she did not love him. It would be a marriage of convenience, undertaken for her people, to bring peace and harmony between the kingdoms of Keladon and Bodengen. It made Sebastian's blood boil because he was convinced that, deep down, Queen Kerin loved him back. But he knew that there was nothing he could do. He would simply have to try and forget her.

Meanwhile Max and Cornelius went right on bickering.

"Perhaps if you put more effort into pulling the caravan and less into moaning all the time, we'd be making better progress. We should have reached the forest of Geltane yesterday afternoon!"

"That's easy for you to say, being carried everywhere by Phantom. I don't see you offering to walk occasionally to give her a rest."

"Perhaps you'd like me to strap the saddle on my back and let her ride me from time to time?"

"Oh, well, now you're just being—"

"Enough!" snapped Sebastian, with such force that both Cornelius and Max turned to look at him. He glared from one to the other, making no attempt to mask his irritation. "Do you think we could journey in silence for a while? Your constant arguing is giving me a headache!"

There was a long pause while his two companions studied him warily. But Max could never stay silent for long.

"Still feeling glum, are we?" he said.

" 'Glum' is not the word I would use," said Sebastian ruefully. " 'Brokenhearted' is closer to it."

"Plenty more fish in the sea," muttered Cornelius.

"Yes, great, if you wish to have a relationship with a *fish*. I, on the other hand, fell in love with a woman—and not just any woman. The most beautiful in all the kingdom."

Max wrinkled his nose. "Hmmph! I didn't think she was that much of a catch," he said.

"Not much of a catch?" Sebastian could scarcely believe his pointed ears. "She was the Princess of Keladon! With our help, she deposed her wicked uncle and became queen. Of *course* she was a catch. If I'd married her, I'd be minted now. I'd never have to lift a finger ever again."

Cornelius edged Phantom closer and reached up to pat Sebastian's hip. "It was never in the cards, my friend," he said, with what sounded like genuine regret. "I *did* try to warn you. Besides, think about what you're saying. You're not the sort who's happy to sit around in the lap of luxury. You're a man for adventure! Just think, if you'd married *her*, there's no way you'd be out here with us on the trail of pirate treasure."

"No," agreed Sebastian wistfully. "I suppose not."

"Imagine," said Cornelius, warming to his theme. "The treasure of Captain Callinestra, lost for centuries . . . and *we* have the map." He patted his breastplate, beneath which, Sebastian knew, he had a hidden pocket where he kept his most precious belongings. "So come on, I vote we crack on and put some more distance behind us before the sun goes down." He pointed across the plains to where the great golden ball of heat was already beginning its slow climb down to the horizon. "We'll want to find a suitable place to put up for the night, won't we?"

Sebastian nodded and slapped the reins against the buffalope's flanks.

"Was that really necessary?" complained Max. "You could just ask!" But he moved obediently toward the trees.

Sebastian looked left and right, searching for a suitable path into the forest, and after a few moments he spied one, a dark opening beneath low-hanging branches. The earth there was lined and rutted with the imprints of many wheels and countless hooves, so it seemed a likely spot.

Max sniffed at the opening suspiciously. "This is not the path we took last time," he observed.

"I'm sure it doesn't matter," said Sebastian. "It's clearly much used."

Max snorted. "I'd forgotten how dark it is in there," he muttered. "Dark and creepy-looking." But he kept going, and soon the caravan and its occupants were moving into the forest. The sun seemed to go out like a snuffed candle.

It was pretty much as Sebastian remembered it, an eternally twilight world, where countless gnarled limbs rose up sheer on either side of them, to lose themselves in a swaying green canopy far overhead. But something was different. This time he was struck by how silent it was in here. Not a single bird sang, not a pair of wings whirred, and even though the foliage stirred restlessly in the wind, not a rustle did it make. It was as though this part of the forest was quite dead. He remembered how, on their previous journey, it had been rich with the sounds of countless birds; and that when darkness fell, there were other sounds, sinister noises and stirrings aplenty.

"I don't like taking a different path," said Max nervously. "How do we know it will get us to the far side of the forest?"

"They say all routes do that eventually," Sebastian told him.

"Yes, well, I've got a bad feeling about this. Couldn't we just go round it?"

"We'd lose too much time," Cornelius assured him. "Geltane forest is the biggest in the Mid Lands. Only the jungles of Mendip to the south are bigger, and they are reputed to go on forever."

"Nothing goes on forever," said Sebastian. And then he added with the ghost of a smile, "Except possibly Max."

"Oh, don't you worry, young master," said Max,

missing the dig completely. "We buffalopes are known for our longevity. I've a good few summers in me yet."

Sebastian and Cornelius exchanged amused glances.

"And a good few complaints, no doubt," murmured Sebastian.

Cornelius chuckled. "Perhaps you are already beginning to heal," he observed.

Sebastian shrugged. "Oh, I don't know," he said. "Sometimes I forget about her for a while and everything seems fine . . . then, all of a sudden, I see her in my mind's eye and I think how it *could* have been."

Cornelius sighed. "Sebastian, it was never in the cards. A commoner and somebody of royal blood— it just wasn't meant to be. You need to set your sights a bit lower, my friend. There are plenty of girls out there. Ordinary girls, who won't look down their noses at you."

"You say that, and yet Princess Kerin never— Shush! Listen!"

There was the sound Sebastian remembered with such dread. A dry rustling noise, as if dead leaves were being dragged slowly across tree bark. He looked this way and that, peering into the gloom, but he could detect no trace of movement anywhere around him. He glanced down at Cornelius.

"You hear it?" he whispered.

Cornelius nodded and listened. He looked decidedly unconcerned. "Tree serpents, I suppose," he said at last.

Max jerked his head round to look at the Golmiran. "Tree serpents?" he echoed. "Are you sure?"

"Not positive, but I've heard of such things. Big snakes. They coil themselves in the branches overhead, waiting to drop down on their prey."

Max swallowed loudly. "And . . . what do they eat, these . . . serpents?"

Cornelius considered for a moment. "Oh . . . pretty much anything that's slow-moving," he said. He rode on for a few moments before elaborating. "You see, they hang there, some distance up, and they fix their gaze on whatever's passing below. But if it's moving too quickly, by the time they've fallen from the heights, their prey has passed. Then they have the irksome task of slithering all the way up the tree again on an empty belly. So you see, if you move briskly enough, you have nothing to fear."

"I see . . ." Max actually picked up his pace dramatically for several steps before something dawned on him.

"Just a moment! This is another of your stories,

isn't it?" he cried. "Like that yarn you spun me about the grundersnat on the road to Keladon. Just a callous trick to make me hurry!"

Cornelius's baby face split into a huge grin. "You should have seen your face!" he cried. "I've never seen anything so funny in all my life." He threw back his head and laughed heartily.

"Cornelius," said Sebastian, puzzled, "you shouldn't make jokes about things like—"

A sharp cracking sound from under the front wheels of the caravan startled him. He glanced over the side and saw that they had just passed over a scattering of dry white sticks. He looked closer. No, not sticks . . . bones . . .

Cornelius suddenly stopped laughing. Sebastian turned back to look at his friend. The little warrior seemed frozen in his saddle, staring up into the trees in apparent astonishment.

"Cornelius?" said Sebastian. "What's wrong?"

And then, with heart-stopping suddenness, a huge snake came hurtling down from the forest canopy, striking Cornelius and knocking him clean out of his saddle.